Walking on My Grave

Walking on My Grave

CAROLYN HART

BERKLEY PRIME CRIME
NEW YORK

BERKLEY PRIME CRIME
Published by Berkley
An imprint of Penguin Random House LLC
375 Hudson Street, New York, New York 10014

Copyright © 2017 by Carolyn G. Hart
Penguin Random House supports copyright. Copyright fuels creativity, encourages diverse
voices, promotes free speech, and creates a vibrant culture. Thank you for buying an authorized
edition of this book and for complying with copyright laws by not reproducing, scanning, or
distributing any part of it in any form without permission. You are supporting writers and
allowing Penguin Random House to continue to publish books for every reader.

BERKLEY is a registered trademark and BERKLEY PRIME CRIME and the B
colophon are trademarks of Penguin Random House LLC.

Library of Congress Cataloging-in-Publication Data

Names: Hart, Carolyn G., author.
Title: Walking on my grave / Carolyn Hart.
Description: First Edition. | New York : Berkley Prime Crime, [2017]
Identifiers: LCCN 2016043581 (print) | LCCN 2016050444 (ebook) | ISBN
9780451488534 (hardcover) | ISBN 9780451488541 (ebook)
Subjects: | GSAFD: Mystery fiction.
Classification: LCC PS3558.A676 W35 2017 (print) | LCC PS3558.A676 (ebook) |
DDC 813/.54—dc23
LC record available at https://lccn.loc.gov/2016043581

First Edition: May 2017

Printed in the United States of America
1   3   5   7   9   10   8   6   4   2

Cover design and art by Daniela Medina
Book design by Laura K. Corless

To Michelle Vega,
in thanks for your kindness and patience.

Cast of Characters

ANNIE DARLING—The tap of a cane sets off a scramble to save a woman's life.

MAX DARLING—Catches a look of fear on a bank teller's face but doesn't know who frightened him.

THE INCREDIBLE TRIO: MYSTERY AUTHOR EMMA CLYDE, CIVIC VOLUNTEER HENNY BRAWLEY, AND ANNIE'S DITZY MOTHER-IN-LAW LAUREL ROETHKE—Use their unusual insights in the search for a would-be murderer.

POLICE CHIEF BILLY CAMERON—He doesn't believe everything he's told.

MAVIS CAMERON—Police dispatcher, crime tech, and Billy's wife.

SARGEANT LOU PIRELLI—A tough cop with a soft heart.

OFFICER HYLA HARRISON—Pays attention to faces.

GAZETTE REPORTER MARIAN KENYON—The first to know.

BAR AND GRILL OWNER BEN PAROTTI—Listens to his customers.

Cast of Characters

VES ROUNDTREE—Knows someone walked on her grave.

KATHERINE FARLEY—Will do anything to save her husband.

BOB FARLEY—Drives to the remote north end of the island on a foggy afternoon.

ADAM NASH—Selling his yacht won't bring in enough money.

FRED BUTLER—Tells Ben Parotti about his future plans.

GRETCHEN ROUNDTREE—Cool, collected, backed into a corner.

CURT ROUNDTREE—Always puts himself first.

JANE WILSON—Dreaming of a June wedding.

TIM HOLT—Wants to buy some property cheap for a can't-miss development.

ESTELLE PARKER—Furious at the idea of suicide.

JOE MACKEY—A neighbor who calls 911.

ROGER CLARK—A business appointment takes a dark turn.

BILL HOGAN—Plays dominoes at Parotti's Bar and Grill on Saturdays.

Timetable

FRIDAY, FEBRUARY 5—Ves hosts a dinner party.

THURSDAY, FEBRUARY 11– Ves hurries up the stairs.

WEDNESDAY, FEBRUARY 17—"I do not intend to die."

FRIDAY, FEBRUARY 19—A discovery on Fish Haul Pier.

MONDAY, FEBRUARY 22—Pirate gold beckons.

TUESDAY, FEBRUARY 23—Blood on a doorjamb.

WEDNESDAY, FEBRUARY 24—Silence in an office.

THURSDAY, FEBRUARY 25—Shots in the night.

FRIDAY, FEBRUARY 26—Billy Cameron hears a confession.

SATURDAY, FEBRUARY 27—The grandfather clock strikes at quarter after seven.

1

Katherine Farley looked down at the bright and inviting bro-chure. Instead of the bamboo forest and charging black rhi-noceros, she pictured Ves Roundtree, springy reddish curls framing a tight narrow face. Ves radiated energy, competence, intensity. Sharp lines at the corners of Ves's eyes and mouth revealed the gnawing mind-set of a worrier, a woman who had scrabbled for what she had and could always imagine disaster looming.

Katherine turned a page of the brochure.

"Doesn't it look great?" Bob's tenor voice was eager.

Katherine smiled at him. She could see herself and Bob in the mirror behind an old saloon bar they'd installed at the end of their long living room, which overlooked the marsh. It had cost a pretty penny to buy the bar and arrange for its shipping, but that was back when they had plenty of money. The bar was a restored relic from a shuttered saloon in an abandoned cattle drive town. Now the golden oak bar and brass footrail gleamed with polish, as bright as when long-ago adventurers, con men, prospectors, and cowboys drank mule kick bourbon and eyed saloon girls. She appraised her reflection clinically, medium height, nice figure, sleek black hair drawn back in a chignon, aristocratic features that were a dime a dozen in period films, dark eyes that had once been merry. Her smile was easy, though that took every ounce of her steel will. She wanted to rush across the room, take his dear face in her hands, love him riotously, ferociously, as if champagne-drenched nights could still be theirs. Nothing would wound him more than to know her thoughts. She was careful to keep her tone light. "You, me, and a herd of gazelles. Add gin and tonic and I'm sold. The safari looks grand." Grand and expensive. Very expensive.

His gaunt face, still handsome despite deep furrows grooved by pain, lighted with an eager smile. For an instant the past overlay the present, and it was like seeing Bob when he was strong and able to walk easily, didn't have to hobble with legs encased in braces, a cane in his left hand. Unchanged was his sandy tousled hair, intelligent dark brown eyes, bony nose, squarish chin. He one-handedly propelled the wheelchair, which he used at home, and rolled up to her. "We get a big discount if I book next week. We'll save a bunch of money."

She listened as if enthralled, hearing the wanderlust, the hunger to go and do and be, the need for variety and new experience despite the maimed right arm that lay useless in his lap and the weakened legs. She listened and knew the cost of such a trip mounted into the thousands, thousands they didn't have, thousands he no longer earned because the hand with fingers locked into a claw had been his painting hand, the thousands she had never earned with her drawings that achieved acclaim but sold for modest sums in the galleries. She was the one good with figures. She took care of bills and investments. Now she scraped to get them from month to month. She'd missed the last mortgage payment. But to see him eager meant everything to her. There were so many dark quiet days when he withdrew, and the dullness in his eyes broke her heart. Ves Roundtree could make the safari possible. She would . . . and if she wouldn't . . .

Jane Wilson cupped her chin in her hand, listened as Tim excitedly described his plan for a shopping center on the mainland " . . . right there on the highway. I've researched the property. A great place to stop between Charleston and Savannah. It can't miss. You and I together can make it happen."

Jane felt the usual bubbling of desire deep inside when she looked at Tim. His strong-boned face enthralled her, thick brown hair above a high forehead, strong nose, chin with a hint of a cleft. His dark eyes held the promise of passion, his full sensuous lips worked magic when he held her. She knew she was nice-looking but no more than that. She was so ordinary compared to Tim. Her mind drifted back in memory to that moment on the beach when they'd met. She'd thought herself alone. She'd stood staring up at the Mediterranean mansion, golden in the sun, tears streaming down her face. He'd loped to her side, face drawn in concern, bronze and muscular in a lifeguard's red swim trunks, binoculars dangling from one large hand. "Hey, what's wrong?" It seemed right to tell him, swiping the tears from her face, about the days when her mother was Mr. Roundtree's secretary and how in the summers Mr. Roundtree insisted Jane was welcome to play in the pool or on the beach and join her mom for lunch. "He was such a good man. When my mom was so sick—she had cancer and the insurance wouldn't cover some of the medicine—Mr. Roundtree helped us out. And he came to her funeral. I didn't even know until after he died that he'd left me some money."

Tim had been so interested. "So you're an heiress. First time I've ever met an heiress. That's neat."

She'd been quick to explain that she didn't get any money when Mr. Roundtree died. "He set up a trust. His sister Ves gets everything for now. When she dies, the money is split up. Originally he included my mom, but after she died, he put my name in instead. I have to be alive when Ves dies or my share goes to the others."

Tim grinned. "Better take care of yourself. How does it feel to be in line for some big-time swag?" She'd laughed and shaken her head. "I'll be an old lady before Ves dies. She's only in her forties and she's a dynamo." To Jane the prospect of lots of money seemed unreal. But she would always appreciate the note sent to her after Mr. Roundtree's death and his tribute to her mom: *Nellie was as fine a person as anyone I've ever known. I wish she could have lived and taken that trip to Ireland she always wanted to. Naming you in the trust is my way of saying thank you to her for years of hard work.* Jane kept the letter in her jewel box. As for the money, it was a gift that might come someday . . .

"Hey, Jane, didn't you hear what I said?" Tim was smiling, but his gaze was intent.

She reached for her glass of wine. Tim had ordered expensive wine. She looked desperately around the crowded dining room for inspiration. He'd brought her all the way to Savannah for a fine dinner, and she'd stopped listening. She felt a moment of confusion, Tim talking about his plans, his big grandiose pie-in-the-sky plans, because how could he ever get enough money to buy that kind of land and build a shopping center? "Oh," she said in a rush, "the center would be wonderful, wouldn't it?"

His face lightened. He reached across the table, took her hand.

"All I need is backing. You can tell Ves Roundtree about the center and we'll promise her a cut of the profits." He was pleased, excited.

She felt a sweep of panic. She didn't want to ask Ves Roundtree for money. "I don't know if she'd be interested." She saw darkness in his eyes. If she made him mad, that warm, intimate smile would disappear. "Oh, I don't know, Tim. I can try"—she didn't want to ask, she had no right—"but I know she'll say no."

Curt Roundtree glared at his mother. "I missed out on a chance to sail to the Bahamas on Buster Gordon's yacht."

Gretchen Roundtree spoke in her usual breathy, catchy voice, but her tone was firm. "We will go to dinner, and I advise you to be charming." She looked at her son and remembered how appealing he'd been as a little boy, reddish hair in shining ringlets, a cherubic face, gurgling laughter. As an adult, in years if not in behavior, he still had reddish curls and a broad, freckled face and he was always ready to laugh or make others laugh. His wanderlust lifestyle was made possible by rich dilettante friends who welcomed him for a stay of a week or a month at no expense to him. A generous monthly check from Gretchen took care of other expenses, but he counted on snagging rides in friends' private planes or on yachts for carefree—accent on *free*—holidays in Snowmass or Bermuda, depending upon the season. Friends assumed he was wealthy, because he had no job.

Gretchen was blunt. "The money spigot is turned off. No more checks from me. I'm working at a cosmetics shop to pay the food bill. Either you sweet-talk Ves out of some money or find a job." She knew the last would get his attention.

Curt's blue eyes were cold. "If the old man hadn't been such a bastard, I'd never have to worry about money."

"But he was, so you better do as I say."

"Where'd your money go?"

Gretchen shrugged. She felt a twinge of the old bitterness. Rufus had been glad to see her go. She'd agreed for $2 million. Curt didn't know how much his father had paid, but he saw her travel in style from Nice to Venice to Bar Harbor to Scottsdale. She, too, was adept at snagging invitations to stay with wealthy friends.

She looked at her son, knew they were two of a kind. Curt took his thrills from diving from a cliff in Acapulco or skiing off trail in avalanche country or daring a night at a seedy bar in Amsterdam.

She enjoyed another kind of daring, but that avenue was closed to her now. Not only closed, but she was pushed to the brink by a blackmailer. All she could do was pay up.

"I had some expenses." Gretchen's voice was tight. A cold-eyed youngish trophy wife had a damning photo in her cell phone, and her price for silence was high. Gretchen had returned to the island and the condo Rufus had provided, taken the job at Perfumerie. She could no longer mail checks to Curt.

She felt the old flash of anger at her former husband. Why couldn't he have left his millions to Curt? It was stupid to expect Curt to become some kind of financial wizard just because Rufus was a success. She still had the letter from Rufus that the lawyer sent after his death: . . . *better for Curt to make his own way, better for him as a man. He should be in his sixties before Ves dies, and by then he will have learned the value of work.*

"The money's gone. I don't have it anymore. I'm going to ask Ves to advance me enough to open a dress shop in Buckhead." Fifty thousand dollars would get her started, fifty thousand and some new credit cards that weren't maxed out. She imagined an elegant shop in Buckhead. If she drew the right kind of women and offered to bring the finest in couture to their homes, she would see the houses, learn enough to engage in her favorite trade. "That's my plan. I suggest you figure out one for yourself."

Adam Nash exuded an aura of success, an aura he'd carefully cultivated over the years. Tall, well built, with a leonine head of silver hair, his chiseled features were quite perfect for a captain of industry, a spellbinding orator, a financial seer. He instilled confidence. His expression was benign, a steady gaze, a slightly raised eyebrow, a pleasant smile, as he listened to the luncheon speaker.

There was no hint of the panic flaring deep inside, like a rat twisting to be free of a trap. He had a couple of weeks at most. He could juggle figures until then, but he must have an infusion of cash no later than the end of February. Eighty-six thousand dollars. It might as well be eighty-six million. He had borrowed on the house. His Lexus was leased. He'd had no luck selling the yacht. Even if it sold, that wouldn't be enough. He'd clear only forty thousand. He needed eighty-six thousand. His credit was no good. He couldn't borrow. He had many high-flying friends but none of them would write him a check for that kind of money. There was no family to call on. His last remaining relative, a down-at-the-heels cousin, died last year. He wished he could demand the return of jewelry he'd lavished on a succession of women, but they cared no more for him than he for them. When there was pleasure, fine. When bad times came, he was alone.

He was at the head table as befitted a leading resident who was currently president of the community drive. He maintained his pleasant expression as he gazed at the audience. He saw Ves Roundtree, wiry reddish hair, nervous gestures, thin bony shoulders hunched as if poised to spring at any moment. She turned toward Ben Parotti, her conversation animated.

Ves Roundtree. She was his only hope.

F red Butler, his round face expressionless, methodically counted out twenties. His hands moved a shade slower than usual, a calculated response to the customer's rudeness. "Nine hundred and sixty. Nine hundred and eighty. One thousand." He took his time as he slipped the bills into a white envelope, pushed the envelope across the wooden counter to a tall, slender woman with upswept dark hair and a supercilious stare, her attitude one of impatience. "Can I do anything else for you, Mrs. Crain?" His tone was bland.

She scooped up the envelope, the emerald on one slim finger gleaming in the beam from the overhead light. She flipped through the bills, turned away without speaking, her Jimmy Choo high heels clicking on the marble floor of the bank.

Fred hated the way he felt diminished. Most of the rich women on the island were nice. Not Viola Crain. She often looked through those she considered her social inferiors or gazed in disdain as if observing some lower life-form. Fred wished he could tell her that someday he'd be rich, too, and, when he was, he'd . . . What would he do? He didn't live in her world. But when he was rich maybe he could join the country club. Or maybe he'd go to Mexico. Americans— rich Americans—lived like princes there.

He looked at Estelle, the other teller, nodded toward an inconspicuous door. She gave him her usual sweet smile. In the right kind of world, people like Estelle would be rich, not Viola Crain. He put the See Next Window sign out and moved quickly. He turned the knob, slipped through the opening, closed the door behind him. He hurried to the break room and poured a mug of coffee. The bank had good coffee. He picked up a glazed doughnut from a half-empty box open on the counter. At the Formica-topped table, he took an end seat. He dunked the doughnut in the coffee, took a bite. The sugar lift was immediate.

He swallowed coffee, felt better. When he was rich, he wouldn't be ignored by people like Viola Crain. People treated you differently if they knew you had money. Or were going to get money. They'd all been nice to him at the dinner in Rufus's memory. When he was rich, he'd enjoy the best of everything, go to a fabulous Caribbean resort. Images of coconut palms swaying in a breeze and azure water soothed him. They would all live high after Ves Roundtree died and the estate was divided.

He didn't understand why Ves kept on working after her brother left her all that money. Or why she hadn't moved to Rufus's mansion on the beach. Instead, she rented out the luxurious home during the season to rich Yankees. He felt his usual spasm of irritation. If she had moved out of the family home, he could pursue his plans without worry. But she hadn't moved. She continued to live in her antebellum home, so he had to slip around her property while she was at her shop. He for sure didn't want Ves to find him in her backyard. She had a sharp tongue. Worst of all, he would have to explain. He'd rather die. As for her brother's money, it would be a long time coming, and by then he was positive he could soon be rich all on his own.

He finished the doughnut. As for Ves, wallowing in all that money, why did she think people wanted to know about money they wouldn't see for years? He wasn't the only one who felt that way. Maybe Ves meant it nicely when she had them all to dinner at her house, the ones who would be rich when she died, but it was a reminder that she wasn't old, that she had years to enjoy all that money. The evening was stiff with uneven bursts of disjointed conversation. Those anointed by Rufus to someday share in his largesse were there. Katherine and Bob Farley, the artists; Jane Wilson, Rufus's secretary's daughter, and her boyfriend, Tim Holt; local financial adviser Adam Nash; Curt Roundtree, Rufus's playboy son; and Gretchen, Rufus's ex-wife. Ves included Gretchen Roundtree and Jane's boyfriend at the dinner even though they weren't in the trust.

Yeah, it was a weird night. He particularly remembered Katherine Farley. She was dramatic in a vivid red-and-yellow dress, flamboyant against the gray walls of the small dining room and the shabby elegance of the old and worn Chippendale dining table. Candles wavered when Ves moved in and out of the kitchen to bring the food. In answer to a question from Bob Farley, she said a seafaring Roundtree had brought back a portion of a Buddhist altar screen that hung over the sideboard. Bob had paused and leaned against his cane to admire the screen before he moved stiffly to his chair at the table. Bob recalled a trip he and Katherine had made to the South Putuo Temple in Xiamen and how he'd love to go back, but he and Katherine were planning a great adventure in Kenya for the fall. Jane Wilson, the daughter of Rufus Roundtree's deceased secretary, listened enthralled as Bob talked about travels, his eyes alight with excitement. Jane was a nice-looking girl, an eager face, curly brown hair, big blue friendly eyes. Her boyfriend spent much of the evening describing some kind of real estate project to Ves, who only occasionally turned to Katherine on her left. Curt Roundtree often looked admiringly at Ves and adroitly drew her out about her shop and her recent trip to Egypt. Adam Nash tried to act like a bon vivant. Fred thought his mellifluous voice was smarmy as he meandered on and on about a Broadway show he'd seen last month and the Degas exhibit in Atlanta. Gretchen Roundtree had been nice to him, but he'd never felt comfortable, not all the long evening. He didn't care that the estate was growing, even more money than when Rufus died. He wanted money now. He gulped the rest of the coffee. He intended to have money now. No one was going to stand in his way, though he'd be careful. Very careful.

Fog curled around a fountain midway to an antebellum house. A marble statue of Diana the huntress faced the back porch. One marble hand held a bow, the other a portion of an arrow pointed skyward. No lights shone in the two-story white frame house. A mourning dove made a low throaty call.

A figure in dark clothing lifted an arm, checked the time. A few minutes before five. Ves Roundtree usually arrived home at a quarter after five. There was plenty of time. The visitor eased through the fog, head swiveling from left to right, backpack shifting from the movement. Confident no one was near, the visitor climbed the back steps, crossed to the door. A gloved hand tugged a ring of keys from a pocket, tried several until one fit. The door opened. The intruder stepped inside, slid the backpack free, closed the door.

In the hallway, gloved hands opened the backpack, lifted out the necessary materials. There was no sound but the ticking of the grandfather clock as the intruder worked swiftly. Perhaps only three minutes passed and the materials were put away, a zipper pulled, and the backpack once again in place. The back door was opened cautiously. The fog was lighter now. A rapid descent of the steps. The figure crossed the yard to a stand of bamboo, stopped in its shadow.

◆ ◆ ◆

Ves Roundtree drove fast, but traffic was sparse on Sunshine Lane. She turned into her long drive, a graveled lane that ran a hundred yards with dense foliage on either side before rounding a curve. The trees thinned here and she could see the house. She relished privacy. Her nearest neighbor was a twelve-foot alligator in a pond a quarter-mile deep into the woods. The van rattled as she stopped a few feet from the stand-alone garage. She needed to take the van, twelve years old now, to Petty's Garage to see if he could do something about the rattle.

She turned off the motor, opened the door, used the hand grip above the door as she slung to the ground. She'd make some spoon bread, reheat chili from earlier in the week. The evening stretched ahead, quiet, comfortable, uneventful. The week had been tiring, prompting her to choose a bright outfit today, a turquoise knit top and gray trousers and matching turquoise heels. She always wore teetering heels to work. They made her feel young and buoyant.

She moved fast, as she always moved, a tight, tense blur of energy, rushing up the back steps. Her heels clattered on the wooden porch. The door opened, closed.

The chill drizzle didn't take the shine from the morning for Annie Darling. Although she was careful in placing her steps, she felt her usual Monday-morning happiness, a new day, a new week, and at the end of the slick boardwalk the best mystery bookstore north of Delray Beach, Florida, her own wonderful Death on Demand. She never tired, not in summer, fall, winter, or spring, of stopping in front of the plate glass window.

She admired the rocking chair with a pink-and-blue afghan casually draped over the armrest, perfect to suggest contentment with a mystery on a drizzly February day. The new titles were tantalizing: *Cometh the Hour* by Jeffrey Archer, *Jane and the Waterloo Map* by Stephanie Barron, *A Turn for the Bad* by Sheila Connolly, *Here Comes the Bribe* by Mary Daheim, *No Shred of Evidence* by Charles Todd, *Time of Fog and Fire* by Rhys Bowen, *The Killing in the Café* by Simon Brett, and *Fool Me Once* by Harlan Coben.

Shoppers were few and far between in February. Perhaps she'd call Max at his office next door. Confidential Commissions would be quiet as well. Max's secretary, Barb, was in the Caribbean. Max usually kept office hours, though this morning he'd murmured something about dropping by the men's grill at the club since not much was shaking at the office. Max was quite willing to consider any interesting task, puzzle, or question brought to him, but he was equally willing to enjoy peaceful hours without a task. He was probably sharing, in a deprecating manner, of course, his recent hole in one on the third green. Her husband considered downtime God's gift to golfers. It was up to her to set a good example. Nose to the grindstone. Hew to the course. As if reading were ever a task and not a pleasure. She'd make a pot of Colombian, heat up a blueberry scone, build a fire in the café area, and settle down with one of the new books. Would she see what Molly Murphy was up to or plunge into Harlan Coben's new novel?

Footsteps sounded behind her. A plethora of footsteps. This was unusual enough at ten A.M. on a drizzly February morning that she turned to look at the hurrying figures. *Oh my.* A quiet, luxurious morning of reading was no longer in her immediate future.

2

Annie Darling maintained a bright smile. The voices rose, the dulcet tone of her ditzy mother-in-law, Laurel Darling Roethke, the gruff bark of renowned mystery author Emma Clyde, the dry, wry contralto of mystery aficionado and indefatigable island volunteer Henny Brawley.

Laurel's husky voice had an otherworldly timbre, as if she conversed with a wise faun in a sun-spangled glen. ". . . swirls of red, white, and blue with stars cascading in the center of the cover, and on the first page of my little publication, it's such a difficult choice, but I believe I will go with *A good friend lifts your heart.*" Laurel's gaze was distant as if she saw beyond the room, the island, perhaps the universe.

Emma spoke with blunt force. "I don't intend to reveal all my secrets in my little booklet, but here's a particular favorite of Marigold's: *A bad dream is your subconscious knocking on the closed door of your mind.* What could be more perfect for a collection of wise observations by my dear Marigold and unflappable Inspector Houlihan?" The mystery writer's strong square face was pugnacious, daring the others to disagree.

Annie's gaze was admiring though she secretly loathed Marigold Rembrandt. Emma's sleuth was an officious busybody with all the charm of a wasp.

Henny was upbeat. "I've never flaunted my mystery knowledge—"

Annie suppressed a smile. Henny Brawley and Emma Clyde delighted in sprinkling their conversation with mystery references that demonstrated mastery of the genre. Recently the tone had been sharp edged when they disagreed about the most memorable quote from Agatha Christie's works. Henny's favorite came from *Towards Zero:* A young nurse tells a would-be suicide bitter at being saved, *It may be just by* being *somewhere—not doing anything—just by being at a certain place at a certain time—oh, I can't say what I mean, but you might just—just walk along a street someday and just by doing that accomplish something terribly important—perhaps without even knowing what it was.* Emma was condescending. "Pretty, but peripheral. In *Ordeal by Innocence*, Hester Argyle says, *It's not the guilty who matter. It's the innocent.* That"—emphatically—"is the essence of Christie."

"—but I can't wait"—Henny's voice was exuberant—"to share my list of favorite mysteries in my pamphlet."

Annie felt caught in a gossamer web, insubstantial but clinging, immobilizing. Of course, sounds didn't make a web. No matter, she felt enmeshed. She recalled a summer day on horseback as she trotted around a curve and almost barged into a twenty-foot web hanging between two live oaks, home to an industrious golden silk spider. She'd gazed in awe before turning to ride back the way she'd come. Unfortunately, she didn't have a horse at hand. There was no escaping her current entrapment and the apparent rock-solid conviction of Laurel,

Emma, and Henny that Annie not only ran a mystery bookstore, she was simply a perfect choice to publish pamphlets.

Laurel waved a graceful hand, nails gleaming with the daintiest of pink polish. "My dears, quiet for a moment."

Emma paused in midbark, raised a demanding eyebrow.

Intelligent, perceptive Henny looked up from her notebook, her expression quizzical.

Annie was resigned to the reality that Laurel's ethereal beauty misled viewers into thinking she was nothing more than a gorgeous blonde. Annie knew better. Her mother-in-law's Nordic blue eyes held a mixture of sublime confidence and wicked mischief that never failed to send chills up Annie's spine. *What was her Laurel thinking? What was she planning? What had she quite possibly already done?*

Silence fell. She and Emma and Henny awaited a Royal Pronouncement.

Laurel's benign gaze settled on Annie. "Dear child, I sense stress."

Emma gave a huff. "Stress? I can tell you about stress. Right now Marigold is trapped in a cave with a marauding bear at the entrance and a nest of cottonmouths—"

Annie loved the idea of a bear looming over Marigold. She was also tempted to point out that cottonmouths, aka water moccasins, were North America's only poisonous water snake and therefore highly unlikely to be found in the depths of a cave, but confronting a bear or even a nest of water moccasins would be preferable to an Emma publicly challenged.

"—and I have to figure out a way for her to escape."

Henny tapped her purse. "If she carries a small atomizer of mace, she's out of the cave in a flash."

Emma's craggy face pursed in thought. She gave an abrupt nod. "Not bad." Her tone was grudging.

"Of course"—Henny was quick to apply balm to an even slightly challenged authorial ego—"I know you'd already thought of mace and likely decided for Marigold to use the emergency food kit she always carries in her purse and toss a honeycomb past the bear to distract him long enough to dart to her car."

Emma's cornflower blue eyes were easily read. *Honeycomb . . . that's a genius ploy . . . I certainly had almost thought of it . . . was thinking of her purse . . . Henny has obviously read my books carefully . . . she's a good sort . . .* Pleased, Emma beamed at Henny. "I was just trying to decide which action offered the reader more excitement. I think, yes, the honeycomb." Clearly Emma was now sure she'd created the clever escape route.

Laurel gave her tinkling laugh that reminded Annie of a pixie playing a marimba.

"We've had such a good visit with Annie and given her much to think about. We hope she will be excited to publish our chapbooks."

Henny clapped. "How perfect to call our little publications *chapbooks*. *Chapbook* used to be the common term for any small pamphlet whatever the subject, not just poetry."

Laurel pushed back her chair, came blithely to her feet. "We've given her a great deal to consider. She has the look of one—"

Annie felt self-conscious as three pairs of eyes settled on her. Was her velour boat neck top too bright a red?

"—needful of a quiet moment to ponder what we've offered. I know we are eager to afford her the solitude necessary for creative genius. I have no doubt"—Laurel's mesmerizing gaze fastened on Annie—"that Annie is already envisioning our chapbooks." A nod at Emma. "*Detecting Wisdom.*" A nod at Henny. "*Classic Crime.*" A modest smile. "And my *Merry Musings, Modest Maxims for Happiness.* I know"—and somehow she was shepherding Emma and Henny down the central corridor toward the door—"we can expect much from our dear Annie."

Annie remained at the table nearest the coffee bar. It seemed hours since the arrival of the Incredible Trio, as she and Max had long ago dubbed his mom, the island author, and mystery guru Henny. Annie glanced at the wall clock. Actually, their visit had lasted less than a half hour. "Why are you such a wimp?" she demanded aloud. Her psyche was defensive, replied hotly, "It would have been rude to refuse to listen." "Did you tell them no?" "How could I tell them no?" But her reply was weak. Just as weak as she was. She might possibly hold up against one of them. When they combined forces, she might as well be an effigy on a tomb. She grinned, picturing herself in marble splendor with three chapbooks clasped to her bosom.

Warm fur brushed against her ankle. She reached down, slipped a hand over Agatha's silky fur. "Do you think I'm talking to you? Of course, I am. Cat's in charge, right?"

In an instant, her sleek black cat landed beside her, turned twice before she settled into a comfortable ball in the center of the table. A throaty purr reverberated.

Annie bent to nuzzle warm fur. "I'm flattered that you waited until they left before you came out. Of course, you were probably eating, and first things first. Agatha, am I a wimp?" Annie lifted her head. The purr increased. "Kind of you to say so. I agree. When the Trio speaks, it's wiser to listen."

She pushed back her chair. Agatha watched with sleepy green eyes as Annie crossed to the coffee bar. She needed a boost. She paused in front of the fireplace to admire the watercolors hanging above the mantel. Each pictured a scene from a mystery novel. The first customer to identify each author and title received a free (noncollectible) book and coffee for a month. As proprietor, it was her pleasure to choose the books. She loved humor, and these books were guaranteed to make readers laugh.

In the first watercolor, a striking young woman in a gypsy dress and an elegant thirtyish blonde in a kimono stared at a heap of dull glassy pebbles lying on a bunk in a luxurious ship cabin. The younger woman looked puzzled and disappointed, but her older companion, who had an air of sophistication, was excited and fascinated.

In the second, a white picket fence gleamed in the moonlight. Four surreptitious figures, each clutching a suitcase, peered over the fence at the unlighted wing of a huge old house. There was an aura of stealth in their posture.

In the third, a sour-faced woman in a business suit teetered on the ledge of a fifth-floor window above a busy street. She clutched a rusty drainpipe with one hand, the other gripped her handbag. A crowd clustered on the sidewalk, faces upturned. Two constables dealt with a traffic jam as gawkers stopped to watch.

In the fourth, a beautiful dark-haired woman lying in a hospital bed stared at an attractive blond nurse, a tall, distinguished man with horn-rimmed glasses and a pipe, a short, pudgy, balding man with a paunch, and a sandy-haired man with a worried face.

In the fifth, a slender middle-aged Asian man stared out the fourth-floor window of a frowsy building at a rusty green crane and the wrecking ball swinging toward the adjacent office windows. Below, a potbellied man with a dirty yellow hard hat and a clipboard appeared to be directing the demolition.

Annie filled a mug. When she settled again in her chair, delectable brew in hand, she was smiling and not only because of the watercolors. She gazed around the table. Although she sold books and didn't publish them, creating pamphlets might be fun. She wondered if the creative trio had illustrators in mind. Laurel excelled at sketches and might already have drawings for her chapbook. Annie reached over Agatha to pick up a pink manuscript box tied with red ribbon and topped with an emerald bow. She untied the ribbon, lifted the lid, pulled out a sheet, and read the author's introduction:

MERRY MUSINGS
MODEST MAXIMS FOR HAPPINESS
by
Laurel Darling Roethke

Merry Musings offers maxims guaranteed to make any life happier. Each is a Signpost on a road that twists and turns, climbs, descends to depths, winds upward once again to touch trailing clouds. Live with élan.

Annie turned the page, nodded approval at Laurel's illustration, a burst of fireworks in a splendid shower of red, gold, and green. *Merry Musing One: Catch a falling star before it knocks you flat.*

Annie pondered. At first glance, the maxim seemed simple. But was it? She had the old familiar sweep of uncertainty she often felt when dealing with her mother-in-law. Was Laurel saying each person must be aware of possibilities, make the right move at the right time? Was she saying—? Annie shook her head. That way lay bewilderment.

Annie replaced the sheets in the pink box, reached around Agatha for a gray folder with a gold-embossed title: *Detecting Wisdom*. Emma, of course, was pleased to share Marigold's dictum: *If you can imagine it, it can happen.* Much as she loathed Marigold, the point was well taken. Quickly, she reached for the sheets prepared by Henny. The introduction to *Classic Crime* was pure Henny, unassuming but potent: *A tribute to memorable mysteries.*

Annie scanned the list. She felt, as always, a tiny chill at *The Franchise Affair* by Josephine Tey. Henny's comment: The Franchise

Affair strips away the comfortable assumption that ordinary, decent people aren't vulnerable to accusations of evil.

As Annie turned over the next sheet, Agatha rolled over on her back, clamped her paws on either side of Annie's right wrist. The cat's green eyes glittered.

"You've already eaten—"

The first tiny tip of claws pricked Annie's skin.

"My mistake." Quickly Annie began to sing, "Chow time for Agatha, chow time for Agatha."

In a smooth undulating move, Agatha loosed her grip, was on her paws, and launched the five feet from the table to the top of the coffee bar.

Annie hurried. Not that her cat bullied her. Of course not. As she poured dry food into the bowl, the front bell rang.

Slow, uneven steps sounded in the central aisle. Ves Roundtree, right arm immobilized in a sling, limped toward her. Ves normally moved swiftly, reddish curls quivering with energy, bright green eyes jerking from face to face, narrow beringed fingers gesturing emphatically.

Annie hurried to pull out a chair. "What happened?"

Ves nodded her thanks as she eased carefully onto the chair, obviously uncomfortable. "A bad fall." She glanced at the table, saw the gray folder, pink manuscript-sized box, and slim sheaf of sheets. "You look busy."

Annie gave a careless wave of her hand. "Nothing that won't keep." Annie knew Ves Roundtree moderately well. Ves's store was at the far end of the boardwalk. She and Ves were active in the Island Council of Retail Merchants. Ves was the current treasurer, Annie the secretary. In good weather, they played tennis on Wednesday afternoons. Ves had a wicked forearm, the arm now cradled to her side. This wasn't the Ves she knew, a woman always in a hurry, bright, so bright she could seem metallic, impatient, never one to curb her tongue, yet a cool thinker on the court, playing each shot to her opponent's weakness.

"I'll get some coffee."

"No." Ves was abrupt in her usual fashion, focused on a goal, not one to waste time. Her reddish hair was drawn back in a bun that emphasized the jut of her cheekbones and the bony point of her chin. "You're sure you have time?"

Annie didn't glance at the clock. It was probably a quarter to eleven, and she'd hoped to call Max and meet for lunch at Parotti's Bar and Grill, but Ves looked upset and worried. Annie gave her a reassuring smile. "Nothing is urgent on a sea island in February. I'm awfully sorry you fell, but if you have to have an accident, now is the time. I don't imagine you have many customers this time of year either."

Ves's stare was hollow. "I didn't have an accident."

Annie sank into the chair opposite Ves. The blunt words hung between them.

Ves talked fast. "I get home about a quarter after five in the winter. There isn't much to do at closing time. I parked in the drive last Thursday. I didn't bother to put the car in the garage. I was in a hurry." A pause, a tight smile. "I guess I'm always in a hurry. Somebody was counting on that. When I get home"—she took a quick breath as if pushing back from a precipice—"I go upstairs to change. The house was just as it always was, a little cool, quiet enough that I could hear the tick of the grandfather clock in the entry hall. I go in the back door and walk to the front of the hall. The house is old and the stairs run right up straight without a turn. There's no carpet on the treads. The steps are wooden. Some of the treads have a kind of hollow in the center. I was almost to the top, maybe four steps, maybe five, and it was as if I stepped on ice. It happened fast. I stepped and my foot slipped. I fell backward." She took another breath. "I ski every January. I close the shop and go to Breckenridge. That's where we always went when I was a kid. I'm a good skier. That saved me. I know how to fall. I turned myself to the right and grabbed at the banister. My hand whacked against the rail, but I hung my fingers around a baluster, caught, held on. I landed on my hip. It hurt like hell. My wrist was bent, but I didn't let go. I huddled there for a few minutes. Finally I got up on one knee and then I was able to stand. I managed to get down the stairs. I grabbed my purse with my left hand, went out the door. I got to the car, drove to the emergency room. Broken collarbone. Dislocated shoulder. Sprained wrist." The clipped words stopped. Her voice was harsh. "I should have been dead."

A slip on slick stairs. A fall. A fortunate twist and grab. "You say it wasn't an accident." Annie's voice rose a little.

"I've had the same housekeeper for fifteen years. Gladys cleans every Monday. She runs a dust mop on the stairs. Those steps are never slick." Ves's lips twisted. "There was no slick step when I went downstairs Thursday morning. There was no one with a legitimate reason to be in my house that day. I didn't spill anything. How did the step turn into a skating rink? Someone made it happen. But there's something worse." Her eyes bored into Annie's. "Someone was waiting outside, watched me come out, get to the car. My appearance must have been a damn big disappointment." The last jerky words were grim.

"You saw someone?" Annie scarcely breathed the question.

Ves shivered. "I saw no one, but I'm sure someone was there, watched me struggle to the van, and, as soon as I left, hurried inside and cleaned up the step. I don't know what was used. Furniture polish maybe. Beeswax maybe. All I know is when I came home from the hospital, I climbed those stairs with a flashlight. I checked every step. The fourth one from the top was clean and dry, not a trace of dust. I ran my hand back and forth, didn't pick up anything. None of the steps"—her voice was heavy—"were slick." She stared at Annie. "I know what happened. I can't prove anything." Her tone was flat. "Something made the step slick. That's why I fell. I've gone up and down those steps for years. Sure, I wear high heels, I move fast. But I didn't trip. My foot came out from underneath me." She gazed at Annie in despair. "You think I'm nuts."

"Of course not." Annie tried to be reassuring. "Obviously something made you fall. Your shoes?"

A tight humorless smile. "I looked at them. I thought if there was something slick on the steps, there should be some residue on the sole of my shoe, but I had walked outside and across the yard. I went to the hospital. By the time I looked, the sole was normal. Then I thought maybe some of the polish, if that's what it was, came off the shoe onto lower steps. Funny thing is, they were really clean, too, but they were last dust mopped Monday. There wasn't a trace of dust on any step."

"Did you call Billy?"

Both she and Ves knew Billy Cameron, the chief of police. Billy was big, stolid, steady, careful, a good man, a good policeman. Ves was an island native. Billy knew her, knew Annie.

Ves turned both hands palms up. "What could he do? There's no evidence of a crime. I know something was put on the step that made me fall, but the step was clean when I came home from the hospital. Billy's a policeman. He needs facts. How do you suppose he'd feel if I gave him a list of names and said one of these people wants to kill me?"

Annie pictured pragmatic Billy Cameron. Billy believed in facts. Accusing people of attempted murder required facts. Ves had no facts.

She had claims. A step was slick. Later the step wasn't slick. Annie didn't look at Ves's feet, but she knew the style of high heels—very high—that Ves preferred. Any man might be forgiven for thinking high heels could cause a fall. Ves spoke of a list. A list? Ves scarcely seemed like the kind of woman to be surrounded by mortal enemies. "A list?" Annie knew she sounded incredulous. A list of would-be assassins plotting death for Ves seemed absurd.

Ves gave a weary head shake. "I shouldn't have come. I guess I wanted to tell someone and you're always reasonable and we've worked together a lot lately on plans for the boardwalk shops this summer. That doesn't mean you want to hear about my troubles." She pushed back her chair, lurched unevenly to her feet. "I shouldn't have bothered you. There isn't anything you can do." She turned away.

Annie started after her. "Ves, wait, you can tell me."

At the front door, Ves looked over her shoulder. "It's all right. I need to think it through. It isn't fair to involve you." She opened the door, gave Annie a twisted smile. "Never mind."

The door shut behind her with finality.

As he came through the front door, Max Darling gave a thumbs-up to Ben Parotti, gnome-sized owner of Parotti's Bar and Grill. Ben looked natty in a blue blazer, striped shirt, and khaki trousers. He'd worn overalls until he met Miss Jolene, owner of a mainland tea shop. Transported to Broward's Rock after their marriage, Miss Jolene added style and class to the rustic restaurant: vases with flowers on the tables and the addition of quiches and gelatin salads to the menu. Unchanged was the attached bait shop, coolers with squid and chicken necks, and sawdust floors.

"The missus coming?" Ben's gravelly voice was genial.

"On her way." Max felt inner happiness spreading across his face. Annie was on her way. He walked to their usual booth, sat where he could see the door. She'd swing through in just a moment, dusty blond hair, steady gray eyes, slim and lovely, kindness in her gaze. His Annie. That was still a miracle to him. They'd met in New York, seen each other across a crowded room. He'd known in that instant that she was his. He'd followed her from New York to Broward's Rock when she inherited a mystery bookstore. In her serious way, she'd decided they weren't well suited. He was rich. She was solidly middle class. He was relaxed. She was intense. He defined himself by what mattered to him, people in all their quirky variety, sun and sand and sea, laughter, moments of ease to remember good days and envision better days. Annie epitomized the work ethic, so many tasks to do, so little time in which to do them. He didn't have to work, felt no need to achieve, but to please her he opened Confidential Commissions and, truth to tell, he enjoyed helping people solve odd and unusual problems, the more odd and unusual the better. At the moment, he had no clients. Maybe Annie would agree to close Death on Demand during the February doldrums and they could take the train from Raleigh to New York, see some plays—

The door opened. Annie saw him, and her face came alight for a moment, followed by a worried frown. She rushed toward the booth.

He stood, reached out. "Hey, what's up?"

Words tumbled, not in her usual happy fashion, but in tight, tense spurts. "Ves Roundtree's in big trouble . . . a list . . . the more I think about it, the scarier it is . . . she told me not to worry. How can I not worry?"

He looked down. "A deep breath." His voice was soothing. "One. Two. Three." He touched her elbow, guided her into the booth, slid onto the opposite bench. "Start at the first."

"The morning started off so quietly. And then . . ."

He listened with an inward smile. Annie was incapable of short-ening a report into a crisp summary. She didn't leave anything out, including the literary aspirations of the Incredible Trio.

Ben stopped for their order. He didn't bother with a pad.

Annie paused in midsentence. "My usual."

Ben glanced at Max. "Grilled flounder, coleslaw?"

Max nodded.

As Ben turned away, Annie called out, "A double shot of Thou-sand Island on my fried oyster sandwich." She swung back to Max. "Anyway, I'd just taken a peek at the copies they left when Ves Roundtree limped in."

When their food arrived, Annie ate as she described Ves's appear-ance and her accident. She concluded, "Worst of all, Ves said she had a list of people who wanted her dead." Annie's gray eyes were stricken. "Ves is nice." Warm emphasis. "How could anyone want to kill her? The idea that she has a list of people who want her dead is awful. Imagine how you'd feel"—her gray eyes were huge—"if you thought people wanted to kill you." She put down her sandwich.

This was also Pure Annie. Whatever happened, she could put herself in another's spot and understand their sadness or anger or, in this case, terror. He tried to picture lurking assassins, had no success. His world was always sunny-side up.

Max reached across the table, placed his hand over hers, realized she was shaking. "You believe her."

Annie gazed at him straight, spoke slowly. "She doesn't make things up. She doesn't exaggerate. She doesn't read fiction." A slight tone of astonishment. "She reads about the Tang dynasty and mon-etary policy and how crows make tools."

Max looked into gray eyes filled with uncertainty and anxiety and understood. In the past she'd often tried to help friends and sometimes she'd been foolhardy, and once she disappeared. The last had shaken him, rocked his world. He'd demanded that she promise never again to become involved in other people's problems. It was a promise she'd tried to keep, hadn't kept. He'd realized she wouldn't be Annie if she turned away from someone in need.

His Annie. Kind, brave, generous. Those steady gray eyes implored him. "I guess," he said gently, "you better go see Ves, find out what's going on."

Annie drove straight to the boardwalk, hurried to Trinkets 'n Treasures, Ves's shop. The front window was dark. A Closed sign hung a little askew on the knobby arm of a wooden chair that might once have been in a monk's spare cell. Ves likely hadn't opened today because she was uncomfortable from her injuries.

Back in her Thunderbird, Annie drove a little too fast, hoping no wandering deer chose this lousy afternoon to cross a road in front of her. It took only five minutes to reach Sunshine Lane and turn into a narrow drive shadowy beneath tree limbs that interlocked. As she came around the last curve, she was relieved to see lights shining on the lower floor of Ves's house. Huge live oaks rose in the front yard. On a misty overcast February day, the gray Spanish moss wavering in the breeze added a melancholy, slightly sinister aura.

The two-story white frame house had upper and lower piazzas with three Ionic columns on either side of the short flight of front steps. Annie pulled up in the single drive and parked behind Ves's van. Out of the car, she walked swiftly on an oyster shell path to the front of the house and climbed the steps. She knocked on the front door.

A clank from inside. A chain being unloosed?

The door eased open, then was pulled wide. "Annie." Ves's tone was surprised, uncertain.

Annie was blunt. "You left because you thought I didn't believe you. I believe you."

Ves's lips quirked in a lopsided grin. "I live on Sunshine Lane, but you're the first ray of sunshine I've seen today. Come in."

Annie stepped into a hallway with a gleaming heart pine floor. Stairs rose old and straight ahead of her. The hallway held a marble-topped side table. Mail lay in a bronze tray. A mahogany grandfather clock sat against the back wall. To the right was a drawing room with a shabby Queen Anne sofa, two Chippendale side chairs, a fireplace with an Adam mantel. To the left was a small dining room with a long table and a glass-door cabinet filled with china.

The door closed. Ves's green eyes might have held a trace of tears. "Thank you for coming. My brother would have said you're a good Joe. Funny expression, isn't it? But it meant a lot to him. And to me. A good Joe." She stood by the door, gave a quick shake of her head, like a terrier coming out of a pond. "What changed your mind?"

Annie kept her gaze steady. "I've been looking over a friend's collection of mystery quotes: *Unlikely melodrama is the likeliest to happen of anything in the world.* That's why I'm here."

Ves's look was peculiar, probably as peculiar as Jerry North's when his ditzy wife, Pam, made the observation in *Death Has a Small Voice* by Frances and Richard Lockridge.

Annie flashed a grin. "I can do lots of quotes. Not just mysteries. *A trouble shared is a trouble halved.*"

Ves's face was transformed, a mixture of delight and amazement. *"Quod in communi, est dimidium malum."* She reached out a thin hand, gripped Annie's elbow. "This calls for a celebration." Talking fast though still moving with a jerky pained gait, she guided Annie down the hallway. "Our dad taught Latin at the high school. Did you know Ves is short for Vesta? She was the goddess in the temple who was keeper of the flame. I shortened it to Ves before I was five, and trust me I've avoided flames ever since. My brother arrived with a mop of red hair and that's why he was named Rufus, 'red haired' in Latin. Dad was irrepressible. Rufus and I could spout Latin quotes like some kids do baseball statistics. *Alis volat propriis.* One of my favorites. *She flies with her own wings.*" She pushed through a swinging door into a bright kitchen, waved Annie to a seat at a maple table in a bay window overlooking the garden. "I have coffee, but how about some egg nog, my own recipe, left over from the Death's Head Feast." At Annie's startled look, she gave a bark of laughter. "More about that anon, as a good Latin scholar would say. I'll bring egg nog with coffee for a chaser."

Ves brought cut glass glasses filled with egg nog and two blue coffee mugs. Annie picked up a crystal glass with golden contents, took a taste. Egg nog could be too sweet, too heavy. This was perfection, and Annie was sure the nutmeg was fresh.

Ves eased into the opposite chair. She, too, took a deep swallow of egg nog. "When in doubt, drink egg nog, and you'll know life is good. That's a quote, too, but nobody famous. My mom was convinced homemade food and drink made any burden lighter." She sipped the egg nog, gazed at Annie. "I'd like to halve my trouble. And"—her face clouded—"I'll feel better if someone else knows what I'm thinking. Just in case." The final sentence was somber. She took a deep breath. "I mentioned Rufus, my brother. A good man. A very good and kind man. After college he went to New York. He was a trader." Her voice was vague. "I don't know what he did exactly, but he made a lot of money. He married fairly late, almost forty. He was quite a bit older than I. It's odd how nice men have a tendency to marry bitches. Gretchen was and is a class A bitch. Gorgeous if you like packaged blondes, always coiffed, sleek as a rat's fur, in my view, never wearing just a dress, always a designer whatever that might as well flaunt a price tag. A tinkling laugh that might have been cute when she was five. She produced an heir, but Curt is lazy on his ass." She gave Annie a quick smile. "I'm telling you my family history because everything's tied up with Rufus. He moved back to the island after he retired."

Annie nodded. She remembered Rufus Roundtree, a big man with a round face, a thatch of red hair salted with white, a booming voice, and a personality that overwhelmed a room. He'd plunged into everything on the island and been generous with donations to the library, the island rec center, the historical society, the art league, and the community charity drive.

"Rufus had a wonderful time. I'm glad about that. He invited me to live with him in his beach mansion, but I've lived in the family house forever. It's home. I don't have a lust for luxury. Anyway, it was grand having him on the island. He died last year."

Annie remembered the headline in the *Gazette*: ISLAND PHILAN-THROPIST FELLED BY HEART ATTACK.

"I wasn't surprised that he made me the life income beneficiary of his estate. I thought it was fair enough that I would enjoy the income and that at my death the estate would be divided equally among six people he chose. It was his money. He earned it. I've enjoyed not having to worry about money for the first time in my life. I know he would be pleased to know—and"—her lips quirked—"maybe he does know—how much pleasure he's given me. I went to Cairo last month and brought back tons of wonderful curios from the Khan el-Khalili bazaar." Her eyes gleamed. "Chess boards with mother-of-pearl inlays, bedouin jewelry, brass hanging lamps . . ." She trailed off. "But"—her voice was ragged—"if he knows how much I've enjoyed the money, he knows what's happening now. I'd hate for him to know that his generosity put me in danger." A somber look. "Last week was the anniversary of Rufus's death. I thought it would be nice to invite the beneficiaries-to-be for a dinner remembering him. I intended to give them an accounting of the estate. Martin Ford at the bank is the trustee—he sends me quarterly updates. He and I have taken good care of the assets. I've had a few extravagances, but the estate is larger than when Rufus died. I took the trip to Cairo, bought a new car and a new furnace for the house, but the estate's grown by almost two hundred thousand. If the remaindermen, as they are called in cold legalese, inherited today, each would receive about three million dollars. There are six of them: Katherine Farley, Bob Farley, Jane Wilson, Curt Roundtree, Adam Nash, and Fred Butler." Ves's face looked thinner, narrower. Her fingers fastened on the coffee mug, but she didn't lift it. "They all came to dinner, plus Gretchen, Rufus's ex, and Jane Wilson's boyfriend. I think Gretchen was especially frosted that Curt didn't inherit immediately and would have to wait for Ves to die. Six million for a couple of artists, no cut for his son. But Gretchen came to the dinner. It's a dinner I'll always remember as the Death's Head Feast. Before that gala evening, most of the beneficiaries had contacted me, asked for money. The exceptions were Bob Farley and Fred Butler. Probably Bob knew Katherine had her hand out. Anyway, I've liked Fred better than the others ever since. I turned them all down. I was bland, said I was honoring Rufus's wish that I enjoy

the estate now, and they would receive their portion on my death."
Ves's chin jutted. "The night of the dinner, we had those stiff ex-
changes, you know the kind. *Are you watching* Downton Abbey? *What
do you think about the plan for a new high school? Which girl-on-a-train book
did you read? Have you priced lobster lately?* I looked around at each one of
them." Abruptly, she pushed back her chair, came to her feet. "Let's
go to the dining room. I want to show you."

3

Ves flicked the switch. The crystal drops of the chandelier glittered. Gray walls emphasized the ruddy richness of the mahogany table and the mauve drapes. Three Chinese plates in brass holders adorned a Hepplewhite sideboard. Above the fireplace hung an oil portrait of Rufus Roundtree, his large face genial.

Ves stood by the end chair. A silver tea urn stood on the dining room table. "There were so many of us, I put in the center leaf. I sat here with three on one side, four on the other." She touched the back of the end chair nearest the kitchen door. "Fred Butler was at the other end. You know Fred—"

Annie did. He was a cashier at the bank and a steady customer at Death on Demand. Annie found customer reading choices fascinating. Fred was an inveterate reader of thrillers with swashbuckling heroes, the more derring-do the better.

"—a dumpy little guy, wispy gray hair that stands up in tufts around his face. He wears bifocals and peers at you over the rims. Rufus met him at Parotti's. A bunch of mostly older men play dominoes at a round table in the bait section." Her nose wrinkled. "Trust men not to mind a stink. I said that to Rufus once and he laughed and insisted a fisherman likes the smell of live shrimp or mullet better than any whiff of cologne. Rufus got a kick out of Fred, said he could surprise you when you got him talking, that his ideas might be crackpot but they put a zing in his life. Fred said almost nothing at the dinner. No repartee from Fred. Adam took up the slack, a torrent of words. He was trying to exude charm. It was wasted effort on me, I can assure you. Put Adam in a brown suit on a platform with a bottle of snake oil and he'd be right at home—senatorial good looks, a plastic face usually wreathed in a smile, a voice so deep and warm you feel like you've pulled on a cashmere coat. Adam spent most of the dinner one-upping Bob Farley with travel tales.

"Bob was next." Her face was suddenly rueful. "Poor devil. They never mention his accident, but you have to wonder why anybody wants to hang glide. Anyway, he did. Ka-boom. Now he can barely manage to walk and his painting arm is useless. He was a superb artist. I have several of his Low Country paintings at the shop. One I especially love, a sunny summer day and an alligator on the bank, but the alligator's eyes are open and he's looking at a man standing by the lagoon." She gave a slight shiver. "Heat. Menace. Power. Danger. I look at the painting and know in an instant the alligator will attack, take the man over the edge and into the water. I hope"—her voice was thoughtful—"that having been a great painter will see him through.

"Katherine Farley was to my left. She's one of those classic beauties, sleek black hair, patrician features, midnight eyes, though she looked haggard, not her usual gorgeous self. She wore a red-and-gold lamé dress. She kept up a pleasant stream of conversation, travel, the new book by Joyce Carol Oates, her recipe for clam chowder, the sketch she'd just finished of a loggerhead turtle in the moonlight just past the high tide line sweeping the sand with a flipper to prepare a nest for her eggs. But"—Ves sounded hollow—"all the while it was as if she and I were pantomimes in a shadowy background. Her attention was focused on her husband. Yet when she turned to him, she spoke casually. I wondered if I was the only person at the table aware of that tension."

For Annie, the dining room was slowly filling with guests, tuft-haired Fred Butler, smooth-talking Adam Nash, crippled Bob Farley, beautiful and passionate Katherine Farley.

Ves looked at the empty place to the right. "If I were doing that honored-guest kind of thing, I should have put my nephew to my right, but Curt drives me nuts because all he does is play. I like people who work whether they have to or not. Rufus tried to fix it where he had to shape up, but Curt sponges off his rich buddies. Gretchen, my ex-sister-in-law, isn't an heir. I called her to ask how to get in touch with Curt, and it would have been rude not to include her. Anyway, I put Tim Holt to my right. I like his get-up-and-go." A smile. "He's one handsome guy. Big, curly brown hair, a lifeguard in the summer. I'm not sure what he's doing now, general handyman work. Ben Parotti uses him for some repairs."

Ben Parotti owned not only Parotti's Bar and Grill and the *Miss Jolene*, the ferry that plied between the island and the mainland, he was involved in several businesses and owned a great deal of property.

"Tim's ambitious. I heard all about the shopping center he wants to build near the ferry landing on the mainland, how the property was available, how he was looking for backers, how much the construction would cost, the possibility of anchoring with a Winn-Dixie, and on and on and on. I already knew about it. Jane came to see me at the shop and finally—she was very diffident, I'm sure he would have been disappointed—she said she wondered if perhaps I might consider investing in a wonderful construction site. I heard her out and gave her my standard reply to all the prospective heirs: no." Ves's chin looked very pointed. "Rufus gave the money to me to enjoy. I intend to do so. But Jane's a nice girl. Her mother was Rufus's secretary and she died of cancer. I remember Jane being at Rufus's big house with her mom during the summers, a little girl with pigtails. Now she's grown up and grown up very nicely, pretty brown hair, a sweet face, beautifully dressed. An Escada blue print sheath dress with cap sleeves. Gorgeous. Nothing she could afford. She works at a secondhand store up the street from Parotti's, and that was someone's discard. Luckily for Jane most rich women are a perfect size eight, so she can enjoy finery as long as she doesn't mind secondhand. She didn't have much to say at dinner. Tim was talking as fast as he could to me. Curt was on her left. He ignored her and put himself out to be nice to me. Gretchen was on her best behavior, favoring me with warm smiles and approving nods when I talked to Curt.

"Gretchen"—Ves's tone was considering—"was her usual vision of perfection. Blond hair gleaming and a face that really didn't look much past thirty. She must spend a fortune on cosmetics. She wore a stunning short-sleeved black lace minidress. She even tried to be charming to Fred. He was on her left at the end of table, but he perched on his chair and stared at her like an urchin meeting high society. She valiantly kept trying." There was grudging appreciation in her tone. "Very unlike her usual disdain for peasants. Believe me, I saw that in operation when she was married to Rufus. I was one of the peasants then."

Annie pictured Ves at one end, fish-out-of-water Fred at the other,

Jane's hunk boyfriend Tim, quiet accommodating Jane, playboy Curt, and sleek Gretchen on one side, vivid Katherine, talkative Bob, and pompous Adam on the other.

"That's the lot. I don't hire a server when I have people for dinner. I cleared the plates. Jane offered to help. As I said, she's a nice girl. I thanked her but said no. I took the dishes out to the kitchen, stacked them in the sink, got the dessert. When I pushed through the swinging door, everyone stopped talking. Their heads turned and they looked at me. I felt like stone. I couldn't move. Time stopped. I started shivering." Ves's green eyes were enormous with a curious emptiness. "My mother always said when out of nowhere you suddenly feel scared, can't breathe, sense darkness and danger, when you feel like that, someone is walking on your grave. That's what happened to me when I came in the dining room with the tray that night. Someone was looking at me and seeing me dead, wanting me dead. Walking on my grave."

". . . and Ves stood in her dining room and saw them looking at her." Fire crackled in the grate. Annie stood in front of the fireplace, but the warmth didn't dispel her inner chill, the same chill she felt that afternoon when she'd seen doom in Ves's eyes. She took a breath, knew her voice was uneven, choked. "Ves said, 'Someone was looking at me and seeing me dead, wanting me dead. Walking on my grave.'"

Max looked at her with concern in his dark blue eyes. Her gaze moved to their guests. Each face reflected an intensity and, more, resolution. Henny Brawley, Laurel Roethke, and Emma Clyde excelled in discovering truth among lies. All three were immersed in island society with knowledge of an astonishing range of personalities from the aristocratic to the disreputable.

Max, relaxed in a plaid flannel shirt and brown corduroy trousers, lounged comfortably in his red leather chair, plump white Dorothy L contentedly asleep in his lap. He stroked her smooth fur. Handsome Max, strong, powerful, gorgeously male. His dark blue eyes said, *Don't be scared, don't worry, I'm here, I'll always be here.*

Henny projected competence, intelligence, wisdom. Silver-streaked dark hair framed a narrow, intent face. She was elegant in a gray turtleneck, cream suede jacket, gray slacks, and ankle-high boots.

Laurel Darling Roethke, golden hair in shining ringlets, lake blue eyes slightly dreamy, had a faraway look of introspection, as if she summoned an inner muse for consultation.

Emma Clyde's primrose blue eyes glowed. She sat with broad stubby hands planted on her knees. "I like it. I like it!" So might the Sphinx appear if garbed in a red velvet caftan: huge, imposing, solid.

Four faces turned toward Emma. Annie frowned. Max's blond brows rose in surprise. Henny's gaze was questioning. Laurel exuded placid understanding.

Emma was not without perception. There might have been a tiny flush in her heavy cheeks. "Not to say I am wishing Ves ill. Certainly not. But don't you see? How often can murder be prevented?" Her spiky hair, a subdued russet tonight, seemed to quiver with eagerness.

Laurel cooed, "Quintessential Emma. Right to the point. A rapier to the heart." A gentle smile for Annie. "Whether you realize it or not"—was there just a hint of a patronizing tone?—"you've come to us to winnow out a Prospective Murderer. That is the only result that will assure Ves's safety." Laurel's smile was confident. "I have no doubt we shall prevail. Now, we have six heirs—"

Max interrupted. "They are actually contingent remaindermen beneficiaries."

Emma was brusque. "They get the money. If they are alive when

Ves dies. If one of them pops off before Ves, the share is divided among the survivors. We can call them heirs no matter what the proper term is."

Laurel gave her son a consoling glance. "So well meant, my dear, so exquisitely legal, but let's keep this simple. Six people will benefit if Ves dies. Gretchen Roundtree and Jane's young man could also profit because of their association with the heirs. Now"—a pause to be sure everyone was attentive—"we know these facts. Each heir except Fred Butler and Bob Farley has asked for money. Ves sees no reason to disburse any sums in advance. One of those who will inherit decided to kill Ves. Last Thursday shortly before five P.M. Prospective Murderer, hereinafter known as PM, entered Ves's house in some fashion"—a careless wave of pink-tipped fingers—"a skeleton key, an unlocked window. Old houses pose no obstacle. PM greased a step on the staircase, exited, waited, observed her arrival, likely heard her cry out, but, and this is a most interesting and curious fact, PM didn't rush to the house immediately to clean the step. PM waited. In a few minutes an injured Ves comes outside, limps to her car. When she was gone, PM entered the house, removed the slick substance from the stairs, departed. What does this behavior tell us?"

Henny's dark eyes gleamed. "PM is agile. We can delete Bob Farley from our suspect list."

Emma was brusque. "Not so fast. Bob gets around on a cane. He has a handicapped-equipped car. Movement takes him longer, but he could have managed." She nodded emphatically, shaggy short cut hair quivering.

Max's admiring nod at his mother was, in Annie's estimation, a trifle overdone.

Laurel's dreamy gaze settled on Annie. "What else can we surmise?"

Annie said uncertainly, "Uh, PM's pretty smart." Annie knew she sounded lame, and Max didn't have to look at her so kindly.

Henny jumped right in. "Annie's right. PM doesn't jump to conclusions."

"Thinks before acting," Emma added.

Laurel was encouraging. "And?" She turned her hands over in a graceful gesture encouraging class participation.

Max punched his right fist into his left palm. "Ves's death has to be an accident." He spoke rapidly. "If Ves is found dead and it's murder, the police immediately want to know cui bono."

Laurel clapped in pretty appreciation of her son's acumen.

With an effort of will born of long practice, Annie maintained an agreeable expression. But honestly, sometimes Max's and Laurel's elevated opinions of each other were a little hard to tolerate.

Emma, never enamored of anyone else's cleverness—after all, she was the clever one—kept to the point. "PM came equipped to get into the house with a substance, possibly furniture polish or floor wax, to smear on an upper step, and cleaning equipment to remove all traces. Likely had a backpack, wore gloves."

Annie tried not to sound grudging. "It does appear that the intruder—"

"PM," Laurel said pleasantly, but firmly.

Annie would have engaged in a verbal joust with Laurel but it would save time to acquiesce. "PM intends for Ves's death to appear accidental."

Laurel nodded approvingly. "And that"—her husky voice was full of cheer—"means we do not have to worry about Ves being knifed or shot. Accidents take time and effort to create. Fortunately, we have no cliffs."

Annie almost mentioned the reddish unstable headland bluffs buffeted by swirling currents, but she understood Laurel's point. The island had no handy canyons or gorges or narrow mountain trails, and Ves would surely not stroll near water's edge alone with any of her recent dinner guests.

Emma's square face folded in a frown. "True enough. Ves may be quite safe, since she survived the fall."

Annie hoped she didn't detect a shade of disappointment in Emma's voice.

Henny's glance at Emma was slightly chiding. "I wish we could be confident no more attempts will be made." Her intelligent face was grave. "We can't make that assumption. But, as Laurel pointed out, accidents require thought, planning, the right particular moment. Failed brakes in a car. Perhaps a shove over the railing of the *Miss Jolene*. I believe Ves is one of the islanders who always gets out of her car and climbs to the upper deck for the crossing. Annie can suggest she not do that until we discover the identity of her attacker."

Annie was cautiously hopeful. "You say that as if you think there is a way to figure out who waxed the step." Annie backed closer to the fireplace, seeking its heat to ward away the cold image of a watcher in the shadows near Ves's backyard.

Henny nodded in agreement. "We know the Prospective Murderer was physically present at Ves's house at approximately five P.M. last Thursday. Where were Katherine and Bob Farley, Jane Wilson and Tim Holt, Curt Roundtree, Gretchen Roundtree, Adam Nash, and Fred Butler at that time? We will find out."

Emma was gruff since she hadn't made the proposal. "Better to have Max nose around their finances, see who needs money now, ASAP. Then we can focus on the likeliest suspect."

Laurel's smile was kindly. "Ranking the depth of monetary desperation can be a challenge. I address that in my collection of *Merry Musings*: *Sufficiency for one is deprivation for another.*" A benign smile. "Or, even more apropos: *Happiness comes from giving, not taking.* However,

Emma's point is well taken. I'm sure Max will see what he can discover about their bank accounts and current financial statuses."

Max's expression was wry. "Easier said than done."

Emma's shoulders squared. "Sounds like shilly-shallying to me. I suggest we lay our cards on the table." A vigorous nod.

Laurel's eyelashes fluttered.

Annie watched in fascination as Laurel murmured, not quite loud enough for Emma to hear, what was clearly another quote from *Merry Musings*: *Indulge a friend's weakness for trite pronouncements.*

"And," Emma continued forcefully, "shoot a warning shot across the bow."

Laurel winced.

Emma bowled ahead. "Just like Inspector Houlihan says to Marigold in the new book: *Don't hesitate to be tough.* It's one of my favorites from *Detecting Wisdom*."

Henny smiled serenely at Emma, but her voice was firm. "A careful perusal of Earl Derr Biggers's *The House Without a Key* yields this observation from Charlie Chan: 'I have many times been witness when the impossible roused itself and occurred.' Our aim is to discover the whereabouts of Ves's guests at the time the step was doctored without their realizing that five P.M. Thursday is important. Let's move with the silence and stealth of a panther so we don't alert our prey that we are in pursuit. There is always time to be tough"—an admiring nod at Emma—"but circumspection will better serve us when we talk to Ves's dinner guests."

4

Laurel sat with a partially open window in her green convertible and observed Tim Holt loading boxes in the back of a black pickup truck. The truck wasn't new but it was clean and well kept. Quite an attractive young man with curly brown hair and strong features. He moved with easy grace. She enjoyed young men, so virile, so . . . She must focus on her task. She smoothed back a curl, opened her oversized calico catchall bag, lifted out a legal pad. She opened it to the first sheet and admired the schedule she had produced quickly and efficiently last night. Dear Max had perhaps been too generous in his praise. She made no claim to brilliance, except perhaps in the sheen of her golden curls. She had never succumbed to an overinflated view of herself. That would never do. After all, when one was fortunate enough to be beautiful, graceful, and perceptive, tributes naturally flowed.

She glanced at her darling serpentine watch, a gold-and-silver band coiled around her forearm from a tail embedded with tiny emeralds to an almond-shaped timepiece, a gift from a young man in Dallas. Texans topped her list of manly men. It was one minute to nine. The plan was as choreographed as a Broadway musical. She, Henny, Emma, Max, and Annie would approach Ves's dinner guests on a precise schedule to be sure their quarries had no opportunity to collaborate on a version of last Thursday afternoon.

Laurel stepped out of her Porsche, welcomed the breeze that fluttered her hair and she knew becomingly molded her pale blue dress against her. She didn't bother to lock the car. She turned to a fresh sheet in her pad, perched the pad against her left arm, and strolled unhurriedly to the recently waxed truck. She noted the painted sign on the driver's door: HOLT ODD JOBS.

A thud as he slid a crate into the bed of the pickup. Despite the chilly temperature, Tim Holt wore a short-sleeved tee. His jeans hung low on his hips and his sneakers were well worn.

Laurel admired the ripple of muscle in his near arm. Very nice. "Tim Holt?"

He turned and looked at her as men usually did. Men were so predictable. He stood a little straighter, brushed a smudge of dust from one arm. "I'm Tim Holt." His voice was low, the kind of voice a man might use in a bar when he turns to a woman sitting alone next to him, an attractive woman who might be willing to play.

Laurel beamed at him and, regretfully, made her tone a trifle arch and definitely not beguiling. "I've been asking around." She gestured vaguely behind her, perhaps implying she'd dropped into some of the downtown shops. "I'm looking for young people for a survey. I'm L. D. Roethke from Consumer Characteristics Commission. I have a few questions and, of course, CCC offers remuneration for your time. Fifty dollars. I do hope you can help us out today."

As she'd expected, his brown eyes glinted at the fifty-dollar offer. "I've got a few minutes. What do you want to know?"

Laurel delved into her bag, pulled out a pen and a crisp fifty-dollar bill. She pinned the bill against the pad with a thumb, held the pen with her other hand. She spoke in a rush, a canvasser with a canned presentation. "A little bit about CCC first. We are seeking to determine buying habits of consumers ages eighteen to thirty with an emphasis on late-afternoon activities. Our specific time frame is from four to six P.M. To avoid the distractions of the incipient weekend, which can easily distort buying patterns, we focus on Thursdays. Now"—she gave him an encouraging look—"please tell me where you were at four P.M. this past Thursday."

He leaned against the back fender. "Thursday." His face crinkled as he concentrated. "Let's see. I needed a battery for my cell phone . . . No, wait, that was Wednesday. Thursday . . . I picked up a riding mower at the inn, took it over to Haney's Repair. Shot the breeze with Big Al in the back shop. That was my last job. I dropped by the fish market at Parotti's around five, got a pound of shrimp, took it over to my girlfriend's house."

"I guess she was glad to see you with something for dinner."

"Yeah. We fixed gumbo."

Laurel leaned nearer as he talked, her eyes widening. "I think I know why you look so familiar. Was it Friday? No. Before that. Oh, Thursday, it must have been Thursday. Where was I?" She pulled out a small notebook, riffled through several pages, looked up in satisfaction. "Sunshine Lane, of course. Did I see you around five o'clock?"

He grinned. "I wasn't anywhere near Sunshine Lane. Jane lives on Bluefish Road close to the church."

At nine A.M. Annie glanced in the display window of You Want It, We Have It. Floor spots angled up to illuminate a tan-and-gold sweater dress draped over a shabby rattan chair, a bright pink suit spread on a worn blue sofa, a man's tweed coat with leather elbow patches dangling from a slightly listing coat tree, and a cocktail dress with spangles pinned to a makeshift clothesline. The effect was cheerful and inviting, the displayed items freshly cleaned and pressed, the window clear and sparkling, the flooring obviously old but gleaming with a high polish. Annie felt a pang. How long had it been since she mopped the flooring of the Death on Demand display window?

She noted the store hours as she opened the door: 9 to 5 winter hours. A bell jangled as she stepped inside. Her nose wrinkled at a combination of potpourri, furniture polish, and dust, not casual house dust but dust embedded in old books, rugs, and cushions.

The store was long and narrow, racks of clothing interspersed with wooden chairs, side tables, sofas, and filled bookcases. A rattle of steps, and a young woman hurried forward. Honey brown hair framed a gentle face with a high forehead, slender nose, generous mouth, and soft chin. A Donna Karan striped pullover sweater was flattering to her willowy figure. Gray wool trousers bunched stylishly over low silver leather boots. The outfit new might have cost around $1,000. Annie wondered what the markdown was in the store.

Big blue eyes were quick, understanding Annie's appreciative glance. "I'm a walking ad for the store. These clothes came in a couple of weeks ago and were priced at twelve dollars each for the top, slacks, and boots. And"—a happy gurgle as she came nearer—"I get an employee discount. If you're interested in clothes, we have some real prizes." She carried a can of furniture polish in one hand, a cloth in the other. "Feel free to browse. Clothing is sorted by size, casual wear in the front, dressier as you go to the back." She skidded to a stop in front of Annie, looked at her with sudden recognition and perhaps a dash of surprise. If she recognized Annie, she knew well enough that Annie had no need to shop for fine clothes at a used store. "Oh, hi. Are you here to check out the books? We have all kinds. Not like your store, of course." A shy smile.

"I'm Jane Wilson. My mom loved mysteries, especially old ones. I used to look for her favorites in your used books. They made her happy."

Annie nodded quickly. "I remember you." Jane's face had been thinner, graver when she used to shop, buying books for a woman who had not long to read. Annie glanced at a nearby bookcase, squinted. Was that an early edition of *The Album* by Mary Roberts Rinehart? She resolutely returned her gaze to the shop assistant. "I wish I were book hunting today. Instead, I'm here for the Island Council of Retail Merchants. We're asking around about store hours, thinking we might come to an agreement for all the shops to close at the same time in the winter. I know you close at five, but I'd like to get your input. We decided to focus on Thursdays. We're asking everyone to give us an estimate of their traffic between four and six." Annie pulled a note card and pen from her purse. "How many customers did you have last Thursday from four o'clock until you closed?"

Jane gestured toward the back of the store. "Come sit down."

As they walked down the center aisle, Annie felt a little ashamed at the subterfuge. Jane Wilson had no reason to suspect this visit was anything other than what it seemed to be, and she was responding quite openly. Would she be this relaxed if she had anything to hide about last Thursday afternoon?

Annie knew the answer. If Jane had crept across Ves's backyard with furniture polish in her hand and murder in her heart, she would have no difficulty presenting an innocent face to the world.

At the end of the corridor, Jane gestured to a blue easy chair for Annie. She put the can of polish and the dustcloth on a table, settled in an upright wooden chair. She crossed one leg over the other, hooked her hands around her knee. "Four to six? Usually it's quiet as a graveyard here from four to five when I close."

"You closed at five Thursday?"

"I stayed a little later. I didn't get away until about ten to six."

There must have been a late customer. This nice girl would have an alibi. Annie was glad. She smiled. "I know how it is. Someone comes in at closing time and they are looking for something and you don't say a word about turning off the lights."

Jane smiled in return. "That happens. But this past Thursday I ducked out in the afternoon. I put up the Back Soon sign. I'm the only one here, but my boss told me at the start if I need to do something, go ahead and just stay open a little later to make up the time. She doesn't live on the island anymore. She moved to Montana. She's trying to sell the store now." Jane looked around. "I like it here. I like seeing the clothes come in. She buys them all over the place. I got a box from Pasadena last week. It's been fun and there's lots of downtime." She gestured at a laptop lying on the table. "I'm taking some classes online until I save enough to go back to school. But Thursday I went to the hospital to visit a friend—well, I think of her as a friend even though she's lots older, but she was so sweet to my mom when she was sick. She came and stayed through some bad days. She doesn't have any family, and I could tell she was kind of blue. She's very nice but very serious."

Annie knew at once. "Pamela Potts?" Annie had been by to see Pamela at the hospital as well. Knee replacement. Pamela, blond, placid, immensely serious, was always the first to bring a casserole or offer to help when trouble struck.

Jane nodded eagerly. "Isn't she swell? I guess most everyone on the island knows Pamela. Anyway I was there longer than I intended so that's why I stayed open late Thursday."

"Did you have any shoppers?"

Jane shook her head. "Nobody came in. I sorted through that box of clothes from Pasadena. I found a gorgeous tulle skirt that needed mending. I wish I had somewhere to wear it. Someone will love it now."

"So you were late getting home."

Jane shrugged. "I got home a little after six."

H enny Brawley followed Emma Clyde's new Rolls-Royce as it turned onto Bayberry Lane, a narrow rutted sandy road. She was perhaps twenty yards behind the crimson Rolls-Royce. Emma's previous Rolls had been bronze. Henny grinned at the contrast between Emma's majestic conveyance and her own shabby old black Dodge. Henny wasn't envious. She enjoyed outings in Emma's chariot, but she knew everything was fleeting. Each moment had a brief life and was gone, never to return. Prized moments were never about riches, not jewels nor silks, not fine cars nor mansions, not stacks of cash nor stock certificates. Prized moments were a look of love, a gentle touch, the sight of a cat's grace, sunlight slanting through a stained glass window. Emma enjoyed her car, but it was a plaything.

Emma's prized moments were the pleasure of crafting a sentence, the joy of creating an illusion that seemed real to her readers. Henny immediately thought of Maureen Summerhayes speaking in *Mrs. McGinty's Dead*: "I never think it matters much *what* one eats . . . or what one wears . . . or what one does. I don't think *things* matter—not really." Maureen Summerhayes would have understood Emma Clyde.

The Rolls glided to a stop in front of a two-story wooden building and parked next to Katherine Farley's gray Lexus. A sign hung above the steps to the piazza: FARLEY STUDIO AND GALLERY.

Henny drove another hundred yards around a grove of pines to a cottage on pilings very similar to her home on a neighboring marsh. She parked on a sandy drive behind a Honda van with a lift on the back for a wheelchair. She noted a similar lift at the top of the steps.

As she shut the door of her Dodge, Henny looked out at the

winter-pale stubble of spartina grass, took a deep breath of the familiar pungent marsh odor. She never tired of the marsh, enjoying the greening grasses in spring, steaming mud flats in summer, migrating birds overhead in autumn, raccoons fishing for clams in winter.

She climbed the stairs to the landing and knocked on a weathered front door.

"Come in." Bob's voice was muffled.

Henny reached for the knob, turned. The door swung in and she stepped inside.

Bob Farley was seated in his wheelchair by the windows overlooking the marsh. He looked at her and there was politeness, but no warmth in his face. He finally managed a cursory smile and seemed to rouse himself. "I haven't seen you in a while. Come in."

Henny had often visited the studio when Bob and Katherine held receptions to display their latest work, his oil paintings of marshes, ocean, beaches, and Low Country wildlife from foraging raccoons to attacking owls, and Katherine's clever pen-and-ink sketches of islanders at work or play. Henny especially treasured two sketches of the *Miss Jolene.* In one, holidayers arrived on the ferry, pale faces eager. In the second, vacationers departed, faces sunburned, noses splotched with zinc oxide, looking back across the water as if trying to hold on to lazy days and wet feet in warm sudsy water and frosty bottles of beer and no thought for tomorrow.

Henny settled on a rattan chair and smiled at Bob, keeping her expression bright and open with no hint of how painful it was to see the gauntness of his face and the immobile arm that had once created such beauty. She hurried to speak. "It's been much too long. Ves Roundtree told me about the safari you're planning to Kenya." She opened her purse, drew out a manila envelope, handed it to Bob. "I wanted to bring you the guidebook from the trip I made last year to Samburu. I hope you can include that reserve in your itinerary.

Absolutely rugged country, but I saw some amazing animals, a herd of Grévy's zebra and more than a dozen Somali ostrich." She chattered on. "Our guide was a Cornell graduate, and he told us the status of endangered animals and especially the need to protect elephants."

Bob pulled out a guidebook, glanced down, made no effort to open it. "A safari. Yes. We've talked about that." His voice was dull. "You're very kind to think of us. I'll show Katherine." The guidebook rested in his lap.

Henny felt as if she pushed against a gate that wouldn't open. "I've been carrying it around ever since last Thursday. I dropped by about five, but you weren't here and Katherine's car was gone, too, so"—a cheerful smile—"I called to be sure you'd be here this morning. I waited a little while Thursday but you didn't come home. What took you out on such a foggy afternoon?"

Bob Farley stared out at the marsh, but Henny knew he wasn't seeing a vee of pelicans or the ripple of the incoming tide. "Thursday." He turned toward her. "I was here Thursday." His expression was remote. "You must have come by Wednesday." He again stared out the windows at the marsh. Sudden deep lines indented his face on either side of his lips. "It was foggy then, too. When the fog hides the marsh, I feel trapped. I got out for a while. I took a drive. Wednesday." He pressed one thin hand against his cheek.

When fog settles on the island, wreathes in the trees like an old woman's straggly gray hair, pools into cottony mounds where roads dip, islanders drive cautiously, if at all.

Henny was casual. "I thought I dropped by Thursday, but perhaps I'm mistaken."

"I was here Thursday." There was the slightest emphasis on *here*.

Henny had a sense that his words meant much more than she

understood. Was his insistence that he was home Thursday an effort to distance himself from Ves's house?

"I don't suppose Katherine was out in the fog either day."

His gaze moved to a photograph of a laughing Katherine on a sunny day, barefoot on the beach, breeze-stirred sea oats behind her. "She hates driving in fog. She hates fog. But she had a delivery Thursday afternoon." A long pause, then he said in a weary tone, "I promised her I'd stay home. So I did."

"The blossoms are always six petaled and a rich cream color." Katherine Farley gestured at a watercolor in the center of one wall. "The flowers bloom from May to July at the top of the stalk. The dagger-shaped leaves at the base have a sharp tip and they really hurt." There was remembered discomfort in her voice. "I was sketching them, my camp stool toppled, and I brushed some spines as I went down. But I love that painting. It was worth the pain."

Emma disliked cold weather. In a puffy quilted beige caftan with occasional chartreuse spots, she resembled a mobile stuffed leopard. That her appearance might amuse some was of no matter to her. She relished comfort and dismissed fashion as irrelevant. She sat with her usual imposing posture in a solid oak Stickley cube chair with a comfortable red leather back and cushion. A number of sketches were spread on a cocktail table in front of her.

Katherine perched on a wooden bench near the table. This morning she was austere in a heather matte knit jersey sweater, blouse, and slacks. With her smooth black hair drawn back in a bun, her chiseled features, and intent expression, she reminded Emma suddenly of a monk in a brown wool robe.

Emma listened to Katherine while she plumbed the vagrant

thought. There was nothing remotely monklike about Katherine. Except, yes, there was an intensity, an almost frightening sense of leashed power focused elsewhere. Although she was making an effort to be charming to a prospective customer, she was jerky in her speech, obviously under some kind of stress.

Emma was brisk. "I'm glad I caught you in the studio today. I dropped by last Thursday around five. I supposed you'd already closed up for the day."

"Thursday? I was making a delivery. I'm sorry I missed you. And glad you came back." Again there was an effort at charm.

"I am, too. Very impressed with your drawings," Emma pointed at a pen-and-ink sketch of a large herring gull, blue-gray wings tipped with white, a white body, a bright yellow beak with a small red dot. Emma knew her seabirds, recognized the herring gull in summer or fall finery, the feather color and red dot beak indicating the season. "I rather fancy a wall of herring gulls. I'd like to commission you to do perhaps a dozen sketches for me. I'd like some of the gulls swimming or cracking clams or nesting. The sooner the better." She spoke with the imperious assurance of a wealthy woman quite willing to pay whatever it might take to achieve her current whim.

Katherine tried to keep her voice even. "A dozen sketches? I'd consider that, though it would require my putting aside some current projects."

Emma placed her square strong hands on the armrests, preparatory to rising. "I don't want to put you behind."

Katherine leaned forward and spoke in a rush. "Oh no, nothing due anytime soon. I'd be delighted to undertake the commission. A dozen sketches?"

Emma nodded. "That's settled, then. Appreciate your cooperation." As she came to her feet, she watched Katherine's taut features relax, saw a tic at the corner of one eye, and knew she was seeing a woman desperate for money, pressed for money, willing to make any accommodation for money. Emma had known hard times. She was rich now. She had not always been rich. She remembered the hollowness when there were bills due and not enough money to pay them. "I understand this may interfere with other projects. Perhaps a thousand dollars a sketch."

Katherine's eyes widened. "A thousand . . ." Twelve thousand dollars.

Emma was gruff. "This means quite a bit to me." If everything worked out and she wasn't talking to a future felon, she would enjoy the herring gull sketches in her terrace room, and she would be glad she'd been able to stave off the dogs of poverty nipping at Katherine for a while.

Emma scooped up her oversized puffy cloth purse, a matching blue with tan spots, fumbled past a notebook, several pens, a cellophane bag of salt water taffy in assorted flavors, an iPad, an iPhone, three copies of her latest Marigold paperback, a change purse and billfold, an island map, an Amtrak schedule, a menu from Paula Deen's restaurant in Savannah, this morning's *Wall Street Journal*, pulled out her checkbook. "Be glad to pay half in advance." She patted a zippered compartment that held a fifty-dollar gold piece now worth $1,500, her nose-thumb to the days when she'd had coffee for breakfast, a candy bar for lunch, and a Big Mac for dinner, when her change stretched that far.

Max skirted his silver Lamborghini, walked to their new runabout, a beige VW that he considered hardy enough for any island road. Its compact size avoided low-hanging branches and spiky underbrush. The car was a recent purchase, an unspoken statement to Annie that Confidential Commissions, his somewhat ambiguous business, would continue.

Not long ago, he'd announced NO MORE: No More trying to solve mysteries, No More danger for Annie. Annie promised to stay out of other people's troubles, but when a close friend was embroiled in a murder, Annie put her promise on hold. That's when he understood that Annie had to be Annie, and he loved her because she cared about him, cared about others, cared about justice and honor and decency. So Confidential Commissions began a new chapter, and he bought the VW knowing there might be times when he wanted to drive about the island without attracting notice. He liked people, was good at finding out information. He understood the logic of checking out everyone who would profit when Ves died, but independent testimony would be definitive. If he found a nosy neighbor who saw one of the dinner guests on Sunshine Lane last Thursday around five P.M., they would have their answer. As he drove, he enjoyed a triumphant moment imagining how he would reveal the perp's identity to Annie and the Incredible Trio and, at their exclamations of amazement, smugly say finding out was just a matter of legwork, good old-fashioned sleuthing.

He drove past the entrance to Sea Side Inn. He reached the main road that looped around the entire island, and turned left, heading for the older residential area where antebellum homes were interspersed with cottages, an occasional doublewide on blocks, and a few modern ranch-style houses.

Since he and Annie had moved to their antebellum house on Bay Road, he'd become familiar with this end of the island. Sunshine Lane intersected Federal near Morgan Manor, one of the island's loveliest old homes, a three-story gray-green tabby home that sat far back on a lot behind several majestic live oaks and huge weeping willows. The house was almost always in shadow. One massive live oak was known as the Hanging Tree. A daughter of the house, learning of her lover's death at the Battle of Honey Hill, took the veil especially made for their planned wedding and hung herself from a high limb.

Max was glad to swing past the house onto Sunshine Lane, leaving behind the looming mansion and long-ago grief. Sunshine Lane was a gravel road. Loblolly pines crowded close on either side. The shadows from the trees belied the name. Every thirty or forty yards white signposts carried house numbers. Ves's address was 207. No houses were visible from the road. Instead, narrow drives plunged into deep woods.

There would be no nosy neighbors to ask if they'd seen anyone near Ves's drive. An Oscar Mayer Wienermobile in all its orange-and-yellow glory could have wallowed up and down Sunshine Lane and never been noticed. No structures were visible from the lane because of the towering pines.

Max reached the end of Sunshine Lane, made a U-turn. Ves's drive mirrored the lane, a narrow road with pines pushing close on either side. He drove slowly, followed a curve into a clearing. He knew from his gardening mother that Ves had used native grasses for the lawn. A single-lane cement drive ended at a separate frame garage. Any car in the drive would be instantly visible to Ves when she arrived home. Max parked and walked around the garage. A neat vegetable garden ran from behind the garage to the woods. No one could have parked there.

Max frowned and returned to the drive, studied the back of the house. The backyard was huge but offered no hiding places for a car. But someone entered the house, applied a slick substance to a step. The intruder had either arrived on foot—very unlikely—in a car, or on a bike. Max walked past the garage. He stopped next to a stand of bamboo and surveyed the yard. He had a good sense of geography. In good weather, he and Annie often took their old-fashioned bikes out for a ride, sometimes following a path down to the sea, sometimes to the marsh, sometimes winding behind homes. He walked swiftly across the back-yard, plunged into the woods, found an asphalt trail about twenty yards from Ves's property line. He remembered this trail. It connected with several paths, making Ves's house easily accessible to anyone with a bike.

He returned to the backyard. A bike would work, but if he planned to arrange a fatal accident for anyone, he thought he'd want to have a car handy for a quick departure. He passed a fountain, noted Diana with a bow and broken arrow, climbed Ves's back steps. He knocked.

No answer.

Ves wasn't home yet. He checked his watch, pulled a ring of keys from one pocket. The fourth key unlocked the back door. He stepped inside, felt an odd sensation knowing he was repeating the actions of Ves's attacker. He walked to the front of the hall, turned to look up the steep stairs. The ticktock of the grandfather clock seemed loud. Max pulled a small laser flashlight from a pocket. He aimed the beam at the worn wooden treads, climbed swiftly. He slowed near the top. The fourth step looked unnaturally clean. He knelt, pantomimed pouring something onto the step, pretended to cap a can or canister, rose, and went down the stairs and outside, locking the door. He strode across the yard to a stand of bamboo that offered a good vantage point to watch for Ves's arrival and be unobserved. He stopped by the bamboo, looked at his watch. Not quite four minutes.

Max folded his arms. The unknown visitor waited for Ves to come home, waited to see what happened. If she hadn't broken her fall, if all had been quiet, the waiting figure would have cautiously eased into the house. If Ves had been lying dead at the foot of the stairs, the mission was a success. If she were injured, unable to move, there would likely have been another blow to her head, one that would appear consistent with a fall.

Instead, Ves limped outside, made it to her car.

The would-be murderer wanted her death to appear accidental, so Ves was allowed to drive away. Then a hurried return to the house to clean the step. Likely the cleanup, while thorough, was done in haste just in case Ves called the police on her cell.

Max frowned as he walked back to the VW. Instead of a triumphant revelation of the attacker's identity, he had paltry bits of information. The house was accessible on a bike. If the attacker drove a car, it must have been hidden somewhere. There were no shoulders on Sunshine Lane, pines thick on either side right up to the graveled road. He was almost to the entrance to Sunshine Lane when he jammed on the brakes, rolled down the window, and backed up a few feet. He stared at a broken frond of a resurrection fern. His gaze dropped. In an instant, the engine was off and he slammed the driver's door shut. Ruts. The indentations were faint but there were definite ruts. There had once been a road here. Traces of it angled past ferns and a bayberry bush. He pushed past the ferns and plunged into gloom. He walked ten feet, twenty, and felt a sense of success. Crushed vegetation indicated a car had come this way, likely stopped where he was standing.

Max was thoughtful as he walked back to the VW. He should have remembered there were many homes on the island where people could come and go and never be noticed. Finding out who wanted Ves dead was not going to be easy. Max checked his time. A quarter to ten. He slid a rarely used prepaid cell from his pocket. He didn't use his regular cell, to avoid being identified on caller ID. The prepaid cell revealed only the caller's number, and that was fine. He dialed.

"Perfumerie. Gretchen speaking. How may I help you?"

Max enjoyed occasional roles in the island's summer theater. He affected a breezy, good ol' boy ebullience. "Goofy Sullivan, pal of Curt's. Here for a spot of golf and somebody gave me a heads-up, said Curt might be here. Like to look him up." He listened. "Thanks a bunch."

5

The sweet scent of gardenia mixed with a hint of ginger pleased Laurel as she stepped inside the elegant small shop on Main Street. Three mirrored kiosks with cushioned stools were arranged in a semiprivate curve to the right. To the left and ahead were counters filled with every variety of cosmetic, probably including the bright green malachite paste used as eye shadow by Cleopatra. A verse from Ecclesiastes was a favorite of Laurel's: "What has been will be again, what has been done will be done again; there is nothing new under the sun." Some might find the message chilling. Laurel in her own mystical way felt part of a continuum of time. Besides, beautiful women owed a duty to themselves to always appear at their best.

Gretchen Roundtree in a becoming pastel blue smock came eagerly around the back counter. "Laurel, I've been thinking about you. We just received the newest Crème de la Mer moisturizing cream." Her smile looked almost genuine.

Laurel chided herself. That beaming smile was likely genuine. A commission on several jars of Crème de la Mer would be a tidy sum for a February sales day.

With murmurs that reminded Laurel of starlings in a cluster, they exchanged pleasantries of the feminine sort—*How lovely you look today. Such a pleasure to see you.*—as Laurel settled on a cushioned stool. While Laurel studied her reflection in the three-way mirror, Gretchen brought a tray with several small jars and tubes, and perched on the next stool. Gretchen gently removed Laurel's makeup. "I have a new ointment you will simply adore, perfect for your flawless complexion."

Laurel selected three lotions, two ointments, and a delicate mauve shade of eye shadow. At the checkout counter, Gretchen swiped the items, rang up the sale. She was so perfectly the well-bred society woman fallen on hard times in a job requiring finesse and charm. The lines near her eyes and lips were a little deeper than when they'd last met. She'd smoothly but determinedly plied Laurel with every possible high-end product. Was Gretchen desperate enough for money to slip through the fog to her ex-sister-in-law's home with murder in mind?

Gretchen looked up and their gazes met.

Before the automatic smile transformed Gretchen's expression, Laurel sensed a crackle of anger and desperation.

Laurel picked up the shopping bag with her purchases. "I'm glad you were here today, Gretchen." A slightly reproachful laugh. "I was soooo disappointed when I came by last Thursday around five and you weren't here. The hours say ten to noon, two to six."

"Thursday." Gretchen's face was utterly still, her blue eyes watchful. "That must have been the afternoon I delivered some purchases to the inn." Her tone was careless, as if it didn't matter.

Laurel remembered, from the last presidential campaign, clips of a politician speaking followed by clips of a dog barking, presumably in response to lies. She smiled at Gretchen. "Do you hear a dog barking?"

Gretchen's eyes were blank. "I don't believe so."

Laurel smiled. "It must just be me. I was sure I heard a dog barking." As she drifted to the door, she mused about the possibilities. Dogs can detect cancer, find the lost, protect the weak, rescue the drowning. Perhaps there was yet a new frontier. Which breed was most likely to detect insincerity, a cardinal sin to dogs? A basset hound? A cocker spaniel? A Labrador retriever?

Laurel smiled as she started her car. Henny had a new dog with a pointed nose, a low-slung body, and a ferocious guttural bark. Cinnamon was an odd mixture of a basset hound and a German shepherd. If only she could be trained to bark at lies.

The island bank was small with a tiny lobby and two tellers. It boasted a marble floor, however, and the bank president's office, behind an oak door to Annie's left, was large and sumptuous. She stood in the center of the lobby on one side of a circular glass counter that held an assortment of slips to make deposits or withdrawals. She wondered what had compelled a half dozen islanders to arrive at the bank promptly at ten A.M. She continued her charade of adding and re-adding figures until there was no line.

Fred looked a bit dazed. She'd overheard several conversations, including a brusque customer who demanded to know why he couldn't get all the cash right now, this was a check from a reputable company, what did he mean it would have to clear, that was a crock, and if there was another bank on the island he'd be the first to sign up, and that's what happened when people had a monopoly.

Annie's tone was commiserating. "Hi, Fred. Always fun to deal with the GP, right?"

He looked frazzled, his tufting hair exaggerated by several frenzied swipes. He poked his bifocals higher on his plump nose and made an effort to smile. "Nice to see you, Annie." He glanced at the checks on the counter. His taut shoulders eased and he took a deep breath. "Got some deposits today."

Annie usually used the bank drive-through. She banked the old-fashioned way. As far as she was concerned, taking a picture of checks and clicking to deposit was an open invitation to a hacker, even though Max insisted mysteries had made her paranoid and she needed to join the electronic world. She insisted she wasn't paranoid, simply careful, and she'd bank electronically when hacking no longer occurred. "All deposits."

Fred turned to his computer. His plump fingers tapped without hesitation.

"I missed seeing you when I was here Thursday afternoon."

She was watching closely and didn't miss the fraction of a second when he stiffened.

"Uh, no."

"Where were you?" Bright, friendly.

A door opened behind him. Quick footsteps sounded. She nodded hello to big, red-faced Martin Ford, the trust officer, lifted her voice just a little. "Yes, I missed you Thursday afternoon. Were you on a holiday?"

Martin stopped behind Fred, gave him a poke in one shoulder. "I'd guess Fred would prefer a holiday. Unless he thinks the dentist is a barrel of fun." Martin gave a deep-throated laugh that sounded like an elephant's trumpet before he swung away to push through a gate into the lobby. He was still laughing as the front door closed behind him.

"Bless your heart." Annie leaned on the ledge. "Who's your dentist, Fred?"

Fred hooked a finger over his collar, tugged. "Nobody on the island. A dental surgeon in Chastain."

Annie was eager. "Someone asked me just the other day if I knew of a dental surgeon. What's his name?"

Fred's voice was thin. "Charles Garcia." He handed her the deposit slip.

On the sidewalk outside the bank, Annie turned to her left, walked briskly past several shops and an old modest hotel with clientele that returned year after year. The wind picked up as she stepped onto the boardwalk. Whitecaps rippled across the harbor. The berth for the ferry was empty, the *Miss Jolene* likely just now reaching the mainland.

Annie reached her goal, a worn phone booth, one of the last public pay phones on the island. Annie pulled, and the door grudgingly opened far enough for her to slide inside. Her nose wrinkled at a sour smell and her right shoe stepped on something sticky. She used her cell to get the number of the office of Charles Garcia, DDS, in Chastain, scrambled for change, dialed, fed the coin slot.

"Dr. Garcia's office. This is Chrissy. How may I help you?" The voice was young and pleasant.

"Hello. Chrissy. This is Agnes Morrison for Cadillac Dental Pan. I'm simply calling to confirm the appointment last Thursday afternoon for Dr. Garcia's patient Fred Butler."

"Hold on."

Annie pictured pinafores as she listened to a sprightly violin rendition of "Hi-Lili, Hi-Lo."

The young voice returned. "Excuse me. What was the patient's name?"

"Fred Butler."

The violin music resumed. Annie hummed along. She didn't mind admitting she loved a great many unsophisticated things, including fried chicken, Edgar Guest, Thorne Smith's Topper books, six-foot-tall sunflowers, week-old kittens, and old June Allyson movies. She sang a verse, broke off when the music was interrupted.

"There appears to be some mistake. Dr. Garcia doesn't have a patient named Fred Butl—"

Annie interrupted with a quick laugh. "I'm in error. I meant to dial the number on the line above. Sorry to have bothered you." She depressed the cradle.

She took a deep breath of the sea-scented air when she stood on the boardwalk, scraped her right shoe bottom on a board. Still sticky. She moved to the sandy border of the walk, swiped her shoe back and forth. Better. She turned to stride back to the bank, ready to confront Fred Butler, ask what he was doing Thursday afternoon since he wasn't at the dentist's office as he claimed. She jolted to a stop. She and Max and the Incredible Trio were trying to garner information without alerting a Prospective Murderer. Fred was safe for the moment.

Henny Brawley looked at Ben Parotti and gestured at the front door. "Here comes Marian. What's her favorite breakfast?" Marian Kenyon, the *Gazette*'s star reporter, was moving fast, her leather shoulder bag banging against one hip.

Ben didn't hesitate. "French toast with whipped cream and caramel syrup, sausage patties, and a side bowl of sliced bananas. Black coffee."

Henny laughed. "And she's skinny enough to fit into a straw. Bring it on. The sliced bananas sound good with some whipped cream."

She'd enjoyed her usual bacon and eggs at shortly after six and watched dawn send fingers of light across the dark marsh. "Coffee black."

Ben didn't bother to write down the order. He waited until Marian plopped into the seat opposite Henny. His smile was fond. "You newlyweds behaving yourselves?"

Marian's narrow face came alight. "We wouldn't dare do otherwise. Those joined in matrimony by Captain Ben Parotti know it would be the brig if we transgressed." She reached up a thin hand, squeezed Ben's wrist. "Oh, Ben—"

He spoke hastily to head off an emotional moment. "I hear Craig's the new City editor."

Diverted, Marian's grin was supercharged. "He started this week. Walt said he'd sweated through his last July here. He's retired to Colorado Springs to write a bodice ripper but I told him those went out with panty hose. Craig's loving the city desk."

"Hope he knows the island's pretty sleepy. Not a lot of news."

Marian shook her head like a terrier with a rag doll. "Not so. There's always news."

As Ben started to turn away, Marian looked surprised.

Henny laughed. "He already has the order. I asked him what you like. I know you're always hungry even though it's midmorning. Consider it a bribe."

"Bribe?" Marian leaned her elbows on the table, dark eyes bright. "What's up?"

Henny picked her words carefully. Marian was smart, quick, always alert for a scoop. "You know more about everybody on the island than anybody but Father Morris, and what he knows never leaves the confessional."

Marian's bony face was intent. "I'm listening."

"I'm looking for gossip, fact, surmise, or questions about several islanders."

"What's in it for me?" Marian had her quid pro quo look.

Henny was grave. "I won't have anything to—"

Ben arrived with a tray, placed a plate before Marian, a bowl and small pitcher of cream before Henny. Steaming mugs for both of them.

"—share with you if your information helps solve a problem. Least said, the better at that point. If things go horribly wrong, I'll tell you everything I know."

Marian dabbed a chunk of French toast in caramel syrup. "Sounds like I get the story if there is a story. Okay. Run the names by me." She spoke with her mouth full. She cut another portion of French toast with the edge of her fork, used her left hand to tug a laptop out of her purse. She set the laptop up to the left of her plate.

"Katherine and Bob Farley."

Marian ignored her laptop. "You consider yourself a friend of theirs?"

Henny was startled. Ves Roundtree's safety was her objective, the objective of Laurel and Emma and Annie and Max. The Farleys? She liked them. If neither had attempted murder, she wished them well. She said the words aloud. "I wish them well." With an unspoken caveat.

"So maybe"—Marian added another splash of caramel syrup—"you're worried about them. I hear a lot of things I never repeat. If someone has a problem according to island know-it-alls, I file it away under Rumors." She pointed her fork at the laptop. "There's nothing but good stuff in the *Gazette* files about Katherine and Bob. But an unnamed source told me Katherine and Bob are broke on their ass and the bank is about to call some loans due." Marian's face scrunched in thought. "I understand people have problems. I've been there.

Maybe it's money. Maybe it's his bunged-up body, but something's wrong big-time with Bob. Somebody I know, a bird-watching nut, was out near Gurney Point Wednesday afternoon."

Henny knew the remote area on the northern tip of the island. Swirling, tricky currents raced against a reddish clay bluff, eroding a foot a year, making the water murky, making a maelstrom at high tide.

Marian looked wry. "The bird-watcher spotted a peregrine falcon and was ecstatic, and here came Hyla Harrison on her yellow scooter."

Police Officer Hyla Harrison was a familiar sight to islanders on her bright yellow scooter.

"My guy was scarcely breathing. And, of course, the put-put of the scooter spooked the falcon. My guy was ready to storm out of his spot behind a pine to ream out Hyla, then he got interested. She rolled the scooter behind a bayberry bush and went up the trail, disappeared in the fog. Then he thought maybe he better stay where he was, maybe she was after someone and something criminal was going on. About this time an SUV pulls around a bend, parks at the foot of the trail. Bob Farley, my guy knows him, got out and somehow, hard to imagine doing it with bum legs and a cane, Bob labors up the trail. My friend said he looked like a crooked scarecrow in the fog, was hardly visible. My friend had binoculars, but the fog got thicker and he couldn't see either Bob or Hyla. A few minutes passed and Bob came hobbling down the trail. Hyla was behind him. He climbed in the SUV, drove away. Hyla got her scooter and left." Marian lifted bony shoulders, let them fall. "Maybe he was out there to look at the water. Not that he could probably see much in the fog. On a clear day you can see the water foam when it hits the rocks, hear it gurgle and suck." Marian speared a piece of banana, dipped it in whipped cream. "Hyla waited until he'd driven away before she left."

Henny felt as if she stood on the bluff and fog swirled around her.

Now she knew where Bob Farley was on Wednesday afternoon. She remembered his bleak expression when he told her he'd promised Katherine he'd stay home Thursday. She'd sensed darkness and now she understood. He claimed he'd stayed home on Thursday. Perhaps that was true.

Marian took a big swallow of coffee. "Who else is on your prom list?"

"Jane Wilson."

Marian looked blank. "Don't know the name." She turned to the laptop, tapped, clicked several times. "Only *Gazette* mention is in the obituary of her mother. I knew her mother. She quilted, won some prizes at the fair."

"Tim Holt."

Marian muttered to herself as she checked. "Rings a bell. Yeah, here it is, arrested in a big melee during a summer beer bust two years ago, no charges filed. Last summer swam out despite shark sighting to rescue a teenager caught in an undertow." Another click. "Good-looking dude. A shot of the lifeguards at the start of the season."

"Adam Nash."

Marian's expression was sardonic. "Best friend to rich old ladies. I'd sooner trust a barracuda. Something about his eyes. Kind of a dull green. They remind me of pond scum. Before Craig and I got back together, I used to go out to the Country Place."

Henny knew about the old plantation house with a roulette wheel, slots, and poker.

"Adam was a regular. He gambled big-time. That's the only thing I know about him that doesn't fit his civic leader profile. So far as I know, he's never landed in any trouble, and I'd know."

"Fred Butler."

Marian rolled her eyes. "Fred reminds me of wilted lettuce. But"—she brightened—"he gets interesting if you ask about Black Jack MacDougal. Fred has a man crush on pirates. Ginger—"

Henny often played bridge with the *Gazette* Lifestyle editor, whose Southern charm masked the instinct of a piranha when she was on a story.

"—did a feature on him about hidden gold on the island. She said he's a little unhinged on the topic. She was kind enough not to point out that pirate maps are an industry and so far as she knows nobody's ever found any buried gold. Otherwise, Fred's a fussy old maid, no wine, no women, no song."

"Curt Roundtree."

"Rufus Roundtree's son?"

Henny nodded.

Marian shrugged. "Never made any waves on the island."

"Gretchen Roundtree."

Marian considered another bite of French toast, regretfully shook her head, put her fork and knife on the plate. "Funny you should ask. This is pure speculation, but I learned about an interesting coincidence. I e-mail with an old friend who works on a Phoenix paper. She said there was a rash of jewel robberies last spring. Rich ladies went beddy-bye, and when they woke up the next morning, jewelry was gone from the boudoir. There were house guests. Turns out Gretchen was in the houses when several robberies occurred. Or had recently been a guest. No one's been arrested. The last robbery was in late April. My friend wanted to know what I could find about Gretchen. I did some checking. Gretchen came back to the island May fourteenth. Also interesting to note, no more jewel thefts have occurred there. But"—a Gallic shrug—"Gretchen has been working in a makeup bar so she's either the world's most cautious thief, frugal with the proceeds, or she's innocent." Marian picked up her coffee mug. "I have to hand it to you. I thought for sure I'd see a connection when I heard all the names. Not so. Are we playing a new version of that brain teaser where you're supposed to spot a common denominator?"

Emma Clyde's sharp blue eyes noted scuff marks on the floor of the poorly lit corridor. Adam Nash's office door needed screws tightened in the upper hasp to right a tilt. She touched the knob, pulled her hand back. She burrowed in her purse for a package of wet wipes, cleaned the knob. She found a Kleenex, wrapped the wipe in a ball.

Opening the door, she stepped inside. No one sat at a receptionist's desk. Emma strode forward, spotted a wastebasket, tossed her trash. Two unoccupied easy chairs sat on either side of a coffee table. She looked past the chairs at a door with a frosted glass panel.

She knocked twice on the door, turned the knob.

Adam Nash looked up with a frown. He was in his shirtsleeves. Interesting. She'd not imagined he wore suspenders. As always, he appeared immaculate. It was surprising he tolerated the slovenliness of a building that needed a better effort from the cleaning crew. Perhaps he was in arrears on his rent and in no position to make demands.

Adam's frown was replaced with an ingratiating smile. He came to his feet. "Emma, it's wonderful to see you. You're looking splendid."

"Glad I found you in." She charged to an apple red chair in front of his desk and plopped down. "The financial news out of China continues to be worrying."

He immediately was judicious, ponderous. "Have to keep a sharp eye on commodities. In times like these, it's good to seek a safe harbor . . ."

Emma listened as he extolled several financial havens he highly recommended, all of which would pay handsome commissions to him. Emma was not a woolly minded writer when it came to investments. She could talk currencies, dividends, and mutual funds with ease, but she kept her gaze wide and admiring. "Oh my, it's all so complicated."

He was instantly reassuring. "You have come to the right place, Emma. I'll be glad to take charge of your portfolio—"

She watched his eyes, saw the eager, hopeful, desperate glint. Pond scum accented by avarice.

"Well"—she tried to sound anxious, not a usual tone for her—"I just haven't made up my mind what to do. I'm talking to several people." She rose. "I'll need a financial statement. Just to be sure your firm is in good order. I know you won't mind sending it. After all"— an arch smile—"if you are to know all about my finances, it seems fair enough for me to know about yours."

Adam pushed back his chair, came to his feet. His face was no longer alight. "That's not customary."

She gave a bark of laughter. "I think you know I don't give a rip about customary. But it's up to you. Send me your financial statement. Or don't." She paused at the door, appraised him with cold blue eyes. "I believe in people keeping office hours. I do when I'm working on a book. You weren't here the day I came by. I decided to give you another chance. But I don't understand why your office was closed a little before five on Thursday."

"Thursday? If you knocked—"

Emma was brusque. "Turned the knob. Door was locked."

"I was here." His voice was flat. "I was working on some figures, didn't want to be disturbed."

◆ ◆ ◆

Max knew a dozen ways in and out of the Sea Side Inn. He parked in the west lot, strolled to the terrace. On a chilly February morning the umbrellas were furled at the tables around the pool. One hardy swimmer stroked methodically. Max used the back entrance. He didn't need to check the note in his pocket. Gretchen hadn't hesitated to give good old Goofy her son's room number. Interesting that he wasn't staying with his mother.

Max walked up to the second floor, stopped at room 227. He held a clipboard in his left hand. knocked with his right. He assumed a pleasant, slightly vacuous expression. He'd taken pains with his choice of clothing, a navy polo that was slightly worn, chinos, loafers.

The door opened. "Put it—" Curt Roundtree's freckled face looked annoyed. "You're not room service."

"Sir, I'm canvassing—"

"Good for you." The door slammed shut.

Henny pulled into the oyster-shell lot north of the police station. She spotted Hyla's yellow scooter parked neatly next to a rack that held several bikes. The island was small enough that it was easy to commute to work in fair weather on a bike. Henny sat with her hands resting lightly on the steering wheel, the driver's window rolled down. She knew and respected Officer Hyla Harrison, who had joined the force a few years ago, seeking a new place, a new life. She'd been an officer in Miami and seen her partner shot and killed. Hyla was reserved, retiring, intelligent. She would never divulge information about an investigation.

But, as Henny had learned long ago in teaching, there are many different paths to the same goal.

Hyla came swinging around a palm tree on the oyster-shell path to the parking lot, slender, trim, moving with a purpose.

Henny opened her door, slammed it shut, turned to the path, her face transforming into recognition. "Hyla." Henny hurried toward her. "I'm glad to see you. I was going to drop by this morning and say hello after I talked to Mavis." Mavis Cameron was Police Chief Billy Cameron's wife as well as a dispatcher and a crime scene tech. Henny patted her purse. "I'm hoping to recruit Mavis to help serve chili at the Friends of the Library supper. Can I can count on you as well?"

Hyla stopped, her freckled face pleasant. As always she was immaculate in a crisp uniform. "Chili supper?"

Henny gave her a brilliant smile. "Two weeks from Tuesday at the library. Two bucks a bowl, corn bread and iced tea free. Can you help? We need servers there at five thirty, doors open at six. Runs to eight o'clock."

Hyla pulled a small notebook from a back pocket, flipped it open. "Will do."

"Wonderful. Free chili for the volunteers. And"—Henny reached out, touched Hyla's sleeve—"on another matter entirely, I like Katherine and Bob Farley. You went above and beyond the call of duty to let Katherine know. I want to thank you."

Hyla's fair cheeks turned pink. "Nothing special for me. Part of the job. Knew it was a near thing. Have to alert a family member."

"Katherine's been worried about him. Their good fortune you took action."

Hyla's narrow face was grave. "I was on my way home and I came up beside his van. I looked up. I saw his face. I saw trouble. Funny thing, when I was in Miami I had a friend in the K9 unit. Her dog always knew when somebody was going to die. That's how I felt. I lagged back, followed him. He wasn't looking in his rearview mirror. I guess he was thinking a lot of things but not about the road behind him. Pretty soon I figured out where he was heading. I went off trail. I got to the point and hid my scooter. I hiked up the trail, waited there in the fog. If he didn't come, well, I was just going to be late getting home, no big deal. But he came. When he got close to the edge, I started talking to him, slow and easy."

Ves Roundtree stood near the mantel, her left hand tight on the ivory head of her cane. Her reddish hair was subdued into a chignon, which emphasized the dark splotches beneath her eyes, the pallor of her fair skin. She had the aura of a woman who'd suffered either a debilitating illness or a psychic shock. She pressed her lips together.

Annie felt sure that in its long history the old house had no doubt witnessed joy and sorrow, but this might be the first time murder was the focus of those gathered.

Emma Clyde, imposing in a maroon velvet caftan, occupied most of the Chippendale sofa. Emma's blunt chin jutted. She was in her combative mode. Laurel Darling Roethke, ethereal in a pale blue dress, perched lightly at one end of the sofa. Her dark blue eyes were concerned. Henny Brawley sat with her usual erect posture in a straight chair near the fireplace. Always intuitive, Henny looked uneasy.

Annie sat stiffly next to Max on the brocaded love seat. She had a sense of something momentous about to happen, like a jagged bolt of lightning when the sky hangs purplish and heavy before a summer storm.

Ves had listened without comment as each of them spoke, her thin face taut and intent. Abruptly, her lips curved in a wry smile. "Clever devils, all of you. If I'd tried to ask each of them where they were at five on Thursday, I'd have asked straight out. Instead, none of them have any idea I'm aware. I suppose my murderer thinks I was so shaken by the fall, I didn't question why I fell. It would have been nice if I could drop a name from the list. I'm inclined to drop Bob Farley. Climbing the stairs to fix a trap and climbing them again to remove any evidence would require a huge effort. But the rest of them"– she ticked them off one by one—"are fair game. Katherine needed money before Bob went to Gurney Point. Now she must be desperate. Fred Butler didn't go to the dentist. Something was important enough to him that he lied to his supervisor. He has a nine-to-five job. If he wanted to get to my house before I got home, he had to get off work. Jane Wilson says she stayed late at work. Was it simply a coincidence her late day was Thursday? Her boyfriend claims he was at her house."

Laurel was pleasant but definite. "It sounded at the time as if she was there, too."

Ves nodded. "To be fair, maybe he didn't intend to imply Jane was there, maybe he has a key. He told you where he was and didn't think her late arrival mattered. He's obsessed with his plan for a shopping center. If he's counting on Jane's inheritance, he must feel very certain she'll marry him. He's a possibility." Ves massaged one cheekbone. "I wish I had a fortune wheel and I could give it a spin and it would stop at the most likely. The arrow might point to Gretchen. She has a substantial monthly income from her divorce settlement. She's always been a big spender, loved going to high-society places, Martha's Vineyard, Scottsdale, Rancho Mirage. When she came back to the island, ended up working at the cosmetics shop, I thought maybe she was trying to set a good example for Curt. But now it looks like she's in big trouble. No wonder she wants money. It looks like she pilfered one time too many, got caught in the act, and came up against somebody as ruthless and greedy as she is. She must be paying big-time blackmail. If she's cut Curt off, that makes two of them that would enjoy my obituary." She glanced at Emma. "I'll be interested if you get a financial statement from Adam. If you do, you can bet it's fake."

"I was quite effective as a possible client." Emma was amused. "In any event, he didn't learn the purpose of my visit. The criminal has no inkling an investigation is underway. I employed a technique I've utilized in many books. As Marigold is quick to say: *Casual conversation has been the undoing of many.*"

Annie was incensed. Emma's authorial ego apparently knew no bounds, but this wasn't the time or place to indulge her. Annie leaned forward. "I think—"

Henny gave Annie a warning glance. "I agree with Annie. We can't do better than to call on Emma for guidance. We are fortunate Emma is sharing with us one of the entries in *Detecting Wisdom.*"

Annie was unimpressed. What did Emma mean? Did she have any idea what she meant? Undoing of whom?

Emma basked in Henny's admiration. "Precisely." Emma nodded approvingly at Henny. "As I reported, either Katherine Farley or Adam Nash could have been here Thursday afternoon. I can't prove it either way. But I can tell you that Katherine Farley is a shaken woman. She looked eons older than when I saw her at the market last week. Eons. Moreover, her conversation was disjointed. She scarcely seemed to pay attention to what I said, though she obviously is desperate to make some sales. Katherine Farley deserves serious consideration." A decisive nod as she scooped up cashews from a pottery bowl.

Ves had insisted on iced tea or sherry for the ladies, a beer for

Max, and had placed bowls on side tables with cashews, walnuts, and spiced pecans.

Ves picked up a glass of sherry with her left hand, lifted it in a toast. *"Quod ad summam illam."*

Annie looked at Max. She depended upon him for Latin translations.

He murmured, "That's the sum of it."

Ves sounded reflective. "One of my father's favorite lamentations when everything's gone to hell. He always said it mournfully when the Dodgers lost. We're talking the Brooklyn Dodgers, and they seemed to love to lose. Dad would murmur, *'Quod ad summam illam.'* That's how I feel, like an old Dodgers fan. You've all gone to bat for me, but we haven't scored a run." Her voice was brittle. "Nobody has an alibi for five o'clock Thursday afternoon. Everybody needs money, even Jane Wilson. She hated asking me, was backing toward the door the whole time, but that young man has her under his thumb." A cold smile. "He doesn't mind asking. He was still pleasant after I said no, I'll give him that. Which means my future—if I have one—is up to me. Someone who ate at my table wants me dead, tried to kill me, slipped away in the fog. So, what am I going to do about it?"

Max was firm. "Go to the police. You should have made a report Thursday."

Ves arched a sardonic brow. "Billy Cameron's a good guy. He'd listen. He'd come out, look at the step, maybe bring a crime tech, check for traces of wax or polish. What if they find it? What's he going to do? Arrest everybody on the island who has some floor wax or furniture polish?" She laughed without humor. "I don't believe in wasting time. His or mine. I've got some ideas. I'm not done. But I want to thank all of you." Her tone softened. "You are my friends. You've tried, done your best. Now it's up to me to spin the wheel. Is it Katherine or Bob Farley, Jane Wilson, her boyfriend, Adam Nash, Fred Butler, Gretchen Roundtree, Rufus's son? I will find out which one came. I will survive."

Again she lifted her glass, her gaze intense, her hand steady. She had the air of a soldier before battle, hearing the far off rattle of guns. *"Audentes fortuna juvat."*

As the Lamborghini leapt forward, Annie turned toward Max. He spoke before she asked. "Fortune favors the bold."

The car plunged deeper into the shadows beneath interlocking tree limbs. Annie stared into the night. "What is Ves going to do?"

6

Annie sketched three chapbook covers, shooting stars for Laurel's *Merry Musings*, a mélange of famous titles like spokes around a wheel for Henny's *Classic Crimes*, and a huge magnifying glass for Emma's *Detecting Wisdom*. This was going to be fun. Each chapbook would be distinctive: pale blue background for Laurel, simulated parchment for Henny, a police blotter format for Emma.

There was silence in Death on Demand except for the rustle of paper and Agatha's purr when Annie paused to stroke her sleek back. Annie enjoyed quiet mornings at the store, though she knew she should be unpacking new books, *Midnight Sun* by Jo Nesbø and *Breakdown* by Jonathan Kellerman. Instead of being relaxed and content, she felt uneasy. Every so often her gaze returned to the first entry in *Detecting Wisdom*: *A scared rat has sharp fangs.*

Maybe she should go see Ves, warn her . . . That was the problem, wasn't it? Ves knew she was in danger. Annie didn't have any bright ideas on what Ves should do.

The front doorbell rang. "Hey, Annie."

She heard Max's voice with delight, came to her feet. Maybe he had thought of something. Somehow she felt sure his morning, too, had been preoccupied with concern for Ves. She met him halfway up the center aisle, gave him a hug. "You know what to do."

He looked startled. "Did Ves call you?"

She had the feeling they weren't communicating. "Call?"

Max hunched his shoulders. "She called the future heirs, plus Gretchen and Jane's boyfriend, said she had an announcement about Rufus's will and to be there at eight o'clock, hung up. I'm supposed to get there a few minutes early."

Annie was eager. "I guess she'll call all of us. That way we can speak up if anyone tries to change their story about Thursday afternoon."

Max looked uncomfortable, stared at a poster for the new Alpine mystery by Mary Daheim, muttered, "I don't think so." He cleared his throat, talked fast. "She wants me to stand next to her, look menacing. She said there's nothing menacing about you or Laurel or Henny or Emma. If she included all of you, the gathering would seem like a party. She said a good time wasn't on her agenda."

A nnie pointed at the yellow walkie-talkie, which looked out of place on the coffee table in their den. "It's set on receive."

Max promised to put the other one in a good spot in Ves's living room. "I wanted to use my cell phone on speaker, but I found the walkie-talkies we take when we camp. The sound should be a lot clearer."

Laurel's smile was approving. "Max thinks of everything."

In the interests of maintaining a cordial relationship with her mother-in-law, Annie did not inform Laurel that her pink cashmere top made her look like a birthday cake and that it was Annie who dug the walkie-talkies out of the attic and insisted Max take one with him.

Emma glowered. In her black—was she making a statement?—caftan, she reminded Annie of an irascible cat when the doorbell rings too many times on Halloween. "Since when is Max menacing?"

"Max is perfectly capable of looking menacing," Annie said hotly.

Laurel no longer looked like a pink confection. Her tone was dulcet with underlying steel. "Max is a blue belt."

There was a moment of silence.

Laurel offered, "Orange belt?"

Henny rushed to the rescue. "Black belt." She laughed, a good-humored laugh. "Face it, ladies. Testosterone counts. Of course Ves wants a tall, strong man at her side when"—a quick breath and the smile was gone—"she confronts a murderer."

Max answered the doorbell. Fred Butler was the last to arrive. When he saw Max, his eyes widened, looked huge behind the thick lenses of his glasses. The breeze lifted the gray tufts on either side of his head, giving him the appearance of a befuddled owl unsure if he'd reached the right roost. "Uh." He started, stopped.

Max held the door wide. "Everyone's in the living room. Come right in."

Fred gave Max one more puzzled glance, moved hesitatingly to the left. The only sound was the slap of his shoes on the heart pine floor. There was silence in the living room.

Ves sat on the brocaded love seat. Her springy reddish curls looked youthful but her face was tight and thin. The dark green of her silk blouse emphasized the brilliance of her eyes. She nodded at Fred, used her cane to gesture at a wooden chair. Fred scuttled to the chair, took his place.

Max stopped just inside the archway, stepped to one side of a wrought iron stand that held a bust of Minerva. Ves had chosen the spot before the company arrived, said, "Whoever waxed the step is a gambler. I don't expect anyone to clutch a hanky and faint when I talk. But it won't hurt for you to be on the lookout for . . ." She'd trailed off. "I don't know, maybe a hint of panic? Anything that doesn't look normal. And you're a big strong man, ready to pounce." He maintained a bland expression and carefully did not look at the walkie-talkie in the bookcase by the fireplace. He'd shoved the unit between two large dark tomes. It would be noticeable only to someone studying the shelves.

Ves used the cane for leverage to rise to her feet. "I have an announcement to make." She moved slowly, the cane thumping with each step. She reached the archway, turned to face the room, standing about two feet from Max.

Every eye followed her. There was a general air of uncertainty and a hint of irritation.

Fred Butler sat with his shoulders rounded and tight, chin low enough to hide his neck. Adam Nash smoothed back a lock of silvered hair, maintained his usual dignified posture, but a reddish flush stained his cheeks. He was accustomed to deference, likely found the assembly odd, the ambience unpleasant. Curt Roundtree, casual in a short-sleeved polo and khakis, slouched comfortably in a wicker chair, but the intensity of his gaze indicated close attention. Gretchen Roundtree nervously fingered a gold filigree necklace, dark brows in a tight frown. Jane Wilson's young, rounded face puckered in concern as if she found herself in the middle of an argument and wished she weren't there. Tim Holt was in his work clothes, a flannel shirt, jeans, and boots. He looked at Jane, gave a shrug as if to ask what the hell was going on. Despite the haggard paleness of Katherine Farley's face and the almost fervid glances she darted at her husband, she was her usual elegant self, dark hair shining, a beige textured top and black slacks and heels. Bob Farley's gaze slid past Ves with every indication of disinterest, a man enduring a social evening until he could go home.

"Each of you will be wealthy when I die." Ves spoke in a thin, clipped voice. "One of you"—she took her time, gazed directly at each in turn—"tried to kill me last Thursday."

This was the moment, if there was to be a moment, the instant when shock might reveal a look of guilt. Max tried to catch a glimpse of each guest. Fred's plump face sagged and he began to shake. Adam leaned forward, looking predatory and wary. Curt gave a low whistle, raised a skeptical eyebrow. Gretchen sat as still as stone, her fingers clamped hard on the necklace. Jane's eyes widened and her lips rounded in an O. Tim looked blank, then his big mouth twisted in a sardonic smile, clearly dismissing Ves as some kind of nut. Katherine's lovely face was rigid. She clutched Bob's arm, held tight. Bob appeared unaffected, a man only minimally aware of his surroundings.

The moment was past.

Adam Nash lifted his leonine head. "You are obviously hysterical. Of course, you're a woman of a certain age." His tone was disparaging.

Ves gave him a cool stare. "A rather curious response, Adam. Instead of asking what happened, you respond with sexism. But perhaps you didn't ask because you know what happened Thursday."

"You are either hysterical or deranged. To accuse one of us"—his big hand gestured at the others—"of murder is absurd."

"The accusation stands. I do not yet know which one of you committed the crime. I have a friend here tonight"—she gestured toward

Max—"as a witness. If I am murdered, he will inform the police about each of you and your motives. Further, I have written an account of Thursday for the police."

Jane Wilson burst out, "Murder? Oh, you must be wrong."

Tim Holt folded his arms, leaned back as if in a theater, a man ready to be entertained. "Are you playing a game with us? I like murder nights, but this is starting to sound kind of crazy."

Gretchen's face was hard. "That is a serious accusation."

"Serious. True. Here's what happened Thursday afternoon . . ." When Ves finished, her mouth twisted in a humorless smile. "What do you do when you know someone tried to arrange a fatal accident? You think, *My God, who wants me dead?* That's where it got easy. Not nice, but easy. I don't have enemies. I never saw any point in quarreling with people. Nobody wants me dead because I cheated them or stole a lover. But when I die, each person in this room will be much, much richer. And"—a slight hesitation, then a shrug—"when I brought the dessert in to the dining room the night we had our dinner, I knew one of you wanted me dead."

Adam sneered. "I suppose one of us stuck pins in a voodoo doll."

Ves lifted a thin hand, rubbed against one cheek. "I grew up here. I can tell you things about voodoo that will make you never want to leave the safety of a lighted room. The room was lighted that night. I had candles in the centerpieces and the chandelier was bright. But one of you had already made the decision that I had to die. I knew it then. I know it now. One of you was here Thursday, came inside, made a high step slicker than a greased pig." She paused, swallowed. "What's worse"—her voice was low—"the murderer waited long enough to watch me limp to my car, then came inside and cleaned the step. I suggest each of you look around because—"

Again Max tried to capture a mélange of faces. As he looked, perhaps too quickly, he had a sense he'd missed something important, an expression, a movement, a glance . . .

"—this may be your only opportunity to say you spent an evening with a murderer. Now I will speak directly to the murderer. I"—she paced her words—"do not intend to die." Her cane thumping, Ves crossed to a marble-topped table. She leaned the cane against the table, used her left hand to lift the lid of a gilt and black japanned box. Her right arm was still in a sling. She reached into the box with her left hand.

Jane Wilson gasped as a gleaming black revolver came into view.

Ves handled the firearm with ease, pointing the barrel away from the guests. "Colt .45, 1911 model. Semiautomatic. The safety is on. At the moment." She was crisp. "I'm ambidextrous so I'm an equally good shot with my left hand. You will notice I am pointing it to one side and at the floor. That's commonsense handling of a gun. But be aware, whoever comes after me will be shot."

Max eased an omelet onto each plate, carried the plates to the kitchen table. "Mushrooms, ham, onions, Monterey Jack jalapeño cheese."

Annie blew him a kiss and pushed the basket with homemade biscuits to the center of the table. "Honestly, sometimes I wonder how I could be so lucky. A handsome hunk who cooks." She admired her plate, a serving of salsa on one side, three strips of bacon, fresh-cut papaya. She speared a piece of fruit.

Max smiled, bent to kiss the top of her head, took the chair opposite her.

Annie waggled the fruit at him. "You had a ringside seat last night. We heard everything, but I wish we could have seen their faces when Ves said one of them was a murderer."

Max cut a piece of omelet, frowned.

Annie felt some of the morning's pleasure, the toasty kitchen, sunlight shining through white curtains, Dorothy L determinedly jumping to the counter and Max as determinedly removing her, seep away when she saw his worried expression.

Max looked across the table, his blue eyes dark with concern. "Ves wanted me there to watch them. I'm afraid I missed something. When Ves told them all to look around because she thought it was the only time they'd ever see a murderer, I think one of them looked—and saw a murderer."

Annie gripped the plastic handle, pulled the razor tip of the box cutter through plastic tape, flipped up the box flaps. Her nose wrinkled in delight. She never tired of the smell of new books. She approved of the large type chosen for the title of *Missing Pieces* by Heather Gudenkauf, sure to catch the eye of browsers. She lifted out five books at a time, transferred them to a dolly, some destined for the shelves, some for an end cap, a good half dozen had been preordered and would await pickup behind the front cash desk.

She worked steadily until midmorning, felt she'd earned a cappuccino. With whipped cream. And a cherry. She settled at the table near the coffee bar, sipped her reward, and faced the fact that she was restless and uneasy.

Agatha landed lightly next to the cup, gave it a dismissive glance, lifted limpid green eyes to stare at Annie.

Annie often shared thoughts with Agatha. "I'm scared for Ves. So she's handy with a gun. How can she be alert twenty-four/seven? She thinks she's warned off an attack. But it looks to me like telling them she knows one of them is after her changes everything. The killer wanted her death to be an accident. No questions. No problems. Now that Ves is making sure the police will know about the trust, the murderer might as well kill her any way possible. He—or she—can lurk in the woods with a rifle and pick Ves off. Or wait until summer and she goes out for a swim and run her down with a motorboat. Or monkey with her brakes. I don't think threats will stop this murderer."

Agatha abruptly crouched, peered down the corridor. In a swift move, she flew through the air, raced in a blur, scooped up a toy mouse, tossed it in the air, caught it.

Annie took a last sip from her mug. Everything was out in the open now. There was no need for subterfuge or subtlety. Annie nodded decisively, pushed back her chair. So far as she knew, only one person had lied about their whereabouts Thursday afternoon. Maybe there was a good reason. Or a very bad one.

Annie stepped into the bank, still uncertain how to approach Fred. He'd had the hunted air of a high schoolboy busted with marijuana when Martin Ford came up behind him and laughed when Annie asked if Fred had been on a holiday Thursday afternoon. If Fred hadn't looked so uncomfortable, she might not have called and discovered that Fred had not been at the office of a dental surgeon as he'd claimed. Should she ask him straight out, say she'd called the dental office and mentioned him and how he'd been there Thursday and thought so highly of Dr. Garcia and been surprised—

Her interior monologue broke off. The only teller on duty was Estelle Parker. Annie hesitated. Maybe Fred was on break. Estelle had a tired but pleasant face. She was nearing retirement and often talked about her plans, she was going to go home to Idaho, live with a younger sister. Annie came up to the counter, was glad there were no other customers. "Hi, Estelle. Looks like you are handling everything alone this morning."

Estelle's placid face was untroubled. "I guess Fred has the day off. Mr. Ford forgot to tell me, and he took the early ferry this morning. He's picking up his wife at the airport. Anyway, it's been pretty quiet. They should have told me." It was as near as Annie had ever heard Estelle sound aggrieved. "Fred didn't say a thing yesterday about not being here. He said he'd see me tomorrow. Meaning today. But"—a shrug—"he's not here. What can I do for you?"

Annie shook her head. "I wanted to tell Fred about a book I thought he'd enjoy. I'll check back another time."

Max drove the VW with the windows down. He braked by the sidewalk in front of the bank

Annie, her curls windblown, her soft tee molded to her by the breeze, pulled open the passenger door. "Do you have the address?" She slid onto the seat, turned toward him.

Max wanted to drive home, fast, and open the windows in their bedroom to welcome in the breeze and turn to Annie—

"You did get the address?" A pause. A swift smile, a head shake. "Max, be serious."

He was serious. Maybe later today . . . Right now Annie was focused on the tuft-haired teller. Okay, they'd go see Fred, then he'd bring her back to her car, suggest they meet at home for lunch. When they were home . . . "I have the address. I'm in the VW, the better to pretend no one sees us. Always glad to drop everything"—his tone implied he'd been hard at work though he suspected Annie knew he was enjoying a cheerful practice session on the indoor golfing green at Confidential Commissions—"and join you in"—a suggestive pause—"the frolic of the moment. But why do you want me to ferry you to Fred's house?"

"You were there."

Max blinked. "At Fred's house?" Sometimes Annie lost him.

She laughed. "At Ves's last night, so Fred knows you're helping Ves."

The VW turned onto a sun-dappled street with modest one-story homes. "Is my presence supposed to instill panic in his heart? Am I the strong silent sidekick and you're the inquisitor? That I can do. What are you going to say? *Fred, I know you were at Ves's house and she told everyone about her fall and you lied to me the other day about going to the dentist on Thursday so what's the deal?*"

"Absolutely." Annie was combative. "It's very strange that he didn't come to work the day after Ves had them to her house."

Max's tone was light. "As in, one action is caused by another? Let me see. It thunders. Dorothy L comes into the room. Dorothy L made it thunder. Ves warns the murderer. Fred doesn't come to work so he's the murderer."

"Maybe." She didn't laugh.

Max slowed, checking addresses. "Here we are." He pulled up in front of a one-story frame house painted a cheerful yellow. A white picket fence enclosed the small yard.

Annie popped out of the car and headed for the gate.

Max caught up with her. He was firm. "You do the talking. Ask the man why he took the day off. I can't wait to hear his answer."

"I'll ask him why he lied about going to the dentist."

"Now that"—the gate clicked shut behind them—"might elicit a sexy answer."

Again, Annie's glance was chiding. "Do you ever think about anything else?"

"Occasionally." He grinned. "Then I get back to what matters."

The porch was shady beneath an overhang. Two wicker chairs looked inviting. Annie stepped forward, punched the bell.

Silence.

Max gestured at the driveway. "No car. But he may always put it in the garage." Annie rang again.

The only answer was the caw of a crow who'd landed on a porch railing to watch them.

Annie knocked, kept on knocking. Finally her hand dropped.

Max leaned against a porch pillar. "Either he's not home or, as they quaintly said in the olden days, he isn't receiving callers."

Annie glanced at the well-kept bed of peonies. "Maybe he's in the backyard. And he's mulching or trimming or whatever it is gardeners do in February. Let's go look." She plunged off the porch in her customary rush.

Max followed at a leisurely pace. He came up beside Annie to gaze at the backyard, which offered proof of Fred's gardening bona fides, clumps of azaleas and a bed with winter-blooming pansies. A wheelbarrow rested beside a small flagstone patio. Cotton gardening gloves rested in the barrow next to clippers. "No Fred." Max knew it was a statement of the obvious. They were the only inhabitants of the backyard except for small gray squirrels that darted about their duties and a trilling cardinal in a magnolia.

Annie spread her hand. "Look at the azaleas. They'll be gorgeous next month. He and Laurel could commune about snails and such. But he isn't here. I'll try the bank again tomorrow."

As they neared the street, he put his arm around her shoulders, gave her a hug. "How about we go home and . . . ?"

7

Henny Brawley enjoyed eating breakfast on her porch that overlooked the marsh. She watched the gold and red of the sun spill across dark water. She chose the porch in all seasons, remaining indoors only when it rained. She was comfortable, despite the fiftyish temperature, in a wool cardigan over a turtleneck, corduroy slacks, thick cotton socks, and ankle-high leather boots. A long twitching grayish nose rose above the glass top of the table. Dark eyes gazed at her hopefully. She sliced a chunk of waffle, offered it. "Good morning to you as well, Cinnamon." The dog slurped the waffle from her hand, leaving moist warmth behind.

Henny smiled, poured a little more syrup on the waffle. She liked Fridays, her usual day to grocery shop, exchange books at the library, tend to errands. She was content. Perhaps this afternoon she and Cinnamon would take the north trail at the nature preserve and Cinnamon could sniff the tracks of raccoons and deer.

A muted trill sounded from the pocket of her cardigan. She felt a flicker of surprise. It was early for a call. She pulled out her cell, recognized the caller, swiped to answer. Her voice was perhaps a shade higher than usual. "What's happened?" She never doubted something had happened. Good news rarely came at odd hours.

"Figured you'd be up." Marian Kenyon talked fast. "An early-morning fisherman at Fish Haul Pier snagged more than he expected. He was looking for dogfish and skates, that's about what you find in February, but he caught a floater. Even worse, a guy he knew, Fred Butler, dead, puffed up from immersion. He—the fisherman, not Fred—called the cops. I got it on the scanner. The body's lying on the pier. Poor guy—the fisherman—was a buddy of Fred's. Tough. Doc Burford—"

Henny pictured the big, rumpled island doctor, chief of staff at the hospital as well as the island medical examiner.

"—is here. He said it looks like a drowning, but he'll do an autopsy. You took me to breakfast and you asked about a bunch of people. One of them was Fred Butler. You also said you and unnamed others were trying to prevent something bad from happening. What would that be? A drowning?"

"No." Henny's reply was swift. "It was something else—someone else—altogether."

There was a doubtful pause. "Are you telling me this is one big coincidence? You want to know about Fred in regard to some unexplained bad scenario and he turns up dead and there's no connection?"

Henny frowned. "I don't know of a connection. There was no threat to Fred Butler."

"That leaves coincidence." Marian's voice was heavy with doubt. "I suppose it's possible. And maybe I'll get a free ticket to the basketball finals because I ate cornflakes this morning. You don't mind if I mention to Billy Cameron that you and unnamed others had an interest in Fred."

Henny was blunt. "Why would he care?"

"Cops like to tidy things up. Did Fred fall, did he jump, was he pushed?"

Henny was firm. "You've read too many headlines. There's no reason to believe Fred's death wasn't an accident. Is there?"

Marian was equally firm. "The guy doesn't have on boat clothes. Or a life vest. Dressy casual. That's a tip-off he wasn't out boating and toppled into the water. Besides, he didn't fish or have a boat. I know because I talk to people everywhere from Parotti's to the bank. It's an occupational disease. If Fred boated I'd know about it. Fred hunted for gold. As in buried treasure, but he was otherwise rational. Anyway, he didn't boat or fish. So what's the occasion in February that he *falls*"—her tone put the verb in italics—"from Fish Haul Pier into the harbor? Did he climb up on the rail and sit there with his feet dangling, enjoying a February breeze? That's an accident that smells like old fish to me. Or maybe he went down the ladder on the south side and jumped in."

Henny remembered the ladder and small landing on the south side of the pier.

"I can see Fred doing a lot of things, grubbing around for gold, working in his yard, volunteering at the rec center. I don't see him going out in a boat on a February night. Nix the idea of a boat. So he comes to the pier. How does he 'accidentally' fall in? If it wasn't an accident, we have to assume he jumped. If so, why? If he didn't willingly jump, somebody pushed him. Why would anyone kill Fred Butler?"

Henny held her cell, stared out at the marsh, a vee of pelicans diving down to murky water seeking their breakfast. She didn't believe in coincidence either. But Marian was right. No explanation made sense. If Fred went to the pier, and that seemed odd in itself, how could he have fallen? But the alternatives, suicide or murder, seemed utterly unlikely.

Marian pounced. "Had you seen Fred lately?"

"Not recently." Henny hadn't seen Fred in several weeks. It wasn't her place to reveal Ves Roundtree's near escape or to describe Annie's talk with Fred or Max at Ves's house with a walkie-talkie in place. There might be a good explanation for Fred's drowning, and she had no reason to connect his death with Ves Roundtree's danger, but just in case, the police should be informed. "Annie and Max Darling might know more."

A nnie pulled her peacoat tighter across her front. "Do you think Fred didn't come to work because he was dead?" She and Max had been lighthearted yesterday. She had wanted to know why Fred lied about that Thursday but she never thought that Fred, mild-mannered, polite Fred, had entered Ves's house and waxed a step high on her staircase. What should she think now?

The breeze tugged at Max's sweater. "It seems likely, doesn't it? Especially if it turns out he didn't ask for a day off." He lifted binoculars. "I can see him—"

Annie jammed her hands deep into the coat pockets and stared at water rippling under a stiff breeze, not at the clutch of uniforms standing in a semicircle.

"—lying on the pier. They haven't covered him yet. Doc Burford's talking to Billy. I see Fred clearly. A tan pullover sweater, white shirt collar showing, dark slacks. That's what he wore at Ves's house."

Annie still didn't look toward the pier. She didn't want to see

Fred's body. If he was dressed as he had been at Ves's house, did that mean he drowned Wednesday night? "If he died Wednesday night . . ." She trailed off.

Max shot her an understanding glance. "Did he leave Ves's and come to the pier? It could be. Doc will figure out whether he died Wednesday night or yesterday."

Annie was glad he didn't go into details about stomach contents and digestion and rigor mortis and the effect of submersion in seawater.

Brakes squealed.

Annie turned. "Ves is here."

Marian Kenyon was at the end of the pier. She turned to look at the van at the curb. Marian's red sweatshirt was ragged at the hem and her gray sweatpants baggy, her ankles bare above leather loafers. Obviously she'd rushed from her house sockless in whatever was handy in response to the alert about a drowning victim. The breeze roiled Marian's short-cut dark hair. She held a pen in one hand, a notebook in the other. A Leica hung from a strap around her neck.

The van door slammed. Ves came limping around the back, cane thumping.

She, too, looked as if she'd thrown on the first clothes at hand, a gray pullover, black slacks. Since her fall, she'd worn dirt-stained sneakers, likely part of her gardening ensemble. Her tight red curls needed a comb. She was breathing jerkily when she came up to them. "Do they know when he drowned?"

Annie understood Ves's unspoken fear. Had Fred Butler come to her house and left it to deliberately die? She reached out, touched a tense arm. "No one knows yet. If it happened after he left your home, it could mean he was the guilty one." Was Fred a failed murderer afraid he was going to be accused? She remembered an entry in Emma's *Detecting Wisdom* from Inspector Houlihan, *When a perp panics, anything can happen.*

"He looked scared Wednesday night. But I can't believe Fred tried to kill me." Her tone was incredulous. "He looked absolutely sick when I told about how I fell. Then I warned them with the gun. I thought the gun upset him."

The sound of footsteps, men's deep voices.

Max looked at the pier. "Here they come."

Billy Cameron was in a brisk conversation with Sergeant Lou Pirelli when they reached the steps. The police chief's short-cut fair hair with a sprinkling of silver was bright in the morning sunlight. A big man, he carried his heft with ease. A pullover sweater emphasized broad shoulders. His navy slacks were freshly pressed. Stocky Lou Pirelli, a good five inches shorter, hurried a little to keep pace. Lou was darkly handsome, a superb swimmer, and a regular at Death on Demand. He loved to reread Ed McBain's 87th Precinct books. Hyla Harrison, ginger hair pulled back in a bun, carried a notebook, made notes as Billy spoke.

Billy's tenor voice carried. ". . . billfold contained a fair amount of cash. Put a call out for his car."

Lou responded. "I already looked it up. A 2006 Camry." He rattled off the license plate.

"Find out who talked to him last, state of mind, could he swim—" Billy saw Annie, Max, and Ves. He paused, studied them intently, then thudded down the pier steps, Lou and Hyla close behind. Billy stopped in front of them. "Are you here because of Fred Butler?" He saw their faces, jerked a big thumb. "I'll see you at the station."

Billy Cameron stood at the end of the stained Formica-topped table in the break room, which was much larger than his office. Lou Pirelli was to his right. Lou held a pen poised over a notebook.

Hyla Harrison was to his left. She'd already clicked on the tape recorder. Annie was next to Hyla, then Max. Across the table, Ves Roundtree sat next to Lou.

Billy kept his expression pleasant, nonthreatening, but he was highly attuned to the faces turned toward him, Annie Darling with sadness and uncertainty in her eyes, Max Darling frowning thoughtfully, always-on-the-move Ves Roundtree oddly subdued. He knew Annie and Max well, had risked his own career to help Annie prove Max's innocence when a young woman was found dead with Max's bloodied tire tool next to her. He liked them. Admired them. Trusted them. Normally Ves Roundtree exuded the fizz of a just-uncapped soda. Not today. That the three of them arrived at Fish Haul Pier in response to news of Fred Butler's death aroused his intense interest. Drownings were usually accidental, a slip on slick wood perhaps compounded by an inability to swim well, or the result of carelessness, venturing into a riptide or not wearing a life preserver out on a boat or too much alcohol. That was his expectation when he arrived at Fish Haul Pier. Now he wondered.

He looked at Annie. "Why did you come to the pier?"

"Marian Kenyon called Henny Brawley. Henny called me."

Another familiar name. Henny Brawley was one of the island's most respected residents.

"Your connection to Fred Butler? Henny's connection?"

Ves clawed through her frizzy hair. "The connection is actually mine. Wednesday night he was at my house. I'll tell you everything." She explained about the brother's estate. Lou interrupted, got the names, repeated them, "Bob and Katherine Farley, Jane Wilson, Adam Nash, Fred Butler, Curt Roundtree."

Ves described the dinner she held to share an account of the estate. "I also invited Gretchen Roundtree and Jane's boyfriend, Tim Holt."

She told how she went to the kitchen for the dessert. "When I came in the dining room, it was like teetering on the edge of a cliff. I was terrified. I knew one of them wanted me dead."

Lou held up a hand. "Let me get the dates. The dinner where you brought the heirs up to date on the estate was Friday, February fifth. You fell the following Thursday, February eleventh. You invited those you suspected to your house Wednesday, February seventeenth."

Billy sorted times and dates in his mind, the dinner, the slick step the following Thursday, her return from the hospital and a clean step, her visit Monday to Death on Demand, Annie going to Ves's house and seeing the dining room where Ves claimed someone walked on her grave, Annie enlisting Max, his mother, Emma Clyde, and Henny Brawley to find out where the dinner guests were at five P.M. Thursday, February 11, their lack of success, Ves's decision to summon the dinner guests to her house on Wednesday, Fred's body found Friday.

Billy wanted clarity. "They came to your house Wednesday, February seventeenth."

"Yes." Ves spoke rapidly. "I also asked Max to come. I told the guests one of them was a murderer and I didn't intend to die. I have a Colt .45. I showed my gun to them."

Billy felt his face tighten. "Attempted murder, but not one of you"—he looked at each in turn—"informed the police."

Ves said wearily, "What could you have done?"

"Quite a bit. We would have investigated. Looked for forensic evidence. Talked to those you suspected." He was brusque. "Fred Butler was one of the suspects. Now he's dead. We don't know how or why he drowned. He may accidentally have fallen from the dock. He may have chosen to die. He may have been killed. If we had been called in to seek the facts about the slick step, it's possible the outcome may have been different." He realized his tone was harsh, regretted his momentary anger, said quickly in a milder voice, "Or possibly not." He looked at Ves. "You have a license for that .45?"

"Yes."

"Very well. Is there any other information that might relate to Fred Butler?"

Annie leaned forward. "Fred claimed he'd gone to the dentist the afternoon Ves fell. But he looked so scared and uneasy that I checked with the dentist's office. Fred lied. He isn't a patient of the dentist he said he was seeing. I went to the bank yesterday morning." Annie's voice was thin. "He wasn't there. I wanted to ask him why he'd lied."

Billy was grim. "We'll find out."

Marian Kenyon still wore the red sweatshirt and baggy sweatpants. "I came straight from the newsroom. I am starving. Do you have anything but those croissants dabbed with chicken salad that you give to old ladies wearing purple hats?" She stood by the coffee bar, looked hopeful, aggravated, pitiful.

Annie was defensive. "They're great croissants. I get them from a French bakery in Savannah."

Marian flung herself into a chair at the nearest table. "Okay, if that's all you can offer, I'll take it."

"I can do better." Annie hurried behind the coffee bar, bent to the small refrigerator, rose with two foil-wrapped oblongs. "Miss Jolene has a special today on pulled pork sandwiches, crusty buns, and mustard BBQ sauce. I bought two of them." She didn't add that she'd intended to ring Max and invite him to join her in sybaritic indulgence, but Marian was in need of sustenance. Annie unwrapped the sandwiches, placed them on a paper plate. "I'll pop them in the microwave."

Annie fixed Marian an espresso, always her jolt of choice, and herself a glass of unsweetened iced tea, added, true to her Texas roots, a basket of corn chips and green chili salsa. The microwave pinged. She served the sandwiches on cheerful yellow plates.

Marian sighed happily. As she ate, she complained. "Henny Brawley is like somebody in witness protection who won't give out a peep unless the DOJ signs on." Another big bite. "Apparently you are the DOJ. When I tracked down Henny, she said to ask you, it wasn't her place to say anything. Something funny, as in *peculiar* not *humorous*, is going on and I want to know the link between now-deceased Fred Butler and the other people Henny asked about. I smell a story like Agatha"—a nod at the black cat regarding them steadily from the counter of the coffee bar—"smells pulled pork." She attacked the remainder of the sandwich. Marian was a dog with a bone and she didn't intend to let go.

Annie cut her sandwich in half, scooped salsa with a chip.

Marian devoured the last of her sandwich, still looked pitiful. "I don't suppose you have another sandwich."

Wiry, bony, fast-moving Marian never gained an ounce, and she was always munching on something. Annie used her knife to slide her untouched half onto Marian's plate.

"Thanks." Another mumble. "Why is Henny mum and what's up? Obviously Henny alerted you to the gathering on Fish Haul Pier unless you have a scanner at your bedside. You must have more than a passing interest in Fred's demise since you and Max showed up this morning."

Annie knew Marian well. Marian could be trusted. "It all started . . ."

Marian's dark eyes widened as she listened. At Annie's conclusion, she immediately fastened on the salient facts. "Fred lied about the afternoon somebody greased a step, and Wednesday night Ves waggled a gun at her chosen suspects." The reporter's gamine face drooped with regret. "I could write a hell of a story about Rufus's estate and the dinner party and the slick step and Ves confronting the heirs, but I can't use any of it, not even as deep background. Not unless I want to see the *Gazette* sued for libel. I can't name people as possible murderers without one of them scurrying to a lawyer, even though it looks like Fred was the perp. You've squelched my hopes for a scoop, but Fred's flop in the harbor may make sense." She wiped a smear of mustard sauce from her chin, leaned back in the chair. "Re: Fred, accident doesn't seem likely. There's no reason to suspect murder. Looks to me like he jumped. The autopsy report won't be out for a couple of days but Doc Burford told Billy unofficially that he estimated the body had been in the water between thirty to thirty-six hours. That puts him in the drink Wednesday night. Do you know what time the confab at Ves's broke up?"

"Max got home about nine twenty."

Marian finished her espresso. "That works for Fred to be at the pier by half past nine. Maybe he hung out there for a while, nerving himself up to take the plunge." Her expressive face was somber. "Jeez. Can you imagine . . . I don't want to imagine. We cling to life like barnacles to a boat bottom. Doesn't matter how rough the water gets, how dirty." A pause. "Most of us."

Annie felt a wash of sadness. What a way for a life to end. "He must have felt pretty desperate."

Marian's eyes narrowed. "I guess he was. Ves confronts the heirs. Fred jumps. Cause and effect. Who goes to the end of Fish Haul Pier on a cold February night? Maybe a hot couple not worried about the weather. Not a middle-aged bank teller fully dressed in casual clothes, no fishing rod, not that people fish there after dark anyway. He had no reason to be on the pier. He either climbed over the railing or he went down that ladder on the south side of the pier. Why? To stick a toe in the water? Not likely. Billy figures he climbed up on the railing at the end of the pier. He had on leather loafers with pretty worn soles and Billy thinks he got up on the railing, teetered there, slipped, and fell to his right."

Annie stared at Marian. "What crystal ball was our police chief consulting?"

Marian gurgled. "I'll share that with him. Actually, it's good old-fashioned cop think. There's a contusion on the right side of Fred's head and that fits with standing on the railing and falling to the right."

Annie was startled. "Maybe somebody hit him and dumped him over the railing."

Marian was dismissive. "Who wanted to kill Fred? A jealous husband? An aggrieved bank customer? Did Fred have a secret life unknown to others? Was Fred a sleeper agent for Red China and he'd decided to turn in his chopsticks? Murder requires a motive."

Annie knew Marian was right. Domino-playing Fred Butler was not a likely candidate for a lurid love affair or nefarious activities. But it was possible there was more to Fred's life than Saturdays at Parotti's and working in a bank.

Marian lifted bony shoulders, let them fall. "I asked, pretty pro forma at this point, but I get paid to ask questions, was it maybe a mugging gone wrong? But who gets mugged at the end of a fishing pier? Billfold was in his back pocket. Forty-two dollars in cash, one credit card. Car keys in left front trouser pocket. Car parked in the Fish Haul Pier, nicely locked, no evidence of any damage." Marian arranged her knife and fork at the side of the empty plate. "Thanks for a lunch befitting a foraging reporter. And now I know a lot more about certain people's financial prospects than they'll ever dream.

But hey, I don't gossip. Just for my own enjoyment. As for Fred, people will wonder why he jumped, and only a few of us will ever know."

Annie tried to concentrate on the chapbooks. Maybe an inner chant would get her in the groove. *Chapbooks, chapbooks, chapbooks.* She knew she was guilty of undisciplined thoughts. She could start off wondering about goldfish and pop to the name of Wiley Post's monoplane the *Winnie Mae* to wondering if panda fur smelled as sweet as a cat's to a passionate diatribe against rosemary as a seasoning ever for anything. At the moment, despite her best effort to focus on Henny's copy: *Juanita Sheridan was as adventurous as any of her fictional heroines . . .* Now her mind tugged at Fred's lie about Thursday. He could have been at Ves's house and when Ves warned them, did he think she would find out and did he decide to jump at that moment?

The front door opened. The ping sounded like a text message. Her thoughts careened again. Death on Demand needed something more dramatic to announce customers. A bugle call? The *Inner Sanctum* creaking door? No, something about the island. Hey, maybe the sound of an alligator. That would be cool, a low, throaty growl, almost like the rumble of distant thunder.

The thump of a cane brought her to her feet. Ves Roundtree came down the center aisle. She looked uncertain of her welcome. "I hate to bother you, but I have to talk to someone." She pulled out a chair, sank into it, leaned the cane against the table. "Billy called and told me Fred's death looks like suicide, that he apparently went from my house to the pier, and jumped. Billy says that makes it likely that Fred was the person who waxed the step, so I can feel safe now. I thanked him, but ever since we talked I've been thinking about it. So here I am, hoping you can help me make sense of everything."

Annie replied quickly, "I'll help if I can."

"I guess I'm looking for someone else's perspective. You may decide I'm nuts. Maybe I am."

Annie shook her head slightly.

"Thanks." A wry smile. "Billy obviously thinks Fred committed suicide because he tried to kill me and he was afraid I was figuring out what happened. That could be true. But I don't believe it. Can't believe it. Maybe I have that thing—what is it?—second sight. Or maybe I'm a melodramatic fool. But I remember the dinner and that awful sensation, someone looking at me and wanting me dead. Fred was his usual self that night, mild, unassuming. I can't believe the death wish came from Fred. If it wasn't Fred, if it was one of the others, and that means Fred committed suicide for some other reason."

"He died Wednesday night." Annie was making the point that Fred drowned after Ves threatened to shoot if attacked.

Ves's face tightened. "I get it. I scared Fred; Fred killed himself." She brushed back a reddish curl. "They think he went from my house to the pier because he was wearing the clothes he wore Wednesday night. Plus something about how many hours he'd been in the water." She talked fast. "You heard everything that happened over the walkie-talkie. I warned them. I was telling the murderer that I was prepared. Obviously I had no idea which one was guilty. Why would Fred kill himself?"

Annie remembered the voices over the walkie-talkie and Ves announcing, *"But be aware, whoever comes after me will be shot."* If Fred was guilty, he saw doom closing in on him.

Ves ran her fingers through her hair. "I was tough. Like a bounty hunter. But I didn't wave the gun at anybody. I handle guns right. I handled the gun like I could shoot someone. That's scary for someone who doesn't do guns. I put on a big show. But you want to know about me and hunting? I've never killed anything. Ever. Dad and Rufus shot deer, squirrels, whatever moved. I wouldn't go out with them. I shot at pop bottles on a fence railing." She gave Annie an embarrassed look. "I can't even kill spiders. You know what I do when a spider gets in the house? I get a cup and a napkin and I catch the spider in the cup and cover the opening with the napkin and go to the garage and put the spider out in a corner to build a web there. That night when I warned them, I was trying to stay alive. I wanted to scare the murderer. If somebody came in my house and crept into my room and I knew it was Death, maybe I could shoot."

Annie, too, found it hard to imagine shooting a living creature. She'd never understood hunting. To lift a rifle and see a live creature drop to the ground and die appalled her. To shoot a human being would either be incredibly hard or horribly easy.

Ves placed her hands on the table. They looked small, defenseless. "I wanted to scare them. Fred looked scared. Now I should feel home free, right? The big bad murderer is dead. But I don't feel home free. I don't believe Fred tried to kill me. I don't know why he jumped off the pier. I don't think he was a murderer running scared. I want you to know that if my body turns up, you can bet it's not suicide." She pushed up from the chair. "Now I'm going to try and act like everything's okay. Maybe the powers that be have it right. Maybe I don't have to be afraid. If I'm alive next month, I'll start to believe Fred was guilty. Until then, I'm looking over my shoulder."

Max lounged in his very comfortable red leather desk chair with his cell phone and listened as his mother recounted a visit to Ves Roundtree's store.

Laurel concluded, "I am concerned about Ves."

"I'll tell Annie."

"Dear Annie." Laurel's tone was affectionate. "How is she?"

"She's fine." He sketched a rainbow. Nice of his mother to always inquire about Annie. "We're going to Parotti's for dinner."

"I'm sure she's very busy with the chapbooks." A rather lengthy pause.

Max refrained from a reply.

"And you are quite busy, too?"

"Busy?" He looked at his desk, bare except for his favorite framed photograph of Annie, dusty blond hair, steady gray eyes, a face that always tugged at his heart. "Working away." He glanced at the yellow pad in his lap, a rather good sketch of Dorothy L on a windowsill, tail vibrating as she stared at a blue jay. Artistic endeavor surely qualified as work.

"Don't overdo. Love you."

"Love you, too." He tapped off, smiled, and picked up his 3B regular pencil. He could always count on his mother for encouragement. He looked at Annie's photo, said conversationally, "Laurel cautioned me not to overdo." Annie would think that suggestion riotously funny. He tilted farther back. Annie loved to quote Laurel's comment the day his mother looked at him admiringly as he relaxed in his big red leather chair and proclaimed, "Truly a chair for a titan of industry. Perfect for you." Annie later asked demurely, "What does the titan desire at the moment?" He'd replied, "Desire? Only you." Her response had been eminently satisfactory.

Annie waved hello at Ben Parotti, hurried across the old wooden floor to the booth where Max stood waiting. She loved the gleam in Max's eyes and looked back signaling *Yes, I love you, later.* She slid into the booth and he settled opposite her.

"Ma sends her regards."

Annie was immediately on full alert. It wasn't that she didn't welcome good wishes from her mother-in-law, but Laurel's contacts with Max often included plans for Annie that she was determined to avoid. "Laurel?"

There was a flurry when Ben arrived with tea for her and beer for Max and took their orders, the usual, grilled flounder for Max, fried oysters for Annie, coleslaw for both, jalapeño corn bread.

Max poured his beer into a frosted mug. He thought it more tactful not to mention Laurel's delicate reference to the chapbooks. "She said she was certainly surprised about Fred Butler. She always thought he was the nicest man. Ma said she believed that an accident occurred. And that's what she'd told Ves. She wanted to know if you'd talked to Ves."

"Ves came by the store." Annie wouldn't forget Ves's tight face as she announced if anyone found her dead, it wasn't suicide.

"Ma went to Ves's shop." His face crinkled in a frown. "She said Ves was a nervous wreck and her hand went down below the counter when the door opened. Ma had a feeling there was a gun down there."

8

Not even the high gleam of his varnished desk looked bright on a cloudy Monday morning. Billy Cameron arranged several folders. He opened Doc Burford's autopsy report.

> White male. Age 46. Height 5'7". Weight 182 pounds. General health excellent. Cause of death: drowning. Body recovered 8:06 A.M. Friday, February 19. Immersion in water estimated at 30 to 35 hours. Puts approximate time of death between 9 P.M. February 17 and 8 A.M. February 18. Slight trauma to right frontal lobe.

At the top of the page, Doc Burford had scrawled in a thick black ink: *Trauma could have been sustained if he balanced on railing, slipped, struck his head on the way down.*

Billy knew Fred Butler as he knew most of the island residents.

He had always found Fred genial and courteous at the bank, friendly at Parotti's on Saturdays. Billy thought of him as steady, dependable, precise, careful. He was not a man who would miscount your money. Billy balanced that picture against Ves Roundtree's claim that Fred was frightened Wednesday night. Why? Was he the kind of person who always thought a barb was directed at him? Did Fred immediately assume the worst—*she doesn't like me, she's angry with me*—when he encountered any kind of snub? Did Fred think Ves was accusing him of waxing the step? That was possible. If Fred took Ves's accusation personally and if he was guilty, had he fled to Fish Haul Pier and, in a distressed state, lost his balance and fallen? Or had he hurried to the pier, frantic that he would be accused of plotting a death, and jumped into dark cold water?

Billy turned his chair toward the window. The sun was bright this morning. A stiff breeze laced the harbor with whitecaps. He considered what he knew. He'd sent officers out across the island seeking information. Fred Butler had no boat. He did not fish. He could not swim. He was not seen, so far as they could discover, after he drove away from Ves Roundtree's house around nine o'clock. Officers had no luck finding anyone who had been in the vicinity of the pier that night. The temperature was in the forties and there was a slight mist, so it wasn't surprising no one was strolling on the boardwalk. Why would anyone go out on the pier on such a night? That question definitely held true for Fred Butler. Why did he go to Fish Haul Pier? He wasn't the outdoor type. But he definitely went to the pier, went into the water from the pier.

Three choices: accident, suicide, murder. Billy shook his head. Accident and homicide seemed unlikely. That left suicide, which strongly suggested he feared exposure as a would-be murderer.

◆ ◆ ◆

Death on Demand bustled with vacationers in June, often painfully sunburned and seeking books to read in the shade of beach umbrellas. Annie wondered if they realized sunlight reflected off sand and an umbrella alone wouldn't suffice. A wide-brimmed hat, filmy long-sleeved white top, and towel-draped legs were also advisable, plus plenty of sunscreen. But it wasn't June. It was a foggy Monday in February and only she and Agatha were in the store. She frowned, pulled her cell from her pocket, swiped, knew caller ID identified her to Marian, dispensed with a greeting. "Anything new about Fred Butler?"

"I just got off the phone with Billy." Marian's raspy voice was matter-of-fact. "Presser at ten A.M. to announce official cause of death: drowning. No judgment as to whether he died accidentally or on purpose. If there's a recent life insurance policy, it might be voided if his death is ruled a suicide. Anyway, the case is closed as far as the police are concerned. Billy will announce that Butler was wearing a dressy casual shirt and slacks and loafers, that his billfold and car keys were recovered, that his body showed no evidence of trauma other than a bruise on one temple that could have resulted from striking the pier railing. The presser wraps it up. I'll write the story and readers can draw their own conclusions. Now I've got to run—an alligator on the back porch of the library. Says he won't leave unless he gets the latest Joyce Carol Oates. I want to get there before the critter guy does. It will make a great photo. Wonder if they'll let me shove a stack of books up by his snout. The alligator's snout, not the critter guy's. I can see it now—Shakespeare's comedies, Edith Wharton, maybe Plato, and, of course, Oates's latest. An erudite alligator. I like it." The connection ended.

Another day, another focus. A man drowned one day, a perambulating alligator the next. This afternoon's *Gazette* would have a fun story by Marian and, if she knew Marian, a photograph of an alligator facing a stack of books. Annie picked up the copy for Henny's *Classic Crimes*. She needed to finish editing the Incredible Trio's manuscripts. Max had found a program that would make printing the chapbooks a snap. Emma's birthday was next week. If she hustled, Max was sure he could get the chapbooks done in time for a party. She looked at Henny's comment about *Rebecca* by Daphne du Maurier. *One of the great opening lines in fiction: "Last night I dreamt I went to Manderley again." The tone captures the foreboding and unease that permeate the story of a second wife who lives in the dead Rebecca's shadow. Brilliant.*

Annie agreed. First sentences could be the topic of a great essay, starting with Mary Roberts Rinehart's "One day last fall I ordered the swimming pool destroyed" in *The Swimming Pool* to Rhys Bowen's "Weather outside: utterly bloody!" in *Malice at the Palace*. Maybe she should put together her own chapbook, *Fabulous Firsts*. The weather had been cool and misty Wednesday night—

She gripped the soft lead pencil. Where had that come from? But she knew. She couldn't push away the fact of Fred Butler's death and Ves's insistence that Fred wasn't the would-be murderer. She glanced up at the wall clock. In a few minutes, Billy Cameron would announce death by drowning. And implicit in the bare facts was the likelihood of suicide. Apparently there was no family to mourn him, to face the misery of what-ifs. Everyone on the island would read this afternoon's *Gazette*, including Ves Roundtree. Ves grappled with a different kind of what-if.

Annie had a sudden clear memory of Fred's round face when she spoke to him at the bank, the widened eyes behind the bifocals, the quick panicked glance at the bank manager. He'd been scared that he would be caught out in a lie about his dental appointment. She wished she had been at Ves's house Wednesday night. Had Fred looked scared in the same way? Maybe he was simply scared of unpleasantness, and what could be more unpleasant than realizing you are a murder suspect? Maybe he was afraid word would get back to the bank. People who worked at banks could never afford a whiff of scandal. She wished she had a better sense of who Fred was. If he committed suicide— She frowned. There was no *if* about it. He committed suicide. The question was why. Unless there was something else going on in his life that led him to the end of the pier, the inescapable conclusion was that he was guilty of the attack on Ves and afraid he'd be caught out.

But Ves was sure she was still in danger.

Annie slapped her hand on the table. Papers slithered. Agatha stared at her reproachfully. "I'm sorry, sweetie. But it's awful to be afraid. If we were positive that Fred jumped because he set the trap, Ves could feel safe again."

Agatha's green eyes were unblinking.

"If we knew what Fred was thinking . . ." Her words trailed off.

Fred's state of mind. Unless something had been troubling him, unless he had been in a depressed mood, then clearly he left Ves's house and jumped because he had tried to kill her. It shouldn't be hard to find out about his demeanor in recent days. Was he happy or grim? If there was no hint of depression, Ves could put her gun back in the closet, not be fearful at every footstep.

Annie picked up her cell to call Billy, slowly put it down. The case was closed. But she wasn't bound by any rules.

Annie felt sadness when she stepped into the bank lobby. Estelle Parker's kind face had a look of shock. She wore a navy silk dress, and Annie was sure the choice was a tribute to Fred, a way of saying, *I'm sorry, I won't wear something cheerful today, the first day here without you.*

Estelle saw Annie, tried to smile, blinked.

Annie hurried across the lobby to the counter. "I wanted to tell you how much we'll miss Fred."

Tears brimmed in Estelle's blue eyes. She snatched a tissue from a box. "I'm just sick. Fred and I have been here for such a long time, almost thirty years. He came two years after I started. My Jim was still alive and Fred was just out of high school and he and Evie were newlyweds. We used to go bowling together." Tears slid down her fair cheeks.

Annie reached out, touched a plump hand. "I suppose he was depressed. Maybe he was sick."

Estelle wadded the tissue into a ball. Pink flooded her cheeks. "There's some awful mistake. Fred was fine. I know he was fine. We told each other things. He'd just got a good report in his checkup. He told me he had low cholesterol and his blood pressure was excellent. He was kind of proud. He was fine except for his teeth, and I don't know how much longer he had to go with that. He'd gone to the dentist every Thursday afternoon for a few weeks. But that's all that was wrong with him." Her face puckered. "He was happy as could be on Wednesday. He said his research—he loved to check through old histories and things like that—finally put him on the right track and he'd have some exciting news for me one of these days and when he did we'd go into Savannah and have a fancy dinner some Saturday. The police have it all wrong. He never jumped into the water. Never. It makes me so mad they are acting like he jumped just because it was odd to go out on the pier. Maybe he felt like a walk. Maybe he got dizzy. But he never jumped in the water. He wouldn't. He never missed Wednesday-night prayer meeting. He kept on going after Evie died—she died having a little girl who didn't live either—so why would he jump into water over anything else? He told me he didn't want to live without her, but he had to do what God said and she and their little girl were in Heaven and someday he'd see them. Oh, it makes me so mad, everybody acting like he committed suicide."

Annie said slowly, "He'd gone to the dentist every Thursday afternoon for a while?"

"Maybe three or four weeks, every Thursday afternoon. He never said exactly what it was. Maybe one of those awful new implant things. I don't know. But other than the dentist, he was fine." Her eyes flashed. "He was happy as could be on Wednesday."

Annie walked slowly across Main Street. The day had turned pleasant and sunny, the temperature nudging into the sixties. Did she need to call the dental office, see if Fred had been there on other Thursdays? The receptionist had been firm. Dr. Garcia had no patient named Fred Butler. Why did Fred leave work early on several Thursday afternoons? Where did he go? What did he do? He wasn't waxing a step on Ves's stairs the other Thursdays. Perhaps this was just an anomaly, a piece of information that led nowhere. The important takeaway from Estelle was Fred's state of mind. He wasn't a man struggling with depression. He was looking forward to the future when something good happened because of his research.

This fact, and she trusted Estelle's judgment, went a long way toward confirming Fred's decision to jump from the pier resulted from the confrontation at Ves's house Wednesday night. She tucked away the knowledge that didn't fit, Fred's false claim to be excused from work on previous Thursdays.

She lifted her hand, pulled open the heavy front door of Parotti's

Bar and Grill. She was just inside when Ben came bustling toward her. Of course, he was on his way to the ferry for the afternoon run to the mainland. She'd arrived just in time. "Ben, I have a quick question."

"Fire away." He teetered on his feet, like a boxer ready for the bell.

She grinned at him. "You love running the *Miss Jolene* better than anything, don't you?"

His leprechaun face crinkled. "Reminds me of the days when I was a young man on freighters. What can I do for you?"

Ben kept his ferry punctual. Annie talked fast. She had a little speech prepared. "I'm putting together a memory book about Fred Butler for Estelle Parker, and I want to talk to some people who knew him well. He played dominoes here, and I wondered if you can give me the names of some of his friends."

"Nice thing to do." Ben patted her shoulder. "Talk to Bill Hogan at Gas 'n Go. He works the afternoon shift." Ben rocked back and forth faster, a man with a job to do. "You can include a tribute from me. Fred ate chili and corn bread here Tuesday nights and we had a right good talk last week. He said he had about decided to run for mayor. He was going to talk to folks, see if he could get support. I told him I'd back him. You know the trouble we have with Cosgrove."

Everyone dislikes somebody, and the penguin-shaped mayor topped Annie's list.

"Fred wanted the town to get behind new basketball courts at the Island Rec Center. Cosgrove opposes it. Fred was a good man and he loved this island and he had lots of hopes and plans for it."

Annie pulled up to the service pump. Gas 'n Go, which belonged to Ben, had two pumps, one self-serve, the other attended. She rolled down her window.

A tall lanky man in overalls approached. "Fill 'er up?"

"With regular. And please check the oil and tires. Are you Bill Hogan?"

"At your service, ma'am."

"Ben Parotti tells me Fred Butler was a friend of yours." She saw acceptance on the long lean face. Ben's name was about the best recommendation she could have. "I'm gathering remembrances about Fred for a friend and I'm hoping you will share some memories."

"Well." He drawled out the word, bushy eyebrows bunched in concentration. "You could count on Fred. When my boy Rick was hurt in a cycle crash, Fred was at the hospital soon as he heard to give blood, and he went out and fed the chickens and took care of my horses while me and my wife was at the hospital."

"Had you seen Fred recently?"

"Saw him every Saturday, rain or shine. We play dominoes at Parotti's."

"Was he cheerful?"

Bill didn't seem to think her question odd. "Yeah." He sounded sad. "We had a beer after we finished. He was in a great mood. He was always nuts about pirate stuff. I don't know how a grown man could believe in old pirate maps. But he did. I never saw it but he used to talk about this yellowed crumbly parchment map and how he'd found it in the bottom of a trunk he picked up at a flea market. I could've told him they churn those out in prints shops and peddle them to suckers. But I never did. Hell, it made him happy, gave him something to think about. I figure everybody has to have something to hope for. Saturday he said he'd figured out what he needed to do, he'd been counting all wrong. Something about so many paces this way, so many that way. He said it was like having a big lightbulb go off in his brain but it was brighter than any old lightbulb, more like

119

a spotlight. He was sure he'd figured everything out, and it depended on where the arrow would land. I don't know what that had to do with pirates, but he was real excited, said he was going to be rich and maybe he'd take a trip to Paris, he'd always wanted to go to Paris." Bill pressed his lips together for an instant. "Anyway"—his voice was gruff—"I'm glad he was happy."

Annie stepped inside Trinkets 'n Treasures. She liked the way Ves had divided the shop. One side was pricey: the gleam of fine porcelain birds, figurines, and plates, a Sheffield silver tea urn, an antique derringer pistol, Chinese plates, an Egyptian chess set in ivory, two Sevres figurines of Napoleonic soldiers. A comfortable sofa faced the display. The other side was for budget shoppers: cookie cutters shaped like starfish, conch shells, salt water taffy, plastic beach buckets and trowels, kites, flip-flops, sunblock lotion, T-shirts with a T 'n T logo in bright pink, synthetic shell necklaces, a manually propelled scooter, an electric-powered scooter, skateboards, foam boogie boards, plastic beach umbrellas.

Ves came around the desk at the back. She moved slowly, but she was no longer using the cane. "Hi, Annie." She smiled but there were dark patches beneath her eyes.

"I have good news." Annie knew she sounded ebullient. She felt ebullient. She was about to give Ves her life back.

Ves gestured at the sofa. "I'm all in for good news. Are politicians being quarantined in Antarctica? Has the state decided to give a sales tax holiday for the summer? Is Jordan Spieth buying a house on the island?"

"I wish." Annie laughed as she settled on the sofa and turned to face Ves. "It's better than all three combined. You don't have to be frightened anymore. Fred Butler was a happy man. There was nothing wrong in his life. He wasn't sick. He wasn't depressed. He had no worries. He was happy and positive Wednesday. Everything in his life was good until he came to your house Wednesday night."

Ves stared, disbelief mixed with the beginnings of hope. "How can you be certain?"

Annie told her about Ben Parotti and Fred's plans to maybe run for mayor and campaign for basketball courts at the Island Rec Center, his announcement to Bill Hogan on Saturday that he'd soon be rich, his promise to Estelle Parker that he'd see her the next day and they would soon go for a celebratory dinner in Savannah.

Ves pounced. "He said he was going to be rich."

"Pirate gold. Nothing to do with you."

"Pirate gold?" Ves spoke as if the words made no sense.

"He believed in pirates." That didn't sound quite right. "He was into hunting for buried treasure." Ves would be well aware the Low Country had seen plenty of pirates in the early 1800s, and there were many tales of hidden loot, including a stash by Blackbeard. "Apparently Fred had a parchment map and he hadn't been following the directions properly and he'd figured out where an arrow would land and all he had to do was dig. He was really upbeat Saturday."

Ves gestured toward the tacky side of her store. "I have an assortment of parchment maps, all printed this year. I could have given him a half dozen different ones. You say he was happy Saturday. Maybe something happened between Saturday and Wednesday."

"He was happy Wednesday." Annie was emphatic. "He was fine." She frowned. "The only thing I can't pin down was why he lied about going to the dentist on Thursday. That was the first thing that made me think he might have been at your house, then Estelle said he'd been going to the dentist for several Thursdays in a row. He lied about the dentist. I don't know where he was the other times unless he was at your house for several Thursdays but didn't nerve himself up to set the trap until that last Thursday."

Ves pressed her fingertips against her cheeks. "Nerve himself up? That wasn't how I felt at the dinner. Whoever wanted me dead wanted it quick, without hesitation. But maybe he was like me. I have a gun. I talk tough. But the idea of shooting anyone scares me. Maybe he came a few times before he waxed the step. I guess he wanted me out of the way so he could really make a search for that treasure."

Annie felt certain that was what happened. All the ends might not be tidily tied, but Ves saw now that there could be only one reason for Fred's death Wednesday night. He went to the pier and jumped in the water because of what he learned at her house.

A nnie sniffed appreciatively. "Mmmm."

Max turned from the pot on the stove. "Coming up soon. Will you check the corn bread?"

She moved to the oven, pulled down the door. The corn bread had a golden crust on top. She used a mitt, set the pan on the granite counter. "Perfection."

Max stirred with a wooden spoon. "I put in lump crabmeat as well as the crab claws." He put down the spoon, picked up a ladle, transferred steaming gumbo to pottery bowls.

The phone rang.

Annie had the corn bread loose and turned it onto a rack.

"Bad time to call. Let it go." Max held a bowl in each hand.

Annie pulled the cell from the pocket of her cardigan and checked caller ID. "It's Ves Roundtree. I better answer."

"Sure." He turned and poured the brown gumbo with crab claws, shrimp, lump crab, sausage, and okra back into the pot.

Annie perched on a stool by the center island, swiped to answer, punched Speakerphone. "Hi, Ves."

Ves's voice was low and hoarse. "It wasn't Fred."

Annie felt as if she'd been struck unexpectedly between her shoulder blades. "Not Fred?" Of course it was Fred who'd jumped from the pier. There was no question about that. Annie said firmly, "Of course it was Fred."

"Fred didn't try to kill me." The words came fast. "I started thinking about what Bill Hogan said. And then it hit me, Fred was going to dig where the arrow landed. I went out in the backyard, and there's Diana in the fountain. A long time ago the arrow broke off but that's the arrow Fred meant. I'm sure that's right because I tracked down Bill Hogan. I asked if he knew the name of the pirate Fred talked about and he said yes." A ragged breath. "Fred was looking for treasure buried by Black Jack MacDougal. I know a lot about Black Jack. Our house was owned by Jeremiah Jemson, and he had this beautiful daughter, Isabel. Black Jack was the second son of some English lord. He had no money but was highborn. Anyway, he had good manners and was a regular at grand dinners and dances in Charleston. Isabel visited some cousins there and she met John, as she called him, at a dance. They fell in love. Supposedly he visited the island several times. He roamed up and down the coast near here in the 1820s. I don't know if the romance really happened. Isabel died of the fever when she was nineteen. Black Jack came to see her before she got sick, and legend says he buried a trunk full of gold in the backyard, but when she died he went off to Barbados and was killed in a duel there. So Fred was looking for treasure in my backyard. The past few weeks I

123

found some odd places in the yard where the dirt was soft and had odd lumps. I couldn't figure out what could have caused it."

Max was standing next to Annie at the island. He silently mouthed, "Gophers."

Annie put a finger to her lips.

Ves barreled ahead. "That explains his lying at work. Fred was coming here on Thursday afternoons before I got home from the shop and digging around in my backyard. I think he was here the Thursday someone came here to set a trap for me. Fred had no right to be here. As soon as he saw someone arrive, he slipped away. He might not have known the person who came inside the house. Don't you see, Fred had no idea what had happened to me, that the step was waxed and I fell, until he came here with the others Wednesday night. That's why he was scared. I told them someone had tried to kill me. Fred looked at someone and he was terrified. He knew who the murderer was. Maybe Fred thought about speaking up but he would have to admit he'd been there. Whomever he accused could say *Oh, I dropped by that afternoon to talk to Ves and I saw Fred and he was on the porch.* There must have been an instant when he almost spoke up, but he was too frightened." Her voice was low. "God, yes, he was right to be frightened."

Annie saw the connections, an arrow, Black Jack MacDougal, lying about Thursdays, lumps in the backyard. Fred could have meant Ves's house when he exulted about buried gold. She wasn't convinced. "Maybe that's true but maybe he decided to try and get rid of you and then he'd inherit from Rufus and he'd have the money to buy your house and it would be hard to sell a house where someone had just died, especially if anyone figured out your fall wasn't an accident."

"I told you how I felt at the dinner, the threat was cold, dangerous, hard. Not Fred."

Annie was skeptical. "Why would he meekly agree to meet this scary person at the end of Fish Haul Pier? In the dark. By himself. If he was scared in your living room, how do you think he'd have felt about meeting a murderer?"

Her answer was slow in coming and her tone sad. "Fred would be afraid no one would believe he was innocent if he admitted he'd been in my yard. Maybe the murderer told him since he hadn't spoken up, he was part of a conspiracy, told him to come to the pier around ten o'clock. Maybe Fred refused and the murderer said *Unless you come, I'll go to the police tomorrow and tell them I thought it over and decided I had to report I'd seen you in Ves's backyard, but if you cooperate no one will ever know.* Maybe the murderer told him all he had to do was sign a paper admitting he was in the yard at that time, and the murderer would keep it as insurance that Fred would keep quiet."

Annie remembered Fred's tension when the bank manager kidded him about the dentist. What would happen to his job if the bank learned he'd lied about dental appointments to dig for gold? "He'd be scared he'd lose his job."

"Fred didn't jump." Ves's voice was shaky. "He was stunned, thrown over the railing."

Annie felt breathless. "We need to tell Billy."

"He'll come back at me with all the objections you had. He won't say so publicly but he thinks Fred committed suicide. Billy will say that now there's a reason why Fred was in my yard. Billy will say Fred had no luck digging and thought it would be easier if I died and the house would be vacant. He could search without worrying about me, plus he'd inherit from Rufus. And I brought out a gun and told them I was ready for a killer, and Fred was afraid I'd hear about Black Jack MacDougal and know he was guilty."

"Billy will listen." Annie knew this was true. "I'll talk to him. I'll call him right now."

"It's after hours. I'll go see him in the morning. I want to think about Wednesday night. I want to remember where Fred sat and where he looked. I haven't had time to really concentrate. Something may come to me. I'll meet you in the morning. Nine o'clock."

Annie spoke quickly before the call could end. "Maybe you should go to the inn to spend the night."

"Don't worry. I have my gun. And believe me, I'll use it now. I liked Fred."

9

Annie parked in the lot north of the police station, rolled down the windows. She breathed deeply, enjoying the faint tang from the sea. The Sound was placid this morning. Puffy white clouds floated in a bright blue sky. She glanced at her watch. Almost nine. Ves didn't think Billy would be impressed that Fred was happy until he came to her house Wednesday evening. Billy could point out that suicides often mask their feelings. Annie intended to insist that Fred's death wasn't suicide. Fred was frightened after he learned of Ves's injury. Why? It was logical to assume he was in Ves's backyard on the Thursday she fell. He was looking for treasure in her yard, had likely been doing so for several Thursdays. He was there and saw someone approach the house. Annie hoped Billy would reopen the inquiry into Fred's death. Billy was painstaking, careful. Even if he wasn't persuaded by Ves's argument, he would surely try to find out where Ves's guests were Wednesday night. Doc Burford estimated Fred had been in the water thirty to thirty-five hours when he was found early Friday morning. Fred was last seen leaving Ves's house shortly after nine. Between then and eight the next morning he went into the water.

A deep throaty whistle announced the nine A.M. departure of the *Miss Jolene* for the mainland. Annie enjoyed the ferry, loved to stand on the upper deck, lean on the railing, and watch passing sailboats and shrimp trawlers and the occasional passenger ship.

Annie twisted to look at the street. Several cars, no familiar van. She hesitated, then fished out her cell, texted Ves: *Waiting for you at the station.* She opened the passenger door, climbed out, walked slowly toward the front steps of the one-story brick building that housed the Broward's Rock Police Station. She reached the steps, yanked out her cell. There had been no ping, no reply to her text. Annie found the number for Trinkets 'n Treasures. After several peals, Ves's voice: *We are sorry to have missed your call. If you'll*— Annie clicked off, tried the home number. The phone rang until it switched to voice mail. Annie clicked off. She hurried up the short flight of steps.

Billy didn't turn on the siren. "Ves Roundtree is all right. Or she's not."

Annie sat tensely in the passenger seat of Billy's Ford sedan. He didn't drive a police car. Maybe most police chiefs used their own cars. She knew she was fastening on an irrelevancy to try and push away fear. Billy had listened to her scrappy recital of what she'd said and what Ves said and responded calmly that more than likely Ves had changed her mind and decided not to show up. Annie knew Ves wasn't eager to talk to the police. She didn't see any point in doing so. "Wouldn't she have called and told me she wasn't coming?"

Billy drove with both hands on the steering wheel. He didn't answer directly. "I'll talk to her."

He swung the wheel, and the Ford turned into Ves's driveway. Annie leaned forward as they came around the curve. She felt a whoosh of relief when she saw Ves's red Dodge van.

Billy pulled up behind the van. Annie scrambled out, came around the car. Billy stood by the Ford, looked carefully at the yard. But Annie was already hurrying toward the back porch. Billy caught up with her. They climbed the steps.

Annie stopped and stared. "The back door's open."

"Right." Billy was calm. "Ves?" He lifted his voice, could likely have been heard from one end of a football field to the other.

Silence.

"Ves?" Annie's voice was sharp.

In two strides, Billy was at the back door. He knocked, a heavy thump that rattled the door, kept on knocking for a minute, possibly more, then let his hand fall.

Silence.

His hand came down, hovered near his holster. "Police. Hands up. Don't move." His voice was deep, commanding. "Police. Hands up. Don't move." He reached out, pulled open the screen door, gazed inside.

Annie saw a brownish smear on the side of the door. "Billy"—she pointed—"that looks like blood."

"Stay there." The order was spoken softly. He stepped inside. "Police." If anyone was inside the house, that shout could not have been missed.

Annie waited uncertainly on the porch. She wanted to follow him. She didn't want to see what might be inside. She heard his progress, repeated shouts of "Police"; "Hands up"; "Don't move."

She waited, hands clenched, listening to Billy's shouts, heard his heavy steps on the stairs. He stepped out on the porch, face creased in a tight frown. "No one's here." He moved past her, thudded down the steps. He strode toward the van.

Annie glanced back at the screen door. Was that blood on the frame? She reached out, then let her hand drop. This might be a crime scene though Billy said the house was empty. She must not touch anything. She hurried down the steps toward the drive.

Billy pulled at the handle of the van door. The driver's door opened and he leaned inside, twisted to look, was out again in a minute. Next came the garage. He slid the door up. It creaked, rose slowly to reveal a dim interior. On the left wall was a workbench, a freezer chest, bike, and a lawn mower.

Billy crossed the concrete floor to the freezer.

Annie tensed as he lifted the lid.

A cursory glance. He lowered the lid.

Annie breathed again. The freezer, of course, was big enough to hold a body. It was horrible to think in terms of a body, Ves's body. But she had to be somewhere. Billy said there was no one in the house. He would have checked every room, the closets, pantry, bathrooms, under the beds. Everywhere. No trace of Ves, and a bloodstain on the frame of the back door.

Billy yanked his cell phone from his pocket, tapped, talked fast. "Possible crime scene. Send Pirelli and Harrison. Bring the forensic van."

Annie knew he was speaking to his wife, Mavis, who worked as both the dispatcher and as a crime scene tech.

He slid the phone into his pocket, looked at Annie. "Will you come to the house with me? You may be able to help." He moved as he spoke.

Annie hurried to keep up with his long strides. As they passed the fountain, she glanced at the statue and Diana's arm drawn back and the small portion of arrow that remained.

Billy held the door. "Don't touch anything."

Annie kept her hands close to her sides.

He stopped in the center of the hall, nodded at the small table with its bronze tray for mail. "Can you identify that purse?"

A green leather tote bag sat on the table. The handles were attached with brass fittings. "That's the purse Ves was carrying yesterday." Annie pointed. "Those are her car keys." The key ring medallion was shaped like a starfish. "If she isn't here, something's very wrong." It wasn't only the smear of blood. "Women don't go out without a purse. If her billfold's in the purse and her cell phone, something's happened to her."

Billy pulled a pair of plastic gloves from a pocket, slipped them on. He stepped to the table, carefully eased the top of the purse apart. "Not zipped. I see a billfold and a cell phone."

"You're sure she isn't here?"

"There is no one in the house." His tone was grim.

"Where can she be?"

A siren sounded in the distance, coming nearer.

Billy Cameron swerved around a bent pine, testament to the force of the wind off the sea. He heard the pound of waves before he reached the edge of the bluff. Twenty feet below, the sea roiled around rocks, hissing and gurgling as the tide went out. Of course Gurney Point has been checked earlier. Searchers covered the island from the northern tip to the marina and shops at the broad southern end. Now the sun was sinking below the western horizon, turning low-lying clouds pink and rose and coral. Volunteers came from all over the island. Boy Scouts rallied. Shops closed. All day searchers drove island roads, hiked paths, rode bicycle trails, checked lagoons. The chatter on cell phones tallied sites visited. The island was searched as well and thoroughly as possible. There was no trace of Ves Roundtree. Ben Parotti swore she had not taken the ferry. The motorboat used primarily by renters of Rufus's mansion was secure in its boathouse. Rufus Roundtree's house showed no sign of occupancy, doors securely locked, drapes drawn, no lights, no cars in the garage. Billy was sure every accessible site had been scoured. But water was all around them and deep lagoons and forests where no one might venture for years. As hope dwindled, as the sun slid lower and dusk turned the world dim, he came back to Gurney Point. The rocks below would be exposed. Earlier the tide had been high, waves crashing against the bluff, only the tips of black rocks visible in the foam. Now he looked down, used his Maglite, played the beam along the rocks. Once, he stopped and tensed. But that was a log lodged below, not a body. Finally, he turned away. He walked slowly, felt heavy and weighted. He'd not protected Ves Roundtree. Now he could find no trace of her body.

Emma Clyde, hair windblown, blue denim caftan wilted, sagged on a red leather sofa. Henny Brawley, equally fatigued, was propped against a wooden arm of a stately Victorian armchair. Henny was in her stocking feet, her mud-stained hiking boots on Emma's front porch. Laurel was pensive, her classic features not so much weary as thoughtful. In a cane chair, she looked safari-ready in an olive top and slacks and hiking boots. Her bush hat lay on the floor beside her.

Annie tried not to be uncharitable, then succumbed. Trust Laurel to be a spot of high fashion during a search of the island. Annie felt Max's gaze, immediately rearranged her face. Bland was always good when glancing at your mother-in-law.

Max's blue eyes were amused. Annie knew she and Max were bedraggled after the long day of looking, he in a flannel shirt and jeans and boots, she in a pink sweatshirt and navy slacks and boots. Their vine-and-bramble-snagged clothing was an odd contrast to the cheerful yellow-and-blue plaid upholstery of Emma's sofa.

"I called ahead." Emma's seaside mansion was well staffed. "We'll have food promptly."

As if on cue, wheels squeaked and the plump, red-faced cook, her blond curls tightly constrained beneath a chef's cap, rolled in a stainless steel serving cart, the three shelves laden. They didn't have to move. An assistant, a muscular teen probably working part-time to save for college, was close behind. He set up teakwood tray tables for each of them, described the offerings, served them.

Annie was voraciously hungry. She bit into a huge French roll jammed with sliced ham, Havarti cheese, and mayonnaise. Chips served as scoops for a generous serving of guacamole. Iced tea was hugely refreshing. There was silence as they ate.

Emma took charge, as might be expected in the spacious terrace room of her home. "I dropped by the station on my way home. Billy has a command center set up in the break room. The island's been combed, as well as you can comb a splotch of land with some impenetrable forests. I know each of us"—she looked around her terrace room—"went with different parties." Her face softened. "Good turnout. Several church groups, Kiwanis, Boy Scouts, Rotary, Friends of the Library." She turned her strong square hands palms up. "Nothing. So we're left with these facts: Ves spoke with Annie at six forty-eight P.M. last night. No other calls are recorded on her cell phone. The landline doesn't show any calls yesterday. Ves said she'd be at the police station at nine A.M. this morning. She didn't come. Billy arrived at her house at approximately nine fifteen." She glanced at Annie.

"That's right." It seemed long ago that she'd jounced in the passenger seat of Billy's car to Ves's house.

"Billy found no one. There was a smear of blood on the frame of the screen door to the back porch. Another smear of blood—"

Annie felt cold. More blood.

"—was found on an overturned straight chair in the living room. Billy declined to say if there appeared to have been a struggle. The search of the island yielded no results."

Henny said quietly, "Remember last August?"

Annie remembered. A birder got off trail in the nature preserve trying for a better view of a reddish egret and wasn't looking down and stumbled over the bones of an Alzheimer patient who had disappeared two years earlier. Search parties set out to look for her as soon as she was reported missing but never found a trace.

Emma's square face was somber. "We have miles of thick woods. A body could lie there forever."

Henny massaged one temple. "Ves left behind her purse, cell phone, car keys. Her van was in the driveway. Bloodstains in the house. I'm afraid we have to conclude she's dead. Her body could have been dumped in the remote woods or in the ocean."

Laurel asked quickly, "Do you know whether the police have the material Ves put together about Rufus's estate and the dinner at her house?"

Emma nodded. "Billy found the sheets upstairs in her bedroom, lying on the dresser." A pause. "The bed was turned down and a cotton nightgown rested on the pillow. The bedroom light was on."

Henny's gaze sharpened. "If one of those present at her house Wednesday night murdered or kidnapped Ves, why was that damning material left behind?"

Annie tried to keep her voice steady. "Murder can't be easy. Those smears of blood, how did they happen? Did Ves struggle? How about the overturned chair? Maybe she was hurt and ran outside. Maybe the killer came after her and caught her and put her in a car and drove away and never thought about the papers."

"Or maybe"—Max concentrated—"the papers were left to suggest her disappearance had nothing to do with her claims about someone trying to kill her. Maybe the killer wants everyone to think she was hysterical and anything she wrote down was unimportant."

Laurel's tone wasn't chiding; after all, she was speaking to Max, but she said firmly, "I doubt in the heat of committing murder that a criminal was quite so clever. It seems more likely the murderer, not wanting to stay there long, made a cursory search downstairs, didn't go upstairs to the bedroom."

Annie thought Laurel was probably right, but loyalty kept her from agreeing. "Whatever happened, we don't know where Ves is."

Emma cleared her throat. "Billy shared one other fact. A thorough search of the house, van, and garage did not reveal a gun."

Annie firmly believed in the magic-carpet ability of many mysteries to plunge readers into a world they would otherwise never know, Nury Vittachi's Singapore, Ellis Peters's twelfth-century Shrewsbury Abbey, John P. Marquand's China in the years leading up to World War II. She went straight to the romantic suspense section, grabbed *Crocodile on the Sandbank* by Elizabeth Peters. She needed comfort after a restless night spent with disturbing dreams, hurrying to Ves's house, finding the open back door, seeing blood stark against white wood. She had woken up exhausted. She knew the right kind of book would make her feel much better. She decided to indulge herself for an hour, then she'd work on the chapbooks. She was luxuriating in the company of insouciant Amelia Peabody in Rome in 1884 when a familiar ring sounded.

She grabbed her cell, expecting bad news. "Have they found Ves?"

Marian's raspy voice was matter-of-fact. "No news. Usually that's good news. But not when you're looking for a body. If they don't find her in the first twenty-four hours, the odds go way down. They brought in some dogs today. Nothing picked up on Fish Haul Pier. Now they're going around to some of the other docks. They think she left the house, by force or on her own, Monday night. Her dinner dishes are in the sink, rinsed but not washed."

Annie remembered the nightgown resting on the pillow. "How about the blood?"

"It's hers. Not much. Traces of her fingerprints in blood smeared on the doorjamb. Billy said so far as they know, no one reports speaking to her or seeing her after you talked to her Monday night. The only new fact is that she was at her shop around nine o'clock Monday night. At least her van was parked in the alley behind the shop and there were lights on in her storeroom. There's a patrol that checks the area—"

As a shopkeeper on the boardwalk, Annie knew all about the patrols, appreciated them though attempted break-ins were rare in winter, happened occasionally in summer.

"—every few hours and the officer knows her van. The alley was empty when he came back around ten. She returned home, because the van is in the drive. Her visit there may have nothing to do with anything. Billy checked and no calls were made or received on the shop phone. Here's what I'm wondering. Ves told you she wanted to wait until morning so she could think about Wednesday night, remember where Fred sat, where he looked. How did she sound?"

Annie could hear Ves's staccato words. "Tense. Sharp. And"—she felt a shiver—"determined."

"Here's my take." Marian sounded sad. "She kept on thinking and she figured out who Fred saw in her yard. And then, hell, I don't know, did she go by and see that person and get fobbed off, you're wrong, wasn't me, hey, we're friends, and she decided she was wrong and came home? I think the killer gave her time to get home, then started after her. I don't see it any other way." A pause. "Somebody got her. I think it was one of the people at her house Wednesday night. Like I told you earlier, I don't gossip. But with Ves missing and Fred likely murdered, Billy needs to know everything about those at Ves's house the night Fred drowned. I told him about the jewel thefts and Gretchen. If she's the thief, she has steel nerves. She looks rich and attractive and she's someone Ves has known for years. How easy would it be for Gretchen to convince Ves that of course Fred hadn't looked at her. Then maybe Gretchen showed up at the house, told Ves she'd been thinking and she was sure she knew who Fred looked at. Once she got inside . . ."

Max tried to appear stalwart. Wasn't that a quality highly prized in the pages of romantic thrillers? "I concentrate better when I'm putting."

Annie's gaze was affectionate and utterly disbelieving.

He plunked his putter into his golf bag and walked to his desk chair with a grin.

She perched on the edge of his desk, which hiked her skirt to her thighs. "I just talked to Marian. She thinks Ves remembered who Fred looked at Wednesday night."

He forced himself to focus on her face. "And?"

"You were there."

He understood. If Fred was a fortune hunter, if Fred crept into Ves's yard that late afternoon seeking treasure, he was innocent. If someone arrived, he likely slipped into the deep shadow of the pines, withdrew silently, probably irritated at losing precious time to search, time made possible by a lie at work. But he definitely didn't want to be discovered trespassing. When Ves described the slick step and her fall, he realized instantly he knew who wanted Ves to die.

Max squeezed his eyes together, tried to remember. Fred was the last to arrive. He hunched in a straight chair, shoulders rounded. Fred's chair was at the end of the semicircle so Fred was half turned toward the others: florid-faced and pompous Adam, playboy Curt, suddenly expressionless Gretchen, wide-eyed Jane Wilson, mocking boyfriend Tim Holt, elegant and haggard Katherine Farley, impervious and distant Bob Farley.

Max felt frustrated. "The answer's there. Fred looked at one of them. His head turned, but I was watching the others. When I looked at Fred, all I saw was fear. Ves was right. He stared at a murderer. They looked at each other, and the murderer knew."

Annie gently tried to move Agatha, who was inelegantly sprawled on her back on top of the copy for Henny's chapbook. A low growl was sufficient. Annie reached for the box tied with a red ribbon and topped with an emerald bow. She wasn't cowardly, but only a fool trifles with a growling cat. It might be cheerful to dwell for a moment in her mother-in-law's madcap mind. There wasn't, so far as she knew, anything she could be doing to help find Ves. It was up to the dogs to find her scent. Or her body might be in the ocean, far from discovery. There were places where currents would pull a body out to sea.

Annie was smiling by the time she'd read several entries in *Merry Musings*: *A dog loves you because you are you. It never hurts to ask. Each person has a story.* And then she read: *Always wonder why.*

Why didn't the killer leave Ves's body where it would be found?

Ves had been adamant that no one had a motive to wish her dead except those who would profit when she died. Yet the lack of a body meant she would not be declared legally dead for seven years. Why remove the body?

Annie frowned, picked up her cell, tapped a Favorite.

Max's voice was warm. "I was thinking about you." A pause, quickly: "You're at the store?"

"Of course. Where else would I be?"

"Anywhere," he answered simply. "Out in a forest hunting for Ves. Nosing somewhere you shouldn't be. Talking to one of her possible murderers."

"That's why I called."

"You're talking to a possible murderer?" His voice rose.

"I'm thinking."

A whoosh of relief. "Think away. That's never a problem."

Annie wasn't sure exactly what he meant, just as she sometimes wasn't sure how a remark from Laurel should be understood. Mother and son often had an uncanny similarity in the innocence shining in dark blue eyes after speaking to her. She rather felt this was one of those times, but this wasn't the moment to delve deeper. "I mean I'm really thinking." She plunged right in. "Is it true that the trust can't be divided unless there's proof of Ves's death?"

"It depends upon how the instrument is written—"

"You sound like a lawyer. I want the bottom line."

He laughed. "If you ask a lawyer, even a nonpracticing one like me, a legal question, you are likely to get a legal answer. In short, no divvying until Ves is declared legally dead. If no body is found, a court can adjudge her legally dead in seven years."

"That's what I thought. So why would the murderer, if it is one of the surviving—what do you call them?"

"Contingent remaindermen beneficiaries."

"Okay. CRBs. A CRB wants a body, right?"

"Presumably."

"Why kill Ves and hide the body?" She pictured a pot of gold at the end of a dark rainbow.

"I see your point. For a con—"

"CRB."

"CRB to inherit, there has to be proof she's dead."

"I thought the whole idea was somebody needed money right now. Seven years is a long time."

Max's tone was thoughtful. "Whether money would be shared before her death was proved is probably up to the trustee. If Ves isn't found and if it seems obvious she's dead, he could choose to make advances to the CRBs and not wait seven years."

"If one of them is counting on that happening, they would have to be pretty savvy. But maybe not. Ves gave money early to Jane to help with her mom. I would guess that portion was subtracted from what Jane will get eventually. The others have asked for money so they knew Ves could make money available and probably think the trustee could do the same if she's still missing in a month or so. But still, why get rid of the body?"

"If there was a struggle"—Max spoke slowly—"the murderer might worry about traces of DNA. Honey, we can't know what happened at her house Monday night. You've done all you can do for Ves. Work on the chapbooks."

Annie nodded approvingly. Laurel's effervescence was on full display in her chapbook. Annie tried to decide which maxim was her favorite. Maybe *Of course there are unicorns.* Or *A seashell is like a memory. The life is gone. The beauty remains.* She had a gold link necklace with an unblemished smooth shiny tan-gray olive shell as the pendant.

Max gave her the necklace to celebrate their first wedding anniversary. They found the shell while walking on the beach. The necklace afforded her both a shell and a memory.

Her cell rang. Marian. She answered with a lilt in her voice, still thinking about Max and the shell. "Hey, Marian."

"No word about Ves, but we got a body." The words came fast. "A client arrived for an appointment, found Adam Nash dead in his office, called 911 at four minutes after eleven this morning. On my way there."

10

"Can't you go faster?"

Max was temperate. "Whether we show up in five minutes or ten won't make a difference to Adam Nash and certainly not to Billy. We don't have any information to add. Crime scenes go on for a long time. I don't see any point in our going there." He did push a little harder on the accelerator, but was ready to brake if a deer bounded across the road.

Annie stared straight ahead. Max was right. But to receive such a call and do nothing seemed an affront to Adam and Ves and Fred. Maybe it was foolish to go to Adam's office, but there had to be a connection between his death and Ves's disappearance. She turned to look at Max. "Maybe Adam killed Ves and then killed himself."

"Maybe."

"Maybe there will be something in his office that will help find Ves."

Max turned onto Main Street. Three police cars, red lights flashing, were stopped in front of a small frame building in the middle of the block. The lane was closed. He took a look behind, began to back up. "I'll park by the pier."

"Hold on a minute. I'll get out here." When the car stopped, she opened the door, popped out, headed for the sidewalk.

Adam's office building, unlike some of its more prosperous neighbors, was unprepossessing. The wood was weathered, the roof lacked some shingles that had blown away in a recent storm, a ground-floor window had a jagged crack.

As she hurried up the sidewalk, she wondered how prosperous Adam Nash had been. If she were looking for a financial adviser, the building wouldn't inspire confidence. An art gallery occupied the cottage next door. Everything was bandbox perfect, from a small brick fountain in front to red shutters to a pale yellow door that looked freshly painted. Laurel had told her, dark blue eyes dreamy, that light yellow was an earth color and one of the best feng shui colors for a west-facing door. On the other side of the building now bracketed by yellow police tape was the cosmetics shop where Gretchen worked. Across the street were several one-story storefront shops, including the secondhand store managed by Jane Wilson, a quilting store closed for winter, and, behind a white picket fence, perhaps half of the pickets newly painted, stood an old house inhabited by two reclusive sisters. A crowd clustered on the sidewalk, watching the activity. A muscular figure holding a paintbrush stood with his back to the fence, also staring. Annie recognized Tim Holt. The front door of the old house opened and a reedy voice called, "You get back to work or I'll dock you for wasting time." Tim slowly turned to the fence, dipped his brush in a bucket of paint.

Marian Kenyon, the harbor breeze stirring her dark curls, stood as near the entrance to Adam's building as possible, a scant inch away from the taut police tape. She was crisp this morning in a plum blouse and black skirt.

Annie hurried to join her. "What's happening?"

Marian jerked a thumb toward Officer Harrison, trim and alert. "Hyla said the ME's there and the chief and the tech crew. Nobody's allowed in or out until— Oh, hey." She leaned forward as a burly gray-haired man with a big face, now creased in a frown, came through the front door. He carried a small black leather satchel. "Hey, Doc, what can you give me?"

Doc Burford stopped a few feet away. "Victim is Adam Nash. Bullet wound to the chest. Likely fatal on impact. Estimated time of death yesterday between three and ten P.M." He started for the sidewalk.

Marian moved along the tape, keeping pace. "Homicide, accident, or suicide?"

"Homicide. No powder residue on his hands. No gun at the scene."

Billy Cameron liked to hold sheets of paper in his hand, easy to make notations, easy to flip back and forth from one fact to another. This afternoon Doc Burford e-mailed a prelim autopsy report, confirmed death by gunshot. Billy knew what a slug could do to a heart. This slug—he glanced at another sheet, a .45 caliber bullet, so plenty of force—had torn through muscle, shattered bone, exploded the right ventricle. Adam Nash as a living creature no longer existed. He checked other facts.

White male. Age 46. 6'2" tall. Weight 210 pounds. Good physical condition. No trauma other than the gunshot wound. Time of death estimated to be between 3 and 10 P.M. Tuesday, February 23. Body discovered at 11:04 A.M. Wednesday, February 24.

He picked up another sheet.

Officer Hyla Harrison: Body discovered shortly after 11 A.M. Wednesday, February 24, by Roger Clark. Clark told officers hall door ajar when he arrived. The light was on in the anteroom. The door to Nash's office was open. That light was also on. Clark called out. He stepped into lobby, called out again, walked to open office door. Clark saw Nash slumped forward on the desk, blood pooled in front of his head. Clark hurried across the room. He touched Nash's arm, found it rigid, immediately left the office. He did not touch anything. He went into the hall and used his cell phone to call 911.

Billy leaned back in his chair. Ves Roundtree told Annie Darling she wanted to figure out who Fred Butler looked at the night he died. Ves agreed to meet at the police station Tuesday morning. She didn't come. Could she have disappeared on purpose? That was possible, but no one on the island admitted seeing her after Monday night. Ben Parotti insisted she'd not taken the ferry Tuesday. She had no money, no car. Billy thumbed through the papers. Yeah. Here it was. Officer Abbott called every rental unit on the island. No check-ins Monday night. Was she abducted and killed? That seemed likely now. Adam Nash was shot Tuesday afternoon. Was he shot because he knew something about the deaths of either Fred Butler or Ves Roundtree or was he shot to increase the portion of those who would ultimately profit from Rufus Roundtree's estate? There was as yet no known link between any of Ves's guests last week to Fish Haul Pier, her house with the smears of blood, or Adam's office with the overhead light bright on a pool of congealed blood. He remembered one hot summer day and a trail through a nature preserve. No-see-ums, mosquitoes, and midges swirled around him obscuring the path. Now conjectures and uncertainties deviled him.

His gaze moved back to the autopsy report. There was one solid fact in the welter of information. Adam Nash was killed by a bullet from a .45. Billy straightened, turned to his computer. He tapped the keyboard. In a few minutes he had the information he sought about Ves Roundtree, Bob and Katherine Farley, Jane Wilson, Tim Holt, Fred Butler, Adam Nash, Gretchen Roundtree, Curt Roundtree. Ves Roundtree and Bob Farley were registered gun owners. Each owned a .45 pistol. No gun was found at Ves's home after her disappearance. He wouldn't know what happened to Ves's gun until her disappearance was solved. Where was the gun owned by Bob Farley? Those not legally registered as gun owners could well possess a gun. Guns were easily come by, legally or not. He picked up another folder. Hyla Harrison had been commended for alerting Katherine Farley about her husband's visit to Gurney Point. The attempt on Ves's life was made the next day. He pushed back his chair.

Emma brandished a rolled-up copy of the *Gazette* as she barreled into Death on Demand. Today's caftan was an eye-popping orange that matched spiky orange hair.

Annie was enjoying the novel pleasure of ringing up a sale to a lean, elderly man who had been excited to find a moderately priced copy of Jack Higgins's first Harry Patterson novel, *Sad Wind from the Sea*. The customer bustled past Emma, cradling his treasure, calling back disjointedly, "Here to visit my sister. I'll be back. You have some fine books."

As the door closed, Emma unrolled the Wednesday issue, slapped it on the counter. "Hot from the print run. Have you seen Marian's story?" She jabbed at the headline.

Before Annie could reply, Emma began to read in her deep voice:

ADAM NASH SHOT TO DEATH

Island financial adviser Adam Nash, 46, was found dead of a gunshot wound this morning at his office, an apparent homicide victim according to police.

Police said Roger Clark, a client, arrived at Nash's office at approximately 11 A.M. today and found Nash's body. The medical examiner estimated that Nash was killed sometime Tuesday between 3 and 10 P.M.

Police interviewed building occupants but no one reported hearing a gunshot. A ground-floor occupant worked late and did not leave the building until shortly after 9 P.M. Anyone in the vicinity of the building at 203 W. Main who heard a gunshot Tuesday between those hours is asked to contact police.

Emma paused in her recital. "Either the gun had a silencer or he was shot at five-oh-five. Surely that's occurred to somebody in the little brick building." *The little brick building* was Emma's designation for the police department.

"Five-oh-five?" Annie repeated blankly.

Emma shot Annie a pitying glance. "The ferry." The tone of her voice made it sound like *The ferry, stupid.*

Annie understood. The *Miss Jolene* departed on her last run to the mainland at 5:05, horn blaring. A half dozen shots could safely be shot before the ferry cleared the harbor.

"I'll text Billy." Emma was brisk. Her gaze returned to the front page. "Here's the rest of Marian's story."

> Police said there was no sign of a break-in at Nash's office nor any disturbance that might indicate a search or robbery. Police said it appears that Nash likely knew his assailant, as Nash was seated in his office chair. Police will interview friends and clients in hopes of discovering a possible motive. Anyone with information about any matter that might have led to his death is asked to contact authorities.
>
> Police declined to speculate whether there is a link between Nash's murder and the disappearance of island shop-keeper Vesta Roundtree. Roundtree did not show up for a scheduled meeting Tuesday morning. Police said a tipped-over chair and two smears of blood in her house suggested a struggle. Roundtree has not been seen or heard from since Monday evening. Her purse, car keys, and van were found at the house. An island-wide search Tuesday yielded no information about her fate. Bloodhounds brought from the mainland had no success in tracing her today.
>
> Police also declined to discuss the drowning death last week of Fred Butler. Butler's body was found near Fish Haul Pier.
>
> Police have not released information about the activities this past week of Butler, Roundtree, or Nash but the *Gazette*

has learned from an unofficial source that Butler and Nash attended a gathering at Roundtree's home last Wednesday. Butler's body was found Friday morning. Time of death is estimated to have occurred between 9 P.M. Wednesday and 8 A.M. Thursday. Also in attendance Wednesday evening at the Roundtree house were Katherine and Bob Farley, Jane Wilson, Tim Holt, Gretchen Roundtree, and Curt Roundtree.

Police have asked anyone with information concerning the death of Nash or the whereabouts of Roundtree to contact authorities.

Emma made an exasperated whuff. "Nothing"—now her voice was a bark—"not a single word about why those people were at Ves's house or Rufus Roundtree's estate or the heirs."

Annie said quickly, "Not heirs. Contingent remaindermen beneficiaries."

"They are suspects. Why doesn't Billy say so?" Her face was red with outrage.

Annie imagined Emma as a scaly orange dragon, fire shooting from her square face. "Billy has to be careful. There are libel laws."

Emma brushed away libel laws with a stubby hand. "There are many ways to say things. Anyway, this"—she tapped the front page with a stubby forefinger—"is police malpractice. There's not a word about Ves figuring out that Fred was digging in her yard on Thursday afternoons and saw the person who waxed the stair tread. Not a word about the fact that Fred was happy as a clam until he got to her house and realized he'd seen a murderer at work. Not a word about Ves trying to remember who Fred looked at that night and next thing you know she's nowhere to be found. As for Adam, I think the killer decided it would be nice to make the pie slice bigger by eliminating another heir. Those people need to be alerted. When you can pinpoint murder to a select circle, don't keep it a secret." She flipped up one stubby finger after another. "Bob Farley. Katherine Farley. Jane Wilson. Tim Holt. Gretchen Roundtree. Curt Roundtree. They need to know. It's up to you and Max."

"Up to us?" Annie was bewildered.

Emma had the grace to look slightly, but only slightly, uncomfortable. "Ves chose Max to be at her house the night she confronted them, so he represents her. These people need to know how all this ties together. I called and told them to come to your house at eight."

"Our house at eight?" Annie knew her voice was high.

Emma tossed her head, and the orange sprigs danced. "Max can report on the status of the investigation. But you know the real reason."

Annie felt like a dazed parrot as she repeated, "The real reason?"

"To warn the damn fools that someone is picking them off, one by one."

B ob Farley looked surprised when he opened the door. "Hi, Billy." Then his face tightened. He looked toward the two-story studio. "Katherine?"

Billy understood. Though he and Bob were friendly, had sailed together before Bob's accident, he knew Billy's job and sometimes that job was delivering bad news, awful news. He spoke quickly, "Katherine's fine. I saw lights in the studio when I drove past."

Bob looked embarrassed. "Sorry. But things have been weird. Fred drowned and Ves missing and Adam shot. I guess that's why you're here." He held the door wide, swung his wheelchair to give Billy space. He continued talking as he gestured for Billy to take a big wing chair, perfect for his solid frame, and turned his chair to face him. "I'm afraid Katherine and I don't know anything that will help. I thought Ves was being hysterical, claiming someone was trying to kill her. The shoes that woman wears would trip anybody. Maybe she was right, but I can't believe someone pushed Fred off the pier and somehow did away with Ves and shot Adam."

Billy kept his voice pleasant, but his eyes never left Bob's face. "You are the registered owner of a JFX5F25 PX4 Storm Type F Beretta handgun. May I see it?"

Bob's eyes widened and then he laughed, a robust laugh that reminded Billy of the old Bob with the spray on his face as he moved a tiller. He couldn't help but smile in return.

"That's a boost for my ego." Abruptly his face was somber. "Not that I think it's funny that somebody shot Adam. But the idea I'm out roaming around with a gun makes me sound damn vigorous." He turned his chair, wheeled across the room. "I keep my gun in the bedside table."

Billy was right behind Bob as they entered a small, Spartan bedroom with a single twin bed next to windows that overlooked the woods. Billy glanced at the closed door to the right, likely a larger master bedroom with a view of the marsh. In the small bedroom, a bedside table, a plain maple dresser, and a leather easy chair were the only other furnishings. A man's room.

Bob saw Billy's glance. "I don't sleep very well these days." Bob's tone was determinedly upbeat. "I have my own burrow so I don't keep Katherine up." He rolled to the bedside table, reached down, pulled open the lower drawer. He pulled out a wooden case, lifted the lid. His shoulders stiffened.

Billy was just behind him. He gazed down. The case was empty.

Bob slowly lowered the lid, returned the case to the drawer. He glanced up at Billy. "I thought that's where we kept it. Katherine must have moved it."

"Let's ask her." Billy was still pleasant. He stepped closer, picked up the receiver from the phone on the bedside table. "I imagine you have an extension for the studio."

"Sure. I can call her." He held out his hand.

"I can do it."

There was an instant of silence. Finally, Bob said roughly. "Five five."

Billy tapped the numbers.

Katherine answered immediately. "Bob?" Was there a breathless quality to her voice? She might well have seen Billy's car parked behind Bob's.

"Hi, Katherine. Billy Cameron here. Bob and I were visiting and I wondered if you could spare a minute and join us."

"Has anyone ever told Emma she's an overbearing old bat?" Max measured coffee into the coffeemaker. His jaw jutted.

"Not to her face." She understood his irritation. As he'd pointed out, Billy Cameron might not be pleased to know the people he intended to interview would have a heads-up on the likelihood the deaths of Fred and Adam and Ves's disappearance were connected. At least, Annie assumed Emma's hope was that Max would not only warn them of danger but urge each to immediately contact the police if they had any sense of who might have killed Fred Butler and Adam Nash.

"Maybe it's time someone told Emma." He poured in water, closed the lid, pushed Start. "All right, fresh coffee coming up. I gather we don't intend to offer liquor or wine?"

"It won't"—she felt a slight shiver—"be a bright gathering."

The doorbell rang.

Annie sat in a wicker chair to the right of the fireplace. Max stood to her left. She knew he wasn't comfortable with his role but that wasn't apparent. He looked relaxed, serious, welcoming. To her, he was always Joe Hardy all grown up, blond, handsome, the man you'd like to have at the tiller in a storm.

"I'm sure some of you were surprised when Emma Clyde asked you to be here tonight. Emma is concerned that some of you might not be aware of the background to Ves Roundtree's disappearance. Although the police did not officially declare Fred Butler's drowning the result of suicide, that was the implication. However, now there is good reason to believe he did not commit suicide."

As he spoke, Annie surveyed his listeners.

Gretchen Roundtree's bony face was blank and unsmiling. The gold medallion pattern of her paisley blouse emphasized the blond sheen of her hair. One hand clutched at the black scarf at her throat.

Curt's relaxed demeanor was in sharp contrast to his mother's. Freckled face skeptical, he lounged on a leather sofa in a preppy plaid cotton shirt, chinos, and tasseled leather loafers.

Jane Wilson's apricot cabled V-neck sweater was perfection above cream wool trousers and cream leather heels with apricot banding, but Jane's sweet face looked troubled.

Tim Holt sat with big strong hands planted squarely on the knees of his jeans. He looked fit and muscular in a wool shirt with the sleeves rolled up almost to his elbows. His strong-boned face creased in a frown.

Bob and Katherine Farley sat side by side on a wooden bench.

Her sleek black hair fell forward on one side, shading her face. Bob's hands were clamped on the head of an oak cane. Katherine would have been her usual stylish self in a plaid jacket with three-quarter-length sleeves except for the rigidity of her posture. Every so often she slid a sideways glance at her husband. He stared straight ahead, lips pressed together.

"Annie discovered Fred was happy and excited. His excitement was based on his expectation of soon finding buried treasure—"

Curt broke in, his tone sneering. "Don't tell us there's a hidden cache of gold and somebody bumped him off to get a map with a huge X that marks the spot."

Max was unruffled. "I'll lay out what we know. Each of you can make your own conclusion. In regard to treasure, it doesn't matter whether it exists or not. What matters is that Fred was searching for a treasure reputedly buried in Ves's backyard by Black Jack MacDougal, and further"—Max's voice was measured—"Fred was searching late on Thursday afternoons. On Monday night Ves concluded that Fred was in her yard when someone arrived there the Thursday she fell. Fred likely hurried away because he had no business being there. He didn't know about her fall until last week's gathering at her house. Ves realized Fred knew who greased the step."

Each person stared at Max. There wasn't a breath of sound.

"That knowledge led to his murder later Wednesday night on Fish Haul Pier."

Jane Wilson held up both hands as if to ward off the words, the knowledge. "It sounded like he committed suicide in the paper."

"He had no reason to jump into the water." Annie was forceful. "I talked to people who knew him. Everything was fine in his life. Ves called me Monday night, said she was sure Fred had been murdered. She said Fred knew who set the trap on her stairs. He could have spoken up that night at her house, but that would mean he had to admit he'd been there. Maybe he was afraid he'd be accused. Maybe he was afraid he would lose his job because he lied to his manager and said he had dental appointments on Thursday afternoons. Ves said she wanted to concentrate, remember everything that happened in her living room, picture where Fred sat and where he looked. She told me she'd meet me at the police station Tuesday morning. She never came. Instead her back door was open, the lights on, some blood smeared on the doorframe, a chair overturned."

Katherine's voice was strained. "You're saying someone killed her Monday night to keep her from going to the police."

Gretchen came to her feet, glared at Annie. "You're saying one of us killed Fred and Ves."

Max's tone was equable. "We aren't accusing anyone. We're telling you that when Fred Butler left Ves's house last Wednesday he had no reason to jump into the ocean. I saw him that night. He looked afraid. It's obvious he had good reason to be afraid. Then Ves figured out what happened to him. Did she talk to the person Fred saw?" He looked from face to face.

Tim Holt stood also, looked belligerent with the same stance as a bull ready to charge. His face was hard. "Wait a minute. This gets ugly. Now that rich guy's dead." Annie realized he was talking about Adam Nash.

"They say somebody shot him sometime Tuesday. Look, people, he stood to get big bucks when the Roundtree woman dies. What happens to his share of that estate? Same with Fred Butler. And maybe Roundtree's dead." His stare at Max was demanding. "You were in Ves Roundtree's pocket, standing there that night like she needed a bodyguard. You seem to know all about everything. We're told to come to your house tonight. So let's get down to business. When one of them dies, do the ones who are left"—he gestured at Jane, Curt, Bob, and Katherine—"get their share?"

Max spoke carefully. "As I understand the provisions of the trust, upon Ves Roundtree's death, the estate will be divided among the living contingent remaindermen beneficiaries."

Tim's voice was harsh. "You mean them?" A big hand waved toward Jane, Bob, Curt, Katherine.

Max nodded.

Tim looked like a man grappling with a realization that death could strike at any time. "That's a hell of a bad deal. Who's going to keep them safe?"

Max put a bowl of fresh-cut papaya in front of Annie, another at his place. "Your favorite."

She smiled her thanks. She'd loved papaya ever since a visit to Mexico City and breakfast at Sanborns near the Zócalo.

Max sat across from her, his sexy morning self with thick blond hair slightly tangled, bristly cheeks, muscular in a T-shirt and plaid boxer shorts. This morning he was exuberant. "Today is going to be fine. No more Sturm und Drang." He was grave for a moment. "It's tough to wonder what happened to Ves but we can't do anything more for her. Or for Fred or Adam. It's time for us to get back to normal, have an ordinary Thursday. How about we take the boat out for some red snapper?"

"I'd love to"—her smile was bright—"but I have to work on the chapbooks." She wondered why Max, usually so perceptive, never detected the insincerity in her voice in regard to all things connected to fishing. It wasn't, she thought defensively, that she was hyper, but spending hours with a rod and a line waiting for a no doubt sneering fish to be dumb enough to glob onto a tidbit slapped on a hook was not her idea of fun. That didn't even take into account going out of sight of land in a boat wallowing like a drunken sailor. A native of landlocked Amarillo, Annie took great comfort from seeing land, however distantly.

Max's eyes had the dreamy look of a fisherman imagining triumphs. "Wish you could come. But you'll have fun, too."

Annie petted Agatha and took an occasional sip of coffee as she learned more about Scottish-born John Buchan, his pleasure in arduous hikes, his recurring stomach ailments, his service as governor general of Canada from 1935 until his death in 1940. Buchan was revered in the mystery world as the creator of Richard Hannay, hero of *The Thirty-Nine Steps*. Buchan's rousing tales featured admirable protagonists and gave a sense of a long-vanished world. It would be great to use the original cover—

The front bell sang.

Annie looked up the central aisle.

Jane Wilson moved with the grace of a model, strikingly attractive in a cranberry velveteen jacket with a starburst on the lapel, a floral silk blouse bright with dashes of silver and cranberry, and slender-legged black trousers above cranberry leather heels. All was perfect except for the haunting paleness of an open and rounded face not suited for drama. She reached the coffee bar area, looked at Annie. "I want your advice. I hope you don't mind. I closed the shop to come. I'm going to owe so many hours."

"Of course I don't mind. I'll get some coffee." Annie gestured at a table nearer the coffee bar that wasn't encumbered by the chapbook manuscripts. Jane sat at the table, looked stiff and uncomfortable.

Annie hurried behind the coffee bar, reached up to the display of mugs emblazoned with mystery titles. She chose *Something Wrong* by Elizabeth Linington for Jane and *The Perilous Country* by John Creasy for herself, filled them, joined Jane at the table.

Jane gripped the mug. "Last night"—her voice was uneven—"Max seemed to be saying that one of us killed Fred and Ves and Mr. Nash. Do you think that's true?"

Annie heard a demand for reassurance. She had to answer honestly. "I'm afraid so. I asked around about Fred. He was a happy man until he went to Ves's house that Wednesday night. When she described how someone tried to kill her, Fred was shocked and frightened. Max saw his reaction. So did Ves. Later she figured out what happened, what must have happened. Fred was in her yard looking for treasure when someone came and waxed the step on her stairs. But Fred didn't know about her fall until the night he died. He came there and he looked at someone. He must have agreed to meet that person on the pier. Ves told me on the phone Monday night she was going to see if she could remember who Fred looked at. No one's seen her since. The next night Adam Nash died. Maybe he knew something or maybe he was killed to increase the others' share, but one way or another, all the deaths have to be connected."

Jane brushed back a soft tangle of brown curls. "Tim says anybody who might get money could be killed. He's furious at me."

Annie was puzzled. If Tim was scared for Jane, she'd understand. Why would he be angry? "Furious at you?"

She lifted her chin. "He wants to get married. Right. Now. Today. Then he can take care of me. Either that or I should let him move into my house. He says I can't live there by myself, that anybody could get in and . . . kill me."

"You live alone?"

Jane's glance skittered away. Her pale cheeks were touched by pink. "Tim and I—well, I'm not in any hurry. I'm nineteen. I want to be able to be myself for a while. Tim is a lot of fun and he's ambitious and maybe he's the right one, but I don't want to decide now. Especially not now. Everything is horrible. That nice Fred is dead and Ves gone and Mr. Nash shot." She pressed her fingertips against her temples for an instant. "It's horrible. I don't want to get married when things are bad."

Weddings should be the happiest of occasions on the happiest of days. Annie remembered Laurel's vision for her and Max's wedding. A red wedding gown. Annie didn't care if that was the custom in China, however nicely Laurel intended her suggestion. Annie wore a soft cream dress of her own choosing. Perhaps the dress had the faintest rose tint. Happiness suffused their day, glorious weather, good friends, a traditional ceremony. *"Do you take this man . . . ?"* Of course Jane wanted to marry in joy, not fear.

Jane hurried ahead. "I want a June wedding. That's what Mom and I talked about. Toward the end"—tears glistened in her eyes—"Mom seemed to like to look ahead and she said, *'You'll marry the nicest boy, I know you will.'* Mom and I figured out what kind of dress, ivory with some lace at the throat, and the flowers. She loved chrysanthemums. I told her—I promised her—when I married it would be just the way we planned." Her gaze met Annie's directly. "A lot of people live together now before they get married but I promised Mom I wouldn't do that. Tim doesn't live with me. He has an apartment on the other side of the woods by the harbor pavilion."

Annie knew the harbor park well and the apartment house separated from the pavilion by thick woods. A path led through the trees to the apartment parking lot.

"He's going crazy. He says we have to get married today or he should

160

come and stay at my house. I told him no. He says he's scared someone will get me. But I told him I promised my mom." She pushed away the mug, her coffee untasted, scooted back the chair, stood. "Thanks for listening. I better get back to the shop. I guess you're right. Fred Butler knew something and Ves figured out who killed him and Mr. Nash was involved somehow. I don't know anything about anyone so I should be safe. I'll be extra careful. I'll lock up real well. And somebody would have to be crazy to keep killing people in Mr. Roundtree's trust."

A sharp nip on one ankle got an immediate response. Annie sped behind the coffee bar and shook dry pellets into a clean bowl. She refreshed Agatha's water bowl, placed it on the newspaper spread out on the floor. She was smiling as she returned to the round table with three separate stacks of manuscript sheets. She was close to completing her copyedit. Next week Max could work his online wonders and soon the chapbooks would be done.

The next author in Henny's list of classics was one of Annie's favorites. John P. Marquand was better known as a literary author but he also wrote thrillers starring Mr. Moto, an elegant Japanese spy who often challenged American adventurers. In the first Mr. Moto, *Ming Yellow*, a sardonic newspaper reporter and a wealthy American heiress faced a ruthless marauding mercenary who killed as thoughtlessly as a housewife swats a fly.

Annie felt a chill. That's what someone was doing. Killing without compunction. There were six guests at their house last night. One of them had killed three times. Who? Which one was a threat?

Annie picked up a pen. What did they know about the murderer? The murderer was calm and cool, remaining at Ves's house after she drove off, entering the house to remove evidence the step had been waxed. That indicated steadiness under pressure. The murderer made quick decisions. When Fred looked across Ves's living room, the murderer decided Fred had to die. Fred died within hours. Ves wanted time to remember the moment when Fred looked at . . . someone. If she remembered and spoke to the murderer, she was somehow convinced she was mistaken. The murderer must have been glib, projected an image of innocence, then followed her in the dark to make sure she never told anyone of her suspicions. The murderer, like the Chinese brigand in *Ming Yellow*, was focused on more money, always more money, and so Adam Nash died.

Which of the six had these qualities?

Jane Wilson. Her visit to Death on Demand might have been a clever pretense, emphasizing that she could be a victim so of course she couldn't be guilty of the crimes. Jane was young. She loved pretty things. Did she want to be able to buy designer clothes, not pick them up secondhand? She seemed sweet. Did she resist Tim moving in to her house because she wanted to be free to go and come as she wished?

Tim Holt. He was smart, ambitious, had big ideas about what he could accomplish but he needed backing. Big money. He pushed Jane to ask Ves for money. Ves said no. Was Tim willing to do whatever was necessary to achieve his goals? He was strong, could move fast. Did he have a gun? So many islanders owned guns, whether legal or not. They were easy to come by.

Gretchen Roundtree. There had to be a reason she'd returned to the island, taken a job at a cosmetics store. If the story Marian picked up from a newspaper friend was right, Gretchen certainly was pressed for money. She liked to live high. If she was also a clandestine thief, she had a penchant for danger, was quick, almost nerveless, and might right now be under enormous pressure to come up with money to hide a secret that could put her in jail.

Curt Roundtree. He chose not to stay at his mother's house when he was on the island. Was that because he wanted to be able to go and come without anyone's notice? He had a reputation for sponging off rich friends. If he'd worn out his welcome at too many places, if his mother no longer sent him regular checks, his cushy lifestyle might be threatened. He had the appealing look of so many reddish-haired men, a freckled face, a genial expression. Had he used his charm to convince Ves he was innocent? He enjoyed hang gliding, which was thrilling and dangerous. The same could be said of murder.

Bob Farley. His struggle to get around made him an unlikely attacker. But he might exaggerate some of his difficulties. He was not the man he'd once been, a successful, admired artist with a six-figure income. If he and Katherine were short on money, and that seemed to be the word around the island, maybe he was willing to kill to make it possible to travel to exotic places on trips that would require huge sums. His physical disability could have served him well, made him seem unlikely to be a danger. Perhaps Fred wouldn't worry about meeting Bob Farley at the end of Fish Haul Pier.

Katherine Farley. Katherine learned the night before Ves's accident that Bob had tried to commit suicide. She would do anything, everything to keep him safe. Did she think he needed travel, something to live for, a reason to keep going? Did Katherine's fear for Bob drive her to set a trap for Ves? Once the trap was set, the rest followed. Fred's knowledge meant he had to be silenced. Adam? Did he know something or was he killed purely for money? Katherine was smart, controlled, implacably devoted to her husband.

If she had to rank them . . .

But any one of them could be guilty. It was up to Billy to discover the truth.

11

Billy Cameron liked the smell of fresh paint. He noted that Tim Holt was doing a careful job for the Misses Quinton on their picket fence, smooth strokes, no paint spattered on the grass. Tim wasn't in painter's white coveralls. As an odd jobber, he chose to work in a red polo and jeans with one worn knee. He listened as Billy pointed out how he had an excellent view of the frame office building where Adam Nash died if Tim looked toward the harbor. Billy intended to visit the secondhand shop next, then cross the street to the cosmetics store. Of those who had gathered in Ves Roundtree's living room, only Tim Holt, Jane Wilson, and Gretchen Roundtree were in close proximity to Adam's office. "Did you see anyone enter the building?"

Tim looked puzzled. "What time? I mean, I'm only here after lunch. I paint in the afternoons except when it's rainy."

Billy studied Tim's face. He was a personable guy. Nice-looking with a clear bright gaze. If he was the perp, this was a smart answer. The innocent would have no idea what time a murderer arrived. "Anytime that afternoon."

Tim nodded sagely. "So he was killed in the afternoon. I didn't hear anything that sounded like a shot but maybe I wouldn't. I'm working on this side of the fence now so my back is to the street. I took a break around three"—he gestured to his left—"dropped into the shop to see Jane, had a Coke with her. I came back and painted until a little before five. I was getting my stuff together and not paying much attention to anything. I picked everything up and walked over there." He pointed at a black pickup parked in a dusty lot at the end of the street. I kind of noticed somebody going inside the building"—he pointed at Adam's office building—"but not enough to know who it was."

"Man? Woman?"

Tim's face creased in tight lines. "Oh hell, I'm sorry. I just got a glimpse. I thought I saw a swish of gray, like maybe a raincoat or something. That's all I remember. A swish of gray." He hesitated. "I kind of thought maybe it was a woman."

Billy watched him closely. "Why?"

Tim's grin was lopsided, engaging. "A guy doesn't walk like a dame. You know what I mean. But that was just a feeling. I sure can't swear to it."

"If anything comes to you, get in touch with me."

"Sure."

Billy knew Tim watched him as he walked toward the door of Jane's shop. He wondered if Tim would follow, and then he heard a high voice calling out, "Young man, we don't pay you to stand and stare."

He didn't envy Tim dealing with the Misses Quinton. Or to be precise, Miss Priscilla Quinton. The other sister—Imogene—never spoke to strangers. Miss Priscilla frequently called the station. There was a cat in her yard. The light at the corner of the street had burned out. The sound of the jukebox at Parotti's Bar and Grill was too loud.

A bell chimed as Billy stepped into You Want It, We Have It.

Hurried steps from the back slowed when Jane Wilson saw him. He admired her sweater. It was—what did Mavis call it?—yeah, a cardigan, white with colored figures of skaters. A turtleneck blouse was in the same shade of apricot as the skaters, and her slacks were white. A mighty pretty outfit.

Jane's eyes widened. "Is it true that someone killed Fred and Ves and Mr. Nash? That's what Max Darling told us last night. He said we all needed to be careful."

Billy gave her an encouraging look as she described the gathering at the Darling house. No harm done. Possibly, it was helpful to encourage them to be wary. As he tried to calm her, he appraised her wide eyes and rounded face. A picture of innocence. Perhaps. Perhaps not. "Investigations are continuing into Fred Butler's and Adam Nash's deaths and we continue to search for Ms. Roundtree. Were you here in your shop Tuesday afternoon?"

"Yes." A slender hand touched her throat.

"Did you leave the shop between one and five?"

She shook her head.

"Did you hear a shot?"

"No." The word was scarcely a breath.

"Do you have any idea who might have shot Adam Nash?"

She took her time in answering. "I don't know. Max thinks it was one of us."

"Us?"

"One of the people at Ves's house the night Fred died."

"What do you think?"

She shook her head again, didn't speak.

"What color dress did you wear on Tuesday?"

Her eyes were huge, frightened. "A jersey floral dress, big red flowers on a black background."

He nodded. "We'll be in touch." He left her standing in the center aisle. As he crossed the street, he frowned. He had trouble believing Jane Wilson slipped into Adam's office, steadied a .45 with two hands, shot Adam Nash dead. But there were killers with sweet young faces.

Billy's nose wrinkled slightly as he stepped into the cosmetics store. Funny how women liked all these smells. He was glad Mavis didn't scatter perfumes and powders across the dresser, and nobody looked nicer than she did. Her complexion was soft and smooth. He liked the pale pink lipstick she wore and her powder had a nice homey gardenia scent.

A curtain parted at the back. Gretchen Roundtree's welcoming smile froze for an instant before she moved forward with a pleasant expression. "Chief Cameron." Even in a blue smock over white slacks, she exuded an aura of wealth and privilege. He bet she'd cost Rufus a pretty penny. Her blond hair seemed to glisten, her black brows were perfectly arched, her face smooth and unwrinkled. She stopped in front of him. It would be easy to dismiss her as just another rich woman, dabbling in a little shop. But he had a different picture of Gretchen Roundtree after he talked to Detective Morales in the burglary unit in Scottsdale. She hadn't, as Marian had been told, actually been present as a guest in all the homes that were robbed. But she had visited the houses recently, was known to the victims. He looked into alert blue eyes and judged she was capable of planning a daring theft, capable of executing a carefully timed crime, capable of selling stones to a well-connected fence, capable of hiding monies that she wouldn't be reporting to the IRS. Detective Morales was curious about Gretchen's return to the island. "Working at a cosmetics shop?" He'd given a low whistle. "Sounds like somebody has the goods on her." A pause. "She was at a weekend blowout at a mansion just before she left town. No robbery. The wife is about thirty years younger than her rich hubby. She loves jewels. She has a ruby necklace supposedly worth four hundred grand. She still has the necklace. Maybe Roundtree tried a grab, got caught. This new wife has a mean mouth. Maybe blackmail is a thrill. Something for her bucket list."

Behind Gretchen's slightly condescending expression was a wary, calculating intelligence. Billy had no doubt she would do whatever she needed to do to save herself. He gave her his most stolid cop look. "Were you here Tuesday afternoon?"

Now there was a slight tilt of amusement to her lips. "I work here. Every day. Yes. If it matters."

"It might matter. Did you hear a shot?"

The tilt of amusement fled. For an instant she looked older. Frightened. "No. When was Adam killed?"

He ignored the question. "Did you leave the shop anytime in the afternoon?"

"I closed over lunch. Went home. Came back at one. I closed up and left around five." She looked at him steadily.

If she was in the shop at five, she was in the clear. When pressed, Doc Burford said, with qualifications, that death likely occurred between four and six. Downtown, while not big-city busy, had plenty of occupants between four and six. Billy was sure Adam was shot as the ferry departed the harbor at five. "Around five? A few minutes before? Or after?"

She appeared to concentrate. "I believe it was a few minutes before five." Then she nodded. "Yes. It must have been. I heard the ferry whistle as I walked to my car."

Was she innocent or enjoying inner pleasure as she used the sound of the ferry horn as an alibi?

Chef Max proudly presented the catch of the day, red snapper baked in white wine with onion, green pepper, and succulent mushroom pieces. Cheese grits and steamed asparagus completed the menu. Max was sympathetic when Annie told him about Jane's visit and her determination not to be pressured into a wedding. As Annie washed the dishes, he opined from a comfortable perch on a stool at the central island. "Tim sounds like he's serious."

"About Jane? Or somebody trying to kill her?"

"About Jane." Max popped a small square of toffee in his mouth.

Annie wasn't one to act as a food gendarme, but toffee seemed a bit of overkill after a spectacular dessert, pineapple cookies crunchy with shredded coconut and homemade vanilla ice cream.

"The man wants her. He's crying wolf to hustle her into marriage. A man will do what a man has to do." There was tacit approval in his tone. "I suppose he may really be scared for her, but I don't see someone stalking the surviving contingent—"

"Heirs," Annie said firmly.

"Oh, ye of little legal knowledge. Anyway, you get my point. Fred had to go because he knew about the step. Then the killer decided to dispatch Ves, and somehow Adam got in the mix. Jane's safe. You want a prediction?"

Annie put the last dish in the dishwasher, poured in detergent, closed the door, and pushed Start. She unloosed the tie to her apron, hung it from a peg at the end of the counter. "Love predictions."

"And this one's about love. I'm surprised you haven't picked up on it." Max grinned. "I admit a mere man cannot be expected to plumb—scratch that—divine the workings of female minds. Greater men than I have tried and failed. But this one's billboard plain. Jane isn't in love with Tim. She won't marry him."

Annie looked at him in surprise. "She cared enough to try and inveigle money out of Ves."

Max shrugged. "They probably have a good time together and she wants to have a boyfriend. She won't marry him."

Annie wasn't so sure. "She's young. She doesn't want to be pressured."

Max looked complacent. "You knew we'd get married."

As they walked into the hall, headed for the den, she looked up at him, thick blond hair, blue eyes, Joe Hardy all grown up and sexy as hell. She remembered the first time she'd seen him. She'd known, perhaps not that she would marry him, but she'd known nothing would ever be the same, he was going to matter to her, her life was going to be different.

He watched her face. His smile was smug. "That's what I thought. Jane doesn't feel that way."

They settled on the couch. Max reached for his iPad, Annie for Charles Todd's new book, then stopped. "I'm in a *Topper* mood." She was happy and she wanted a little frosting on that cake.

Max bypassed the iPad, picked up the remote. "Your favorite ghosts, sophisticated and fun. Coming right up."

Annie loved the beginning, the ebullient married couple racing along in George's car, a crash into a tree. Was there ever a cooler couple than Cary Grant as George Kerby and Constance Bennett as Marion Kerby? She knew the dialogue after the crash by heart:

Marion: "Oh, George, you're getting transparent. You're fading."

George: "Say, that's funny. I can see through you, too. Say, who's that?"

Their bodies are lying by the wrecked car.

Marion: "It's us. You know something, George? I think we're dead."

George: "I think you're right. Funny, I don't feel—"

The ringtone "Happy Days Are Here Again" announced a call from Marian. Annie had changed the ringtone after Marian and Craig remarried. But Marian wasn't likely to be calling with happy news, not with everything that had happened the past few days.

Annie tapped Speaker. "Marian?"

"Just got it on the scanner. Shots fired. 225 Bluefish Road. On my way there. Jane Wilson's house. Right around the corner from you."

S irens squealed behind them. Annie twisted to look. "Police cars. Maybe three."

The Lamborghini squealed around the corner onto Bluefish. Lights blazed from a house midway up the block. Lighted windows marked several houses on the even-numbered side of the street. On the odd-numbered side, two houses were dark. Only the house in the middle had a small light shining from a front window. In the glare of Maglites, Annie saw the gilt numbers, 225, Jane's house.

"We're here first." Annie's voice rose. "Marian got the report at the same time as the call to the police and she was on her way when she called me." The police station was a good six blocks north and east of their house and even farther from 225 Bluefish.

Sirens blared. Flashing red lights whirled. Max pulled to the curb. Police cars raced past, screeched to a stop in front of the house with a dim light shining through a living room window. Police spilled out, took cover behind their vehicles. Shouts. "Police. Hands up. Throw down your weapons. Police."

Max rolled down the driver's window.

Annie felt sick inside. Jane was upset when she came to the store this morning, but she was alive, alive and thinking about the wedding that someday she hoped to have, a June wedding and an ivory dress with lace at the throat. Annie strained to see, yet she looked with dread. Her gaze traveled across the front lawn. Nothing. Which meant she didn't see a body lying on the grass. The steps . . . Nothing there, but to the left of the steps, a huge fern looked askew, its fronds bent and tangled.

Maglites illuminated the yard. The house was well kept, a one-story yellow cottage with a magnolia tree to one side of the gravel drive. A green Honda was in the drive.

Annie scarcely breathed as she stared at a huge royal fern to the left of the front steps. Portions of the fern looked crushed. It was a still night and the flower bed was sheltered from wind. Some of the lower fronds of the fern moved.

A uniformed figure darted forward. Annie recognized Lou Pirelli's stocky, muscular build. He moved fast, gun in hand, weaving to avoid providing an easy target. He thudded across the drive, hunkered behind the magnolia tree. "Police. Hands up. Out from behind that fern. Now."

Hyla Harrison, gun in hand, covered Lou. She held the gun with both hands, the barrel aimed at the quivering fronds. A swarm of officers fanned out to form a backup perimeter. Billy Cameron's old sedan pulled up behind the police cars. Billy swung out of the car, strode forward, big, strong, imposing.

Marian's VW nosed past the Lamborghini, jolted to a stop. The driver's door was flung open. Marian popped out, lean in a navy turtleneck sweater and black jeans.

One of the officers—he was young with short brown hair and an unlined face—yelled, "Take cover. Active shooter at large."

Marian ran to the far side of her car, knelt, but she had the Leica in her hands, ready to take a series of photographs.

Annie reached for the door handle.

Max grabbed her arm. "Wait."

"I don't see Jane anywhere." Annie's voice shook.

"Maybe she's in the house. Maybe she's all right." Max gave her arm a reassuring squeeze.

Lou Pirelli's voice was deep, harsh. "We have you covered. Come out from behind that fern, hands up." He left his cover, eased toward the flower bed, alert, ready to fire.

The fern fronds quivered again, parted. Jane Wilson was on her hands and knees, crawling forward. In the glare of Maglites, she was pale, hair tousled, a purplish bruise on the left side her face, her velveteen jacket snagged. She pushed herself up, stood, looked small in the glare of the lights. "Don't shoot. Please." Her voice was high and shaky. She held out empty hands half raised, eyes blinking against the glare of the flashlights. "Someone shot at me."

Lou Pirelli came out of his crouch, stared. "Janey? Janey Wilson?"

She squinted to see. Her face changed. "Is it Lou? Angie's big brother?"

He hurried to her, putting his gun in his holster. "Yeah. I'm Lou."

Billy Cameron was directing officers. "Sweep the area. Be careful not to mess up any footprints. The call came in twelve minutes ago. It looks like the shooter got away."

Annie opened the car door, jumped out. Max was right behind her as they crossed the street. She stopped on the sidewalk.

"Lou." Jane wavered unsteadily.

Without fanfare, as if it were the most natural thing in the world, he spread an arm around her shoulders. "You're safe now."

A barefoot man in a Braves sweatshirt and gym shorts stood on the opposite curb. "Somebody shot a gun. Eight past nine. I called 911. I looked out and didn't see anybody."

Billy joined Jane and Lou, spoke to her quietly. "Are you hurt?"

"I tried to duck and fell. I hit my face on something." She began to shake, perhaps a delayed reaction to shock, lifted a trembling hand to the bruised portion of her face.

Lou tightened his grasp. "Don't worry. We're here. I'll take care of you. What happened?"

She looked up at him. "I was late getting home. I usually get home before dark. But I owed some hours at the store so I stayed late."

Billy was encouraging. "You arrived here a few minutes after nine. What happened?"

Her blue eyes were huge. She took a deep breath, tried to stop trembling.

Maglites swung back and forth across the yard, around the house, into the woods. Officers moved cautiously, shouting, "Police. Come out with your hands up. Police."

The neighbor joined Annie and Max and Marian on the sidewalk. "I thought she was a goner after I heard the shots. I knew they were across the street. Had to be her house. The Jenkinses"—he jerked a thumb to his left—"are out of town, and"—he pointed to his right—"that house is empty."

"How many shots?" Marian held her pen over a sheaf of folded copy paper.

His red face was pugnacious. "Three. Three for sure. After I called 911, I got my gun out. But when I snuck out on the porch, I didn't see a soul. Not anywhere."

Jane's voice was thin but steady. "It happened so fast. I parked in the drive and got out. I walked across the yard and started up the steps, and all of a sudden there were shots. I knew what they were. I tried to get out of the way, and that's when I fell." She reached down, touched an ankle. "I twisted my ankle and my head hit something. There's a wisteria bush next to the fern with knobby branches and that's how I hurt my face. I stayed really still and burrowed down behind the fern. I was afraid whoever shot at me would come and find me."

"Did you hear anything?"

She looked at Billy blankly. "The shots."

"After the shots."

She clasped her hands tightly together. "I don't know."

The neighbor took a couple of steps forward. "Hey, Billy. Joe Mackey here. I heard the shots, came out right after I called 911. I didn't see anybody. I didn't hear a car. I was on the porch soon enough to hear a motor and see taillights."

An engine gunned and a rusted black pickup squealed to a stop. The cab door opened and Tim Holt was out and running toward the house. "What the hell's going on here?" He hurtled toward Jane and Lou, glaring at Lou. "Get your damn hands off her. What the hell do you think you're doing?"

"Tim." Jane slipped free of Lou's support, stepped forward, one hand outstretched in front of Lou. "Someone shot at me a little while ago and they came to help."

Tim checked himself midstride, looked like he'd been body slammed. "Shot at you?"

Billy Cameron moved closer. "Miss Wilson is unharmed. She sustained a bruise when she took cover behind a fern. She's safe now."

Tim's face twisted in fury. "I told everybody she could be in danger. Like the others are. I called you this afternoon, told you people you needed to get this thing solved. So now somebody's shot at her. No thanks to you she isn't dead." His head swung around. "Where is he? I'll kill the—"

Billy's tone was sharp. "The shooter escaped before we arrived. You are impeding our investigation."

"'Impeding our investigation.'" Tim's voice was heavy with sarcasm. "What investigation? Now they say somebody pushed poor old Fred off the pier and Ves Roundtree's dead somewhere and Mr. Nash is on a slab. What investigation?"

"Tim, hush." Jane was angry. "It doesn't help to come here and act ugly. Please be quiet." She turned back to Billy. "I didn't hear a car. I didn't hear anything but the shots."

On the front steps, Hyla Harrison aimed a Maglite at the clapboard siding to the right of the front door. "Bullet holes here, Chief. Estimate six feet from the ground. If I stand on the second step, it looks like the shots were just above and to the right of the target. Maybe not a real good shot. Or shot from a pistol, not a rifle."

Billy nodded. "Get photos. Mavis can remove the slugs after you've measured." He turned back to Jane. "Would you like for a paramedic to check you?" He gestured at the flashing light of an ambulance that had pulled up behind the police cars.

Jane touched the bruise. "I'm not really hurt."

Only hurt emotionally, Annie thought. Jane could no longer go in or come out without a flicker of fear. To know another person deliberately aimed a gun at you, intended to take away your life, was as devastating as solid earth turning to quicksand beneath your feet, sucking you to oblivion.

"We will complete our search. You may wish to go inside."

Jane's eyes slid toward the door, where Hyla was photographing the evidence of metal tearing into wood.

Tim bulled forward. "No two ways about it. Thank God I decided to check on you. I'll go get my gear."

Annie saw the recoil in her eyes. Jane didn't want him to stay all night. She'd promised her mom. Jane wanted love, if that's what they had, to bloom in happy times, not when death lurked. Annie rushed forward. "Come home with us." She looked at Billy. "She will be much safer. No one can get at her at our house."

Annie reached sleepily for the phone on her bedside table. "Hello."

"Annie, my dear. Still in bed." Laurel's husky voice faintly accusing. "On such a troubled Friday morning. But that suggests all is well. Or as well as it can be. I just heard about the shots at Jane Wilson. We need to rally round to keep her safe. I've texted Emma and Henny. Both are quite bright and shining in the morning."

Annie decided it would not be a good start to her day to take umbrage at the implication that she and Max were derelict as adults to still be in bed at, she squinted at the clock, six A.M. She swung her legs over the side of the bed. "Good for them." She managed to sound cheery.

Max rolled up on one elbow, hair mussed, expression muzzy.

She mouthed, "Your mother. Worried about Jane."

Laurel's tone was a shade stiff. "To think of that young woman all alone."

Annie said quickly, "She's here. We brought her home with us."

"Splendid. That's the very best solution. I'll let Henny and Emma know all is well. Call us if there is anything we can offer, though it does seem now that Billy is best equipped to discover what happened." The call ended.

♦ ♦ ♦

Annie knocked gently on the guest room door, spoke loud enough to be heard. "Breakfast will be ready in half an hour. Come down whenever you wish." Max was already downstairs, cleaning strawberries.

The door opened. Jane looked out shyly. "I hope I'm not a huge bother." Although Jane had taken only a few minutes last night to pack a bag, she was certainly lovely this morning in a beige Windsor plaid sheath dress and double strap bronze heels. A necklace with several strands of amber, black, and crystal beads sparkled.

Annie smiled. "You're no bother. Max loves to cook and he especially loves to cook for guests. He's already in the kitchen."

Annie led the way downstairs and they settled at the kitchen table.

Max brought coffee and orange juice, served bowls with freshly sliced strawberries. "The quiche will be ready in a moment." He turned back to the stove.

Annie offered sour cream and brown sugar to Jane, who chose sour cream.

As they ate, Annie carefully avoided any reference to murder and gunshots, talked brightly about the latest Hannah Dennison book. "Her characters are fabulous. I love"—she took a bite of a succulent strawberry, savored the sprinkle of brown sugar—"the way a really good book could only have been written by that particular author. Good books are never copycat." She chattered on as Max brought them each a plate with a generous slice of quiche. She wished she could do something to erase the dark smudges beneath Jane's eyes, restore an eager bloom to her rounded face, remove the memory of shots in the darkness.

As Max replenished their coffee cups, a knock sounded at the back door.

He looked surprised, walked to the door, opened it. "Hey, Lou. Come in."

Jane twisted a little in her chair. She looked pleased, surprised, uncertain.

Lou Pirelli stepped into the kitchen, looked immediately toward the table. "Morning." His gaze settled on Jane. "I wanted to check in with you. I'll be going to work with you. We thought it would be a good idea for someone to be on hand for a while." Lou spoke with the easy drawl of a native islander. He wasn't in uniform today. He wore a soft blue polo and khaki slacks and tasseled loafers. A uniform tended to create a sameness in appearance. In civvies, Lou's curly dark hair, handsome face, and athletic build made him distinctive. "If you don't mind."

Annie saw relief in Jane's rounded face. And pleasure. How nice for Jane. She looked at Lou. Oh. And oh.

Annie felt restless, popping up and down every few minutes to check her e-mails, to place orders, to make phone calls for a committee meeting for Friends of the Library. When the radio news announcer led the top of the hour with a breathless description of a shooting on Bluefish Road, she switched to a cool jazz station.

Agatha watched with glowing green eyes and a tail that flicked irritably.

Annie returned to the table determined to focus on the chapbooks. She picked up Laurel's *Merry Musings*. She smiled in agreement as she read: *If an elephant's in the way, find another path*. Excellent advice. Her present elephant was her inability to immerse herself in the ordinary life of the store and her job and committees and volunteering and tennis and—

"Happy Days Are Here Again" rang.

Annie answered. "Is everything okay?" So much had not been okay in recent days.

Marian spoke in a staccato rush. "Heads-up. Bob Farley just thumped into the station, told Mavis he was turning himself in. I was there, checking the overnights, everything from the shooting on Bluefish Road to a stolen chicken coop out on Bidwell Lane. The TV reporter from Savannah was refreshing her makeup, waiting to see Billy. I swung around to be sure I'd heard right. It was Bob Farley. Not the man he once was, too thin now, but impressive, thick sandy hair, chiseled features, would still look good on a *GQ* cover even though he's too gaunt. There's an air about Bob. He was dressed like a *GQ* guy, blue blazer, a triple-stripe dress shirt, no tie, chinos, loafers. I guess you dress up to go to jail. He said, 'I killed Fred Butler, Ves Roundtree, and Adam Nash. I tried to kill Jane Wilson.' He was composed, but his face had an empty look. I whipped out my Leica. The TV blonde moved like a tigress, motioning her camera guy to whir. I was shooting photos of Bob. The door to the offices opened and Billy walked out. Mavis must have buzzed him the minute Bob started talking. The TV gal yelled at Bob, pushed a mic in his face. 'Statement for the press.' Bob ignored her. Billy came up to the counter. Bob said it all again, same words, nothing more, nothing less. The TV gal's mic was right in his face. Bob wasn't emotional. His voice was kind of tired. Billy never changed expression. The TV gal's yelling like a banshee at this point. 'Are the murders solved? Three crimes? Bob what? What's your last name?' Bob half turned, said formally, 'Robert J. Farley,' turned back to Billy. Billy said, 'Come this way,' and held the gate open. I called out, 'Where's Ves Roundtree's body?' No answer. Billy yanked open the door to the back. They started down the corridor and the door shut. I was going nuts. I kept pestering Mavis. I wanted a statement. Finally the printer started clacking. She went over to check, picked up a sheet, handed one copy to me, one to the TV reporter, who moved so the light was better, and started talking as her cameraman filmed. 'A reign of terror ended shockingly this morning on Broward's Rock, a sleepy resort island off the coast of South Carolina, when . . .'"

Marian took a breath. "Probably been picked up coast to coast at this point. Murder with your morning coffee. Here's the statement: *Broward's Rock police announced that Robert J. Farley is a person of interest in the deaths of Fred Butler and Adam Nash and in the disappearance of Vesta Roundtree. Farley was taken into custody when he claimed to be responsible for the crimes. He's being held on suspicion of murder.* That's it. Nada mas. Nothing about an arraignment."

Marian cleared her throat. "Talk about dancing on the head of a pin. I don't get what Billy's doing. Why wasn't Bob arrested for murder, plain and simple? If murder is ever plain and simple. Anyway, I used my cell to record Bob's repeat. TV will run with the film, which also got him admitting to the murders. I know Billy doesn't like to show his hand but this time I don't see where he's going. I wrote the story, pulled up the stuff on all the deaths. But I had a couple of hours before my deadline. I knew what I had to do. I went out to the studio. Katherine was working on a watercolor. When I walked in, she turned and smiled. She's truly beautiful, that sleek dark hair and classic features. Or maybe I should say she would be beautiful if she didn't sag like she'd been pressed through a wringer. She looks haunted. Not even the smile hid her stress. I know her fairly well because she teaches classes at the Haven. David's taken oil painting from her and she's encouraged him."

Marian's son was gifted, loved art, planned to be an artist.

182

"Anyway, Katherine gave me a sweet smile, asked, 'How's my favorite young painter?'

"I said, 'He's doing fine and working hard.' I felt like a rat dripping slime. I walked up, stopped a foot away from the easel. She looked at me and knew I had bad news. Her face went blank. I saw terror in her eyes. I said, 'Billy Cameron issued a statement announcing Bob is a person of interest in three murders. Bob's being held on suspicion of murder.' It was like watching a hurricane surge destroy dunes. One minute everything is beautiful. The next, the sea oats are a memory and the dune isn't there. She gave a low moan and she was running past me, the brush flung on the floor, still wearing her painting smock. The door slammed and she was gone." A pause. "I'd imagine she's at the station."

Annie drove too fast, made it to the station in just under four minutes. She slammed out of her car, yanked out her cell phone. Max was likely on the back nine. He'd insisted today was a day to enjoy living, and he lived to golf. She texted: *At police station. Bob Farley confessed, arrested. Will try to help Katherine.*

Annie hurried up the path, stopped by a young palmetto palm a half dozen yards from the station. Katherine Farley stood next to the trunk with its jagged thatched covering, the remnants of dead fronds. The wind rippled her paint-spattered smock. Her face was white as alabaster. A faint tracery of veins was apparent on one temple. Katherine held out a hand. "You heard?" Her voice was dull, defeated. Agonized.

"Marian called. She thought"—it had not been said but Annie knew it was so—"you needed someone."

"I need Bob." Katherine shivered. "Bob didn't kill anyone." She spoke with the intonation of a child repeating words she doesn't understand. "They were nice to me. Billy took me into his office and he told me what Bob said. I told him it couldn't be true, wasn't true, Bob would never hurt any living thing. He wouldn't." Her luminous brown eyes brimmed with tears. "Billy was nice to me. He said he was sorry. I told him I had to talk to Bob. He said he'd go see. It seemed to me he was gone such a long time, and when he came back inside the office, he stood with his back to the door and I knew he didn't want to tell me." Tears trickled down her cheeks. "Bob won't see me. But I know Bob was at home that Thursday when someone tried to kill Ves. I was gone then. I told Bob I was delivering a watercolor across the island. When I got home, his car was exactly where it was when I left." She spoke emphatically, trying to convince Annie. "I know that's so because there was a huge pinecone by the back right wheel when I left. The pinecone was lying in the same place when I got home. It would have been smashed if he'd gone anywhere."

Annie said nothing, but her face must have revealed her thought.

"You think he wouldn't confess to murders he didn't commit. But he did. He lied. I know why." Now her eyes were dry, her face drawn. "He's lying to protect me. Bob thinks I killed them."

The sea breeze was picking up. Katherine's smock billowed. She brushed back a dark tangle of curls, stirred by the wind from the harbor. "I told him I was delivering a watercolor I'd just finished, an alligator on the bank. But he came down to the studio and saw the painting was still there. I knew he was puzzled. He looked at the watercolor, then at me. I started talking about something else. He didn't ask me. But he was right. I didn't make a delivery that Thursday. I went to Ves's house." She took a deep breath. "I have to tell Billy. Will you come with me?"

12

Annie loved the view of the harbor from Billy's office window. February offered days that hinted of spring to come, shining blue sky, puffy white clouds, silvery porpoises leaping as if for joy. A brisk onshore breeze trimmed jade green water with whitecaps. A shrimp boat moved steadily past. An iceberg-white yacht glided south.

Annie turned her gaze to Billy, sitting stolidly behind his shiny yellow oak desk. His stepson Kevin had made the desk. The varnish was sticky and there was a slight list to Billy's right. Billy's face was expressionless, but his eyes were intent.

Katherine leaned forward. She looked insubstantial in the smock, but her voice was clipped and urgent. "I want you to understand why I was upset. Bob, oh God, he went to Gurney Point and I think he would have jumped into the water if your officer hadn't followed him. I tried to thank her and she was matter-of-fact, said, 'Ma'am, it's my job to see that people are safe.'" Katherine's voice quivered. She pressed her lips together for an instant, managed to keep going. "That's what I was carrying with me. I talked to Bob. I told him"— the planes of her face sharpened—"I can't live without you. Oh, I'd live. But it wouldn't be life. There wouldn't be joy or meaning, only one dead dull day after another. I told him he must never never never think he's a burden. That's what I was dealing with the next day, the Thursday that someone set the trap for Ves."

Katherine looked out the window at the harbor, but Annie knew she didn't see blue skies or puffy white clouds.

"Bob went to Gurney Point Wednesday. The next day was the Thursday Ves fell." Billy spoke quietly.

Katherine faced him. A pulse fluttered in her slender throat. "All day I tried to think what I could do. There isn't much money now. I can't earn what Bob did. And"—her tone was fierce—"I won't sell his paintings. He'll never paint again. I can't sell his paintings. I decided to go see Ves." She brushed back a swoop of dark hair. "I thought she'd help me. She's—" A breath. "She was kind. I was going to tell her how I'd nearly lost Bob. I was going to ask her for twenty thousand, tell her somehow to subtract it from whatever we'd get someday, and I would promise never to tell any of the others. They all wanted money from her. I could see why she felt like she was surrounded by crabs with their claws grasping. But this was Bob's life." She stared at Billy, her eyes huge. "I drove to her house."

Billy held up his hand. He opened a drawer, lifted out a recorder, placed it on the desk, turned it on. He looked at Katherine and recited the Miranda warning.

She stared for an instant, gave a strangled laugh. "I don't care. I'm trying to tell you what happened."

Billy nodded. "Police Chief Billy Cameron. Friday, February twenty-sixth, interrogating Katherine Farley, a possible person of interest in the murders of Fred Butler and Adam Nash and the disappearance of Vesta Roundtree. Now—"

Annie heard Billy's words, was puzzled. Billy talked about Ves's disappearance, but Bob admitted he'd murdered her.

"—Mrs. Farley, what time did you arrive at Ves Roundtree's house on Thursday, February eleventh?"

Katherine pleated her fingers together. "About twenty after five."

"Did you see any cars?"

For an instant, she looked surprised. "No. I suppose that should have told me she wasn't there. I didn't think about it. I wanted to see her. I thought she'd put her car in the garage. I pulled up on the drive. I started to walk back to the front of the house, but as I came even with the porch I saw the back door was open. I veered that way, went up the back steps. I was right, the back door was open."

"Ajar or fully open?"

"Wide open. I hurried up the back steps, came to the door, knocked on the jamb." For the first time, the rush of words slowed. "I pulled open the screen, stepped into the back hallway."

"Could you see the stairs?"

Katherine's nod was impatient. "The hallway extends from the front door to the back door. The stairs were to my left. I would have had to go to the front of the hall to go up the stairs. Or to look up the stairs."

"Did you?"

"No." Her voice was flat.

"What did you do?"

"I stopped inside the screen door and called out. There was no answer." Now her words came slowly. "I don't know if I can make you understand, but suddenly I was afraid. It was quiet. Terribly quiet. The back door open. Calling for Ves and no answer. I started backing up and then I was at the door and outside and running for my car. I don't know why I ran. But I did. I slammed in the car and got out of there as fast as I could."

Billy's gaze was considering.

Annie wondered if Billy felt he was hearing the truth, a woman who likely had entered a house where a killer lurked and interrupted the cleaning of a slick step or a woman spinning a tale to divert an investigator. Had she walked into the hallway and the sound of the door and her call sent a killer scurrying upstairs and out of sight?

"Did you tell anyone of this experience?"

"No."

"Why are you telling me now?"

Her shoulders tightened. "The next week on Wednesday we went to Ves's house."

Billy nodded. "That was the day Ms. Roundtree told you how she'd been hurt, the day Fred Butler died."

She nodded. "That night, after we got home, Bob went to his room." For an instant she looked defensive. "He has his own room now. He sleeps poorly and he doesn't want to keep me awake."

Annie heard more than the halting explanation, wondered if Bob Farley resisted closeness because he was no longer able to make love to his wife.

"I was restless. I couldn't seem to read. I decided to go to the studio. I didn't come back to the house until a little after midnight. Bob was in the living room. I told him I'd been working."

"Did you meet Fred Butler?"

"No." A steady gaze. "I did not meet Fred. I had nothing to do with Ves's disappearance on Monday or Adam's death on Tuesday." A pause. "I was working in the studio Monday night. I delivered the alligator painting Tuesday afternoon." She looked defiant. She had good explanations for her whereabouts at all the critical times, but that didn't change the fact she had the opportunity to have been on the pier or at Ves's house or in Adam's office.

"Did you go to Adam's office?"

"I did not."

"Did you shoot him?"

"No."

"Your husband's gun was gone when I came to your house Wednesday. I called you on the extension. When you joined us, you claimed you had no idea where the gun was. Is that true?"

Her shoulders bowed. "I took the gun from the bedside table the day after Bob tried to jump into the water. Bob was in his shower. I slipped downstairs and put the gun in my trunk. I was afraid to keep it where he could get it."

"What did you do with the gun?"

"I went to Blackbeard Beach and threw the gun as far as I could."

Billy made a notation. "Convenient that you claim to have disposed of the gun long before Adam Nash was killed or shots were fired at Jane Wilson."

"Not convenient. True." Katherine's stare was straight. "I wasn't home last night when someone shot at Jane. I was working in the studio. I'm trying to finish a commission. We need the money. I didn't come back to the house until ten or so. This morning we had the radio on and heard that shots were fired at Jane last night. Bob looked upset. I told him I thought it was awful. She's so young and so nice. I thought he looked at me strangely, but everything has been so odd. I asked him if he wanted to do anything this morning and he shook his head, said he was tired, thought he'd read, so I went to the studio.

I heard Bob's car leave." She looked defiant. "I'd fixed it where I can track his cell on GPS. If he'd started for somewhere solitary, I would have followed. He parked downtown so I didn't worry."

"He came here. He confessed."

"He's lying." There was pain in her voice. "He thinks he's saving me. He knows I could have killed them. I was out at the times the paper said they died. Worst of all, he knew the gun was gone, and I was the only person who could have taken it."

Billy said smoothly, "Unless you were as surprised as you seemed when I was at your house and Bob took the gun, used it, hid it or threw it away."

"Not Bob." It was a cry of despair. Her mouth twisted. "You think I'm lying to protect him. I would lie for him. But I'm not. He's lying for me, and I didn't kill them. Neither of us killed them. Don't you see, Bob knew I lied about the delivery. He wouldn't understand why I'd tell a lie unless I had something to hide. I did have something to hide. I didn't want to admit I'd gone to Ves's house, especially not after she told us someone tried to kill her. Bob knew I was out at all the times that mattered. This morning, after I went to the studio, he thought about the times and my lies and decided I'd tried to kill Ves, and Fred saw me so I had to kill him. He knew the only reason I would hurt anyone would be for him, so he came here, claimed he'd killed them." Katherine's face was no longer defiant or hopeful or anxious. She looked like a woman driven to despair. "Please tell Bob I didn't shoot anyone. Tell him everything is all right. Let him go."

Billy's face furrowed. "I told your husband he could call, arrange for a lawyer to come. He insisted he did not want a lawyer."

Katherine was adamant. "He must have a lawyer."

"I agree. He confessed to a series of crimes. I have taken him into custody." Billy's expression was odd, part exasperation, part dismay.

"Normally I wouldn't disclose his response, but you are his wife. As I locked the cell, I told him again that he could remain silent and call a lawyer. He hooked one hand around a bar and said, 'I don't want a lawyer. I have nothing to say. Not to a lawyer. Not to you. Not to anybody. I'm keeping it for the judge. When I go to court, I'll tell the judge I'm guilty. End of story. Until then, I intend to relax.' He turned his back on me and limped to the cot."

"He lied about the murders." Katherine's voice was shrill. "He thinks he's protecting me. Tell him I'm here and that I've told you everything. Tell him I will get a lawyer. Tell him"—her voice shook—"I want to see him."

"I will tell him." Billy's face was expressionless.

Annie thought his voice was uncommonly gentle.

When the door closed behind him, Katherine turned to Annie. "He has to see me."

Annie wanted to reassure Katherine, but she could hear Billy's voice, stolid and uninflected as he quoted Bob Farley: "I'll tell the judge I'm guilty. End of story." "Perhaps tomorrow he'll talk to you."

Katherine spoke rapidly. "I'll get a lawyer. Jed Lowery handles things for us. The minute I get out of here, I'll go straight to his office."

Annie knew Jed, who wrote wills and handled probates and real estate law. He was pleasant, intelligent, and had likely handled criminal matters only if appointed by the court. "There's a wonderful defense attorney in Savannah. Handler Jones."

Katherine came to her feet, paced to the window. She whirled to look at Annie. "How can it be such a beautiful day and my whole life is falling part?"

The door opened. Billy stepped inside, closed the door behind him, remained standing. He was an imposing figure, tall, solid, powerfully built. Slowly he shook his head. Annie saw sadness in his eyes, sadness at bringing hurtful news to a woman desperately afraid for the man she loved.

Annie watched Katherine's car bolt out of the police lot. She felt empty and sad. How did lives get so tangled? Bob and Katherine. Before his accident, they'd been a golden couple, the envy of many, physically attractive, full of charm and life, gifted, busy, successful. Now Bob was in a cell and Katherine was frantically trying to save him. What was the truth? Was Bob lying to protect her? Or was he quite certain that Katherine went to Ves's house, made the step slick, and when threatened by Fred's knowledge met him on the pier and pushed him to his death? Fred would not have been afraid for his safety with a woman. She could have convinced him that she wanted to talk, that they could reach an understanding. After that, perhaps it seemed easy to go see Ves, perhaps force her to leave the house at gunpoint. Had Ves died in the woods or was her body somewhere in the sea? As for Adam, was his murder simply to increase the size of the pot or had he become a danger?

The fact that Bob was in a cell meant either he was guilty or Katherine was guilty. No matter how much Katherine loved him, admitting her guilt would not help him. He would obviously claim she was making it up to protect him.

Katherine had the opportunity to commit the crimes.

Bob or Katherine? Katherine or Bob?

Annie looked out at the harbor. She didn't know when the water had ever seemed more beautiful, its color a rich jade green and above, a bright sky full of promise. A yacht neared shore, its hull a gleaming white. A man and woman stood near the prow. They looked young and happy, coming to the island for a holiday.

It was unsettling to juxtapose her memory of Katherine's face and the beauty of the day. Her cell phone rang, the tune for Max. As always, she felt a surge of happiness.

Hyla Harrison, crisp as always in her french blue uniform, pointed at the chair Katherine had occupied.

Billy nodded. "Pick up what prints you can. Check them against the unidentified prints on the screen door at the Roundtree house."

Hyla's green eyes were alert. "She can claim she touched the door when she came to dinner there or the night that Ms. Roundtree called them there to warn them."

"The prints may be among the most recent, overlaying other prints. It's been several days since she was there as a guest. And"—his blue eyes were grim—"her husband may use a cane, but I imagine I can prove he customarily opened doors for her."

Hyla's gaze was admiring.

Annie hurried along the sidewalk toward You Want It, We Have It, the secondhand store where Jane Wilson worked. Max's call to arrange lunch at Parotti's had given her some perspective. It was up to Billy to decide whether Bob or Katherine was guilty. But Bob in jail likely meant the danger was over. If Katherine was the murderer, she would not attack anyone now. Jane Wilson no longer needed to be afraid. Annie was eager to bring her that good news. The bell sang a cheerful song as she opened the shop door. She stepped into the center aisle, looked about.

Jane came hurrying up the aisle, her bronze heels making a sharp tattoo as she hurried forward. Close behind her loomed Lou, broad face easing into a warm smile. "Hey, Annie."

Annie smiled in return. What a handsome couple they made, sturdy muscular Lou, sweet-faced Jane with her cloud of soft brown hair. That sheath dress set off her willowy figure quite perfectly.

Lou was in charge. He made a high five. "Have you heard the news? Bob Farley's in jail."

Annie knew neither Lou nor Jane was thinking of what that reality meant to Bob and Katherine. Understandably, they were elated that Jane was safe from attack.

Jane's sweet face was suddenly somber. "It's dreadful for Katherine to know that Bob did such terrible things."

"Katherine says he's innocent."

Lou was sardonic. "What else is she going to say?" His face brightened. "Hey, Annie, put in a good word for me. I'm trying to persuade Jane to close down the shop, come out on my boat with me."

Jane gave him a cheerful smile. "I can go with you Sunday. I can't close down. I owe too many hours anyway."

"I'll get my sister Maggie to take over." He was determined. "She used to work at Walmart in Hilton Head. She knows how to handle a cash register." He pulled out his cell. "I'll call her right now."

Annie was surprised. Obviously the station would alert him that he no longer needed to protect Jane, but didn't he need to get back to work? She blurted out, "Don't you have to work, too, Lou?"

He gave her an impish grin. "The chief was going to have a patrol keep an eye on the shop today, but I was due a few days off so I decided to take them. Jane and my sis Angie were really good friends in high school. The least I could do."

Jane's cheeks were pink. "Isn't that sweet of Lou?"

"So"—his tone was teasing—"you owe me. I don't want to waste my time off, and boating alone is no fun. I'll get Maggie over here ASAP." He pulled his cell phone out of his pocket. "I'll step outside," he said, and he hurried toward the front door.

Annie suspected he intended to tell Maggie she had to help him out, it was big-time important.

The door closed behind him. Annie turned to Jane. "I know it's a huge relief. You can tell Tim he can relax."

For an instant, her face was still. "Oh. I suppose I should call Tim." The front door began to open. "But not right now."

H yla Harrison reported in her usual crisp fashion. "I checked the prints we made on the screen door Tuesday. Several correspond with those left on the chair by Katherine Farley. However, they are overlain by prints from Ves Roundtree."

Billy Cameron asked quickly. "Are any Farley prints on top of other prints?"

"No, sir. I picked up fragments of her prints below Ms. Roundtree's prints."

"Are any of the prints on the screen door smudged?"

Hyla's eyes narrowed. "I would not describe them as 'smudged.' Portions of prints overlay prints but there is no indication, for example, that a gloved hand gripped the panel."

"Good work, Officer."

As the door closed behind Hyla, he faced an unpalatable truth. He had a perilous course to navigate. A buzz. He flicked on the intercom.

Mavis's voice was uninflected, but he knew she was stressed. "The mayor called again. Demands that you return his call. Now."

"Thanks." He clicked off, glanced at the clock. A quarter to five.

His smile was humorless. What if he told the mayor it was quitting time and he had the weekend off and he'd get back to him on Monday? Sometimes he thought it would be nice to have a workday that started at nine, ended at five. He'd had an offer last year from an island boat builder to join his crew. For a millisecond he imagined the smell of sawdust, cutting a plank of Douglas fir to the right specifications, ending up with a hull that was seaworthy and fine. He picked up the phone, called.

There was no salutation. "You missed the press conference. I spoke with reporters an hour ago. They're here from all over. One TV crew helicoptered in from Atlanta. It would have been helpful if you'd been here. *Triple Murderer Confesses*. I told them you were busy wrapping up the case. I guess you were, though what you have to do escapes me since Farley's confessed. None of that matters now. We'll make the five o'clock news big. Very big. The message will be loud and clear. The murders were the work of one possibly deranged individual, and Broward's Rock, the loveliest sea island off the coast of South Carolina, is safe. Absolutely safe. Revelers welcome. Old ladies. Kids. Honeymooners. The arrest didn't happen a minute too soon. The PGA tournament is here next month, and for sure we don't want nationwide coverage of Murder Island. That would kill the tourist trade. You should have called and filled me in. My secretary saw the feed about Farley on TV and ran in to tell me. I'm sure you intended to keep mc informed. I had to wing it from what I picked up on TV." Mayor Cosgrove's voice wasn't the mellifluous tenor known to island residents. It was clipped and sharp edged.

In the privacy of his office, Billy's face was hard, but he kept his tone pleasant. "This is a complex investigation—"

The mayor interrupted. "What investigation? The man confessed."

"People confess. Sometimes they're lying—"

The mayor broke in again, and now his voice was rough. "Don't screw this up, Cameron. The murders are solved. Period. I've already talked to the circuit solicitor. I told him you'd be in Beaufort for the arraignment Monday. Ten A.M. Be there." The phone was slammed in the cradle.

Murder Island. A reporter or newscaster must have used the phrase, and it rankled Mayor Cosgrove. His main focus was bringing visitors to the island. The more tourists, the more money in local coffers, and Cosgrove liked spending money. Billy was all for art, but he thought the town could have found a better use for money paid a local artist—young, sexy, and voluptuous—for a series of red-and-purple rectangles that now graced the harbor front and, according to the artist, represented eons past, present, and future. There had been rumors that the married mayor and the artist had a "close" relationship.

Billy yanked his mind back to business. To be fair, the mayor had a point. Bob Farley had confessed. Presto. Case solved. Island's resort reputation shiny again. The majestic reach of the law reassuringly restored.

Billy knew what the mayor expected. Wrap up the case. Get the evidence to the circuit solicitor. There was enough evidence for a charge, likely enough for conviction. Brice Willard Posey, the overbearing ham-faced posturing circuit solicitor, would love leading the charge. Lots of newspaper attention. Maybe even make the cable news. Farley might be guilty, but his car with the hitch for a wheelchair was distinctive, and careful inquiry found no witness who saw that car or a man with a cane near Adam Nash's office late Tuesday afternoon. Still, it was a gray February day, not many out and about. By Monday he needed to bring a murder charge or free Bob.

Billy leaned back in his chair. He had to find out the truth about Bob Farley.

Annie heard the ping of her cell phone, picked it up. A message to her, Max, Henny, and Laurel from Emma.

Emma: *TV running a feed on Bob: Triple Murderer Confesses. Crime spree ended. Arraignment scheduled Monday.*

Laurel: *Katherine's arranged for Handler Jones to come to the island tomorrow.*

Henny: *Fred's killer needed the strength to heave his body off the pier. Bob?*

Annie didn't chime in. What was left to say? Instead, she looked again at Laurel's text. Kind Laurel had obviously gone to the Farley house or studio, found Katherine, offered support, and was glad to learn Katherine had hired wonderful Handler Jones. Annie pushed away the memory of the night she'd entered the jail, using the code for the entry pad courtesy of Billy, and whispered in darkness to Max in his cell. Dark days. The dead days of summer. She had come so near to losing Max, because appearances can deceive and lies can endanger the innocent.

Bob Farley confessed.

Katherine claimed innocence.

Who was telling the truth?

13

Max added a new log. The fire crackled, sparks flying. Annie glanced at the flames, then at Max as he settled back on the leather sofa. He felt her glance, looked her way, smiled, then picked up his book, a new Brad Meltzer novel. Dorothy L curled beside him. He stroked her soft white fur. A contented purr rumbled loud enough for Annie to hear.

Annie had a sudden chill vision of Katherine Farley's studio. Likely it was dark now. Annie looked at the clock. A little after eight. Velvet night pressed against the windows. They hadn't drawn the curtains because they had no near neighbors. In a moment, she'd get up, put her book aside, an Alafair Tucker title by Donis Casey, and pull the cords, make the serene room even more cozy.

A distant rattle, a knock at the back door, brought Max's head up. "I'll go see." Friends often came to the back door instead of the front. He pushed up from the sofa. Dorothy L jumped down and padded after him.

"Hey, good cat."

Annie recognized Billy Cameron's voice, came to her feet.

Billy walked to the fireplace, turned, stood with his back to the warmth. "Sorry to bother you tonight." He looked weary. His posture was straight as always, but lines grooved in his face.

Annie hurried to speak. "You are never a bother." Her voice was firm and her gaze said more. *You are our friend. We will always owe you. You know you can call on me or Max. Anytime. Anywhere.*

He understood, nodded gravely. He walked to the sofa, sat beside Max. He spoke quietly. "I find Bob Farley's confession suspicious. I may be wrong. Maybe he killed the three of them. But I've never dealt with a confessed murderer who didn't talk and talk and talk. Bob says he killed them, but that's all he'll say. No details. What time did he meet Fred on the pier? Did he hit him with his cane, stun him? How did he get him over the railing? Or did he pull the body to the opening for the ladder down to the side dock. If so, how did he have the strength to shove him past the platform? Where is Ves's body? How did she die? What time did he go to Adam's office? Why kill Adam? Why shoot at Jane Wilson? How did he miss? I checked: Bob's a sharpshooter. We estimate the bullets traveled about thirty yards before they slammed into the house. Bob Farley shouldn't miss at thirty yards. What does Bob say? Monotone: 'I killed Fred Butler, Ves Roundtree, and Adam Nash.' Period."

Max looked at him steadily. "You think he's lying."

"I do. I've done everything I can to encourage him to talk. I have one last hope." He turned to Annie. "Will you help me?"

Annie's breath caught when she reached the back steps of the station. She'd been this way only once before, the night Billy gave her the entry pad code so that she could talk to Max, alone in a cell, accused of the murder of a beautiful young woman he'd never known. As she tapped the numbers, she was grateful for the chill breeze from the harbor. It would be too much to bear if the air had been hot and heavy and sultry as it had been on the August night her life crumbled around her.

She pulled open the door, stepped into the quiet corridor of the cell block. The ceiling inset lights were muted. She stepped inside. The door closed behind her. She walked forward.

A dimly seen figure came up to the bars of the third cell. Most visible was the blob that was Bob's white face.

Annie came even with the cell, uncertain how to begin, what to say. The words came slowly. "Katherine wants you to know she's innocent."

"How did you get in?" His head turned as he peered up and down the cement corridor.

"I know a way." If she told him Billy had given her the code, he would say nothing. Yet she was speaking truth, even if not all the truth. "When Max was arrested, a friend gave me the code to the entry pad at the back door." Billy was her friend. "I'm here because Katherine knows you are innocent."

Thin hands gripped the bars, but his face was a pale blob in the shadowy cell. "She knows I'm innocent." There was no joy in his response. Instead, there was grimness.

Annie hurried to offset the implicit assumption that Katherine's knowledge was based on her guilt. "Katherine is innocent, too. She went to Ves's house that Thursday but Ves wasn't there. Katherine went in the house and found no one there. She suddenly felt afraid and she rushed outside. She didn't know about Ves's fall until the following Wednesday."

His fingers locked tighter around the steel rods. "She told me she was making a delivery. She lied."

"She didn't tell you where she was going because you would have wanted to know why she planned to see Ves. She didn't want to tell you that she was going to ask for money. She thought Ves would help, that Ves was kind."

"Katherine wanted money for me, didn't she? Katherine never cared about money. She wanted to make things better for me. Take the cripple here and there, pretty things to see." His tone was bitter.

Annie didn't think he was bitter with Katherine. He was bitter with the fact of his injuries, his incapacity.

"Katherine loves you." Annie spoke with all her heart.

"Yes." The single word was bleak.

"She knows you're innocent. She swears she's innocent. You don't need to lie to protect her."

He spoke at a rapid clip. "The police know—or they'll find out— she was in her studio the night Fred was killed and the afternoon Adam was shot. She was alone. She was in the studio when shots were fired at Jane."

"There are others who don't have alibis." Annie was sure this was a fact.

"The gun is gone." There was a note of finality in his voice.

"She threw the gun in the ocean after you went to Gurney Point." Silence.

Annie put her heart into her voice. "Tell Billy you made a mistake."

Bob's voice was harsh. "He'll arrest Katherine."

Annie was startled. Perhaps Bob was right. Perhaps Billy believed Katherine committed the murders. Billy had a passion for justice. Would he use Annie to save Bob and then charge Katherine? Billy was tough.

"That's how it is." Bob's voice was grim. "Tell Katherine—" His hands dropped from the bars. He was tall and thin, too thin, a shadowy figure. "—I love her." He turned away, limped to the cot.

B illy always drove the speed limit. The headlights did little to pierce the pall of darkness that swathed the island at night.

Annie described the conversation. Her voice broke as she quoted Bob's final words: "Tell Katherine I love her."

Billy loomed big and solid in the driver's seat. He slowed for a deer bounding across the road, picked up speed. "Bob knows Katherine. Until my dying day I'll carry with me the certainty that he's lying to save her. I don't like for perps to walk. But if she's guilty, she's built her own hell. The only thing that matters to her in life is Bob. She would live and die for him. I think she killed for him. I know murderers. They come in all stripes. People kill because of pride, fear, anger, greed, passion. Most of all, greed or passion. Some people want money or power enough to destroy any obstacle in the way. Katherine's driven by passion. She will do whatever she has to do to make Bob's life better. Now he'll go to prison. Or be executed."

B illy sat cross-legged on the floor, his little blond daughter next to him. She moved her piece and gave a shrill whoop. He threw up his hands in surrender. "You did it!" She hopped up, ran toward the kitchen. "Mommy, I won, I won!"

He folded the Chutes and Ladders board and reached for the box. He was still smiling as his cell phone rang. He glanced at caller ID, stiffened. What the hell? He swiped. "Billy Cameron."

• • •

The jacket of Billy's Windbreaker sagged from the weight of his gun. He rarely carried a gun. There shouldn't be danger. Not if the hurried words were true. Anger was hot deep inside. Billy knew the back of his neck was reddening. He drove at his usual pace, the headlight beams no match for the pool of darkness beneath overhanging tree limbs. Why Gurney Point? But the remote far north end of the island at half past nine should be inhabited only by owls, foxes, deer, raccoons. He came around the last twist in the road, glimpsed windbent pines but no car in the turnaround space at the end of the road. He cut the lights, glided to a stop, another twenty feet. No reason to make himself an easy target. The windows were rolled down. He listened intently, heard the soughing of tree limbs in a stiff breeze, the whoo of an owl, and, distantly, the rush of water at the base of the bluff.

He was ready to ease out through the window when he heard his name called.

"Billy, I'm over here." A flashlight flickered on, was turned up, revealing a face he knew, then the beam swept over his car.

Billy opened the door, moving fast, his hand firm on the butt of his gun.

Annie thought Billy Cameron looked tired as he held the door of his office open. Of course, he didn't usually work on Saturdays, though the police station was always in operation. This morning his shirt was crisp, his brown slacks creased, his loafers well shined, but his face was weary. Bluish shadows marked the hollows below his eyes, and there was a small spot of tape on his chin where he'd likely nicked himself shaving.

Annie moved ahead of Max, took the chair nearest the window that overlooked the bay. She glanced outside at puffy white clouds in a robin's-egg blue sky, lacy whitecaps on pea green water, and outriggers with the nets lowered on a passing shrimp trawler. Max sat in the chair next to her.

Billy closed the door, moved behind his desk.

Max was curious. "It looks like you're stuck with Bob. Will the arraignment be Monday?"

Billy settled behind his desk. "There have been some further developments. There may be an arraignment Monday. I would like to arrange a meeting at Ves Roundtree's house under your auspices, Max."

Max looked surprised. "My auspices?"

Billy spoke matter-of-factly, but his dark blue eyes stared intently at Max. "Ves contacted you, asked you to assist her the evening she invited the Farleys, Curt and Gretchen Roundtree, Jane Wilson and Tim Holt, Adam Nash, and Fred Butler to her house to inform them of her fall and to warn one of them that she had a gun and didn't intend to die."

Max nodded. "Ves wanted me there as a witness, although I wasn't the only one who helped her. She first talked to Annie. Annie drew me in and then my mom and Henny Brawley and Emma Clyde. We were all involved."

"But as far as the guests are concerned, you were there as Ves's agent."

"That's right."

"That gives you the status"—Billy sounded pleased—"to contact those with an interest in the investigation on behalf of Ves Roundtree."

Max looked bewildered, but he heard his cue. "I will be glad to do anything I can on behalf of Ves."

Billy gazed at them without expression, spoke as if thinking aloud. "Obviously, this won't be your usual Saturday evening. But I certainly understand that you feel an obligation to Ves and have decided to contact everyone involved and invite them to come to Ves's home at seven o'clock tonight. Since Ves sought your help before she disappeared, you know she would want everyone informed about the arrest and scheduled arraignment. The police are glad to cooperate and relinquished the house key to you as Ves's agent. You spoke with the chief and he agreed to come and present the facts."

Annie blurted, "What about Bob Farley?"

"He'll be there." He pushed back his chair and stood. "The department is always eager to work with the community."

Annie had a pen-and-ink sketch of a champion seal point Siamese. She thought Billy's face was similarly inscrutable. Apparently he'd told them as much as he intended to reveal.

As they rose, he said casually, as if in afterthought, "It might be as well to invite Emma, Henny, and Laurel since they assisted you earlier. Ask them to be there at seven and tell them they should direct their complete attention to the person with whom they spoke. Let me see"—a pause as if recalling names—"Emma spoke to Katherine Farley, Henny to Bob Farley, Laurel to Tim Holt, Max to Curt Roundtree, and Annie to Gretchen Roundtree." His face was bland. "At a quarter after seven, I want each one of you to watch that particular individual." On that pronouncement, he moved to the door, held it open for them to step in the hall, closed it firmly.

As the Lamborghini picked up speed, Annie twisted to look back at the station. "Billy's up to something. Did you notice when he talked about watching people he left out Jane Wilson?"

"I noticed. Maybe Billy feels she's innocent because someone shot at her. But that doesn't give us any idea why he wants anyone watched. He said the arraignment is on for Monday. What's the point of getting everyone together tonight?" He shrugged. "Anyway, it's up to us to persuade people who don't want to have anything to do with the police to show up. I'll call them. You can text the Incredible Trio and invite them over for shrimp creole at six. That gives us plenty of time to explain. Not that we can explain much. Henny will have a dozen questions about our assignment to watch a particular person. Emma will probably quote from either Marigold or Inspector Houlihan. And Ma, who knows"—a quick smile—"what she will think. Or say. Anyway, we'll follow Billy's script, pretend the gathering is my idea."

Annie perched on the edge of Max's desk. It was odd to be there on a Saturday morning. Death on Demand, of course, was usually open. She'd hung the Back Soon sign in the window. It would be wonderful to have Ingrid Webb, the world's best clerk, back from her vacation Monday. Max looked comfortable in his large leather chair, holding a legal pad, making notations. He scanned what he'd written, gave her a thumbs-up, put the pad on his desk. She glanced at the index card in her hand as he punched a number, then speakerphone. She liked lists. This one was short if not sweet—Jane Wilson and Tim Holt, Gretchen Roundtree, Curt Roundtree, Katherine and Bob Farley. Not that she needed a list to remember these names. One of her favorite lines from *Casablanca* was Captain Renault's bland directive on the airport tarmac: "Round up the usual suspects."

"Don't miss our special on eyeliner today." Gretchen's voice as she answered the phone was as smooth as honey. "How may I help you?"

Max was equally smooth. "Gretchen, Max Darling. I'm calling a meeting at seven tonight at Ves Roundtree's to bring everyone up to date on the investigations into the deaths of Fred Butler, Ves Roundtree, and Adam Nash."

"Why?" Her tone was flat, almost hostile.

Max was unruffled. "There's been a lot of loose speculation about the status of the case and some errors in television reports. However, the police have reached a conclusion and Chief Cameron has agreed to share that information."

"Do you mean we can get this all behind us? Get our lives back?"

Annie thought about three lives lost. Fred, Ves, and Adam wouldn't get their lives back.

"That's my understanding. I look forward to seeing you at seven."

"I'll be there." Gretchen's voice still held a note of anger.

Max clicked off, looked thoughtful. "She sounds innocent. I'd still put my money on her as the killer. Though"—his expression was wry—"if she was going in for homicide as well as jewel thefts, you'd think she'd take out her blackmailer." He punched a number.

"Sea Side Inn. How may I direct your call?"

"Curt Roundtree, please."

As the room telephone rang, Max lounged back in his chair. "I doubt we'll find sonny boy hunkered in his room—"

"Hello." Curt's voice was wary.

"Max Darling call—"

"Not int—"

Before he could finish, Max interrupted. "You'll be interested. The murder case will be closed tonight and the disposition of your father's estate discussed. Seven o'clock. Ves Roundtree's house." Max punched Off. "I don't much like sonny boy. And"—a huge smile—"since the call came through the switchboard, he can't call back. I doubt he has any idea about Confidential Commissions. Stew, baby, stew." Max punched a number.

"You Want It, We Have It." Jane's voice was cheerful.

"Hi, Jane. Max Darling."

"What's happened?" Now her voice was thin.

Annie understood that visceral response.

"Everything's fine. I wanted to let you know I've called a meeting of everyone who was at Ves's house that Wednesday." There was no need to explain which Wednesday. Jane would well remember the last time she saw Fred Butler. "Chief Cameron has agreed to give a final report on the crimes."

"It's over, then." Her voice was odd. "Bob Farley killed them?"

"It's over." Max said nothing about Bob.

"Ves's house? I don't know if I can bear to be there again. I'll remember Ves at her shop, those frizzy red curls and the way she had so much energy. I don't know if I can bear it."

"Please come. She'd want you to be there. Ask Tim Holt to come with you."

There was a pause. "Tim? I haven't seen him for a day or so. I told him I needed some quiet time. You can call him." She rattled off a number. "Do they know what happened to Ves?"

"I believe the chief will answer all questions."

"She was kind to my mother. I'll come."

"Seven o'clock."

"Seven o'clock." Her voice was heavy as she repeated the time.

"We'll see you then." Max clicked Off. He gave Annie a quick look. "You have a soft spot for birds who fall out of nests, even for baby alligators. I'm glad Jane's innocent." He was already punching the number.

"Tim Holt." His voice was strong and pleasant.

"Max Darling." He repeated the by-now-familiar pitch.

"I saw on TV that Bob Farley's in jail. Why meet?" He sounded puzzled and not particularly interested. Old news was old news.

"There will be some information that hasn't been released to the press."

"Yeah? Well, I'd just as soon forget about the whole thing. And Jane's sick of it."

"She's coming."

"Oh. If she said she's coming, I'll bring her."

"Thanks. We'll see you then." He clicked Off.

Annie shook her head. "I don't think Jane wants to deal with Tim." Had she told Tim she wanted some space because she was reeling from murders and Ves's disappearance and gunshots in the night? Annie remembered the sound of her voice when she answered the phone. Full of cheer. Annie had a clear picture of that moment in their kitchen when Lou looked at Jane.

But Max was staring at the phone. "One more call. This one's tough."

Annie understood. His bland come-over-to-Ves's-for-the-latest-on-the-murders spiel was a nonstarter with Katherine Farley.

"Hello." Katherine's voice was deep, brusque.

"Max Darling. As you know, I tried to help Ves when she said she was in danger. I've arranged for the police to provide the latest information about the crimes. Everyone is coming to Ves's house at seven, and Billy Cameron will describe the results of the investigation."

"What investigation? There's no investigation. Billy's jailed an innocent man, a man obviously disturbed. But that's the easy way out, isn't it? An arrest makes the police look good. Three murders solved. Billy Cameron accepted a confession he knows is fake. He'll put Bob on trial, kill him." Her voice shook with rage. "And you want me to be there? Hear all about that dangerous killer, Bob Farley, who can barely walk with a cane, who doesn't have the strength to lift a bag of groceries. Go to hell." The connection ended.

Annie was already heading for the door. "I'll talk to her."

Max was on his feet. "Billy said for Emma to watch Katherine tonight. She may have killed all of them. I'm coming with you."

Annie stood in the doorway. "She won't see you. You're an enemy now. I'll go." She had a sudden sense of certainty. "I'll be safe."

Sometimes men made things too complicated. Annie held tight to that thought as she walked up the steps to Katherine's studio. She turned the old-fashioned brass doorknob, stepped inside. She wasn't sure why she chose the studio rather than the Farley house on its stilts with a view of the lagoon. When she was inside in the entry area, now unlit, she looked past easels and tables littered with paints and brushes and jars. Light streamed through the skylight, illuminating a cream leather sofa where Katherine sat, holding a small painting.

Annie's shoes made a hollow sound as she crossed the old wooden floor.

Katherine turned a pale, hard face. "Leave me alone."

"Bob will be at Ves's house tonight."

For an instant, Katherine sat rigid, the painting clutched in her hands. "Bob will be there?"

Annie came nearer, sat down on the sofa. "Billy doesn't think Bob is guilty. Last night he let me into the jail and I talked to Bob. I don't think he's guilty either."

Katherine's burning stare into Annie's eyes never wavered. "Billy thinks he's innocent?" There was a rising note of hope. "Why did he arrest him?"

"He hasn't actually arrested him yet. He's holding him for investigation, and he had no choice after Bob said he killed them. I told Bob you were innocent."

"Did he believe you?"

Annie wasn't sure. But she would never make that admission. "Yes, but he's afraid Billy will arrest you because you were at Ves's house that Thursday and you were out the other times. And the gun is gone."

Katherine rested the painting on her lap and pressed her hands hard against her cheeks. "Oh God, I wish I hadn't thrown it away. But I did. I threw it away before Adam was killed or someone shot at Jane. But I can't prove that's what I did."

Annie glanced down at the painting. Bob had often painted vivid splashes of color with the vigor of a carnival or swirling dancers or pulsing rhythm. This painting, an eight by twelve, was muted, the faint violet of sunrise, a hint of the ocean below, the promise of new beginning.

Katherine once again held tight to the frame as if a lifeline. "Bob's afraid for me. But he knows I'm innocent." Tears slid down her cheeks. "We have to tell Billy."

"He knows. It's Billy who wants everyone to be at Ves's house tonight. He asked Max to arrange the evening, make it look like Max was in charge. Billy has something planned. I'm sure of it. He believes Bob is innocent."

"That's all that matters." Katherine's face was still haggard but now there was hope. "Bob will be there. I'll come."

Annie hoped deep inside that she hadn't held out a hand to pull Katherine aboard a tumbrel to her destruction.

Emma sipped espresso. "Damn good. I'll have another macaroon. You're a dandy cook, Max." Emma's emerald green caftan and sandals matched the glow of the massive stone in a ring on her right hand.

"Chef," Laurel corrected. Laurel's beige cable sweater and chocolate brown slacks emphasized the golden sheen of her hair and the Nordic blue of her eyes. She took a dainty nibble of a raspberry truffle.

"Whatever." Emma waved a stubby hand, and the emerald flashed.

Henny used a spoon to retrieve the maraschino cherry from the mound of whipped cream on her cappuccino. "We are grateful to Max for a wonderful dinner and to Annie for a great dessert selection. We have dutifully refrained from talk of murder but"—she glanced at the clock—"we leave here soon to go to Ves Roundtree's house. As I understand our instructions, at precisely a quarter after seven I fasten my eyes on Bob Farley, Emma observes Katherine Farley, Max watches Curt Roundtree, Laurel stares at Tim Holt, and Annie gazes at Gretchen Roundtree. May I ask what we are looking for?"

Max turned his hands over, palms up. "My guess is that Billy will announce something, and he wants a witness who can testify about a particular person's response."

Emma nodded sagely. "As Marigold says, *Even a clever criminal isn't always on guard.*"

Laurel put down her piece of candy, half eaten. Her dark blue eyes were grave. "I don't feel comfortable about this evening." She quoted from her chapbook, "*In rattlesnake country, watch where you step.*"

Henny looked from one to another. "I share Laurel's uneasiness." She rose. "It reminds me of *Rebecca*. Foreboding, uncertainty, suspicion, a sense that life is a quicksand, insubstantial and treacherous. Perhaps tonight nothing will be what it seems to be."

14

Annie loved dancing at the country club on Saturday evenings. The music was different each Saturday night. She'd circled this date because Max loved the latest in pop, and the band was sure to play "Happy" and "Walking on a Dream." Annie wished they were on their way to dance. Instead, Max followed the now familiar route to Sunshine Lane, turned into the drive to Ves Roundtree's house.

The Lamborghini's headlights didn't dispel the gloom of the tree-shrouded drive. He pulled up behind Ves's van. Annie felt cold. The van was precisely where it had been parked when she and Billy came looking for Ves. The house was dark. Max turned off the headlights. There wasn't a glimmer of light until he opened the driver's door. He pulled a small laser flashlight from the pocket of his blazer, turned it on. He held the light until Annie stepped out and came around the car to join him.

She put a hand on his arm. "I don't like this."

The little laser beam illuminated the flagstones to the back porch, emphasized the surrounding dark, the unlit looming house. "We'll light the place up." His tone was easy.

Annie understood she was reacting to Ves's disappearance, to a sense that evil lurked. She hurried to keep up with Max. He thudded up the back steps, opened the screen door, tried several keys, found the one that fit. The door opened. More darkness. Max flipped switches, and light, wonderful, warm, glowing light, shone on the porch and in the hallway and living room and dining room. The house smelled stale. Dust dulled the surface of the marble-topped hallway table and the tall mahogany grandfather clock. Max stepped to the thermostat near the clock, tapped. The fan whirred into action.

Annie checked the time. Last spring Ves's house was included in a tour of old homes. Ves proudly recited the provenance of the antique, a Roxbury tall clock made by Simon Willard in 1795. That lovely day Ves was at her most energetic, talking fast, her reddish curls quivering as she gestured. Now the clock was dusty and it was ten minutes before seven.

The clock chimed seven o'clock as Jane Wilson and Tim Holt, the first to arrive, came through the front door. They stopped uncertainly in the archway to the living room.

Max gestured to the far side of the room. "Sit anywhere you like."

Jane touched the scarf at the throat of a white silk blouse. The scarf, a gorgeous floral weave azure paisley, matched the blue of slim-legged wool slacks accented by white leather ankle boots. "I wish I hadn't come." Her voice wobbled.

"Hey, Jane." Tim was hearty. "We'll see what the cop has to say, then go to Whistler's for a drink."

"I don't want a drink." Her voice was still tremulous. "I want to go home."

Annie moved nearer. "Thanks for coming. We know everyone is concerned about what's happened, and now we can find out what's true and what isn't true."

Tim shrugged. "I thought everything was already definite. That crippled guy confessed. What else is there to say?" His face darkened. "I don't care if he is a cripple, I'd punch him if I had a chance." He grabbed Jane's hand. "Scared the hell out of me that night. I turned into your street and there's cop cars everywhere and somebody shot at you." He looked at her with his brows drawn, his face jutting. "But you're okay, and I won't ever let anyone hurt you. And now we can plan our wedding."

Jane gave him a quick glance. "Shh. Not in front of everybody. And you're hurting my hand."

He loosed his grip. "I get mad whenever I think about him shooting at you. He's lucky I won't be able to get my hands on him. Where is everybody? We"—he took Jane's arm again—"want to get out of here as soon as we can, do something fun." He led her to an Empire-style carved mahogany sofa, the bolstered ends upholstered in red satin with a gold medallion pattern. Jane slid close to one end, pressed against the pillows. Tim plopped next to her, bent near to murmur something. She shook her head, made no response. For an instant, his face was hard, then he again began to talk softly. The sound of his voice was warm, entreating. Her posture remained rigid and she never took her eyes away from the opening to the hall.

A rattle as someone knocked. Max pulled the front door open. Katherine stepped inside, hurried to the archway, looking quickly around the room. She whirled toward Max. "Where's Bob?"

"Billy's bringing him."

Annie felt a twist inside. So much was the same, sleek black hair in a chignon, aristocratic features, but now Katherine's face was tight and hard and her thin shoulders hunched. She wore unrelieved black—black silk blouse, black wool trousers, black leather ballet flats. No jewelry. Perhaps a dash of makeup. She surveyed the room again, her gaze cold and hostile, acknowledged no one, strode to a small settee with room for two.

Another knock, voices, steps in the hallway. Gretchen Roundtree brought with her a faint exotic scent. Her blond hair glistened and her smooth face looked confident. A pearl necklace glowed softly against a pale rose cashmere sweater. Her cream skirt was short and stylish. Curt was casual in a blue-and-yellow plaid cotton shirt, khaki slacks, and sneakers. He glanced around the room. "Where are the gendarmes?"

Max was pleasant. "Chief Cameron will be here soon."

Curt looked combative, ready for a quarrel. "I'll give him five minutes, then I'm out of here. I'm damn tired of the island, this house, and everybody here." He dropped into a wicker chair, stuck his legs out straight, bored and resentful. Gretchen shot her son an irritated glance, then her face was once again smooth. She sat in a chair near the fireplace. Her gaze moved to Katherine. Gretchen's smooth face altered for an instant. The lacquer of self-absorption was pierced by Katherine's despair. She took a tiny breath, was once again self-possessed.

The back door opened. Heavier steps sounded. And the faint tap of a cane.

Katherine came to her feet, eyes wide, lips trembling.

Billy Cameron, big and powerfully built, reached the archway. Bob Farley came up beside him. He looked frail and tired.

Annie wasn't surprised to see Billy wearing a white shirt and gray trousers and loafers, but Bob wasn't dressed in the orange jail coveralls. She remembered Marian's description as Bob came into the police station. Tonight he was wearing the blue blazer, triple-stripe dress shirt without a tie, chinos, and loafers he'd worn Friday when he confessed. Bob's hands were not manacled.

Katherine was running across the room. "Bob, oh, Bob." She wrapped her arms around him. Bob stood stiffly for a moment, then a hand lifted to gently smooth her sleek hair. He bent to rest his face against her head.

Billy watched them, his face expressionless. He cleared his throat. "If you'll take your seats now."

Katherine lifted a tear-stained face, looked into Bob's eyes. "I was afraid I'd never have you near again. Bob, please tell them the truth."

Bob pulled away. He looked around the room. "I didn't know we were coming here." He glared at Billy. "What's the point? Take me back to that damn cell. I told you I killed them."

"Bob." Katherine's cry was anguished.

There was a flash of pity in Billy's eyes.

Annie saw that look, quickly gone. She was afraid she knew what was going to happen. Billy brought Bob here, a Bob not in prisoner's clothes, a Bob without handcuffs, but Billy intended to leave with a murderer. And he felt sorry for Bob.

Katherine tugged at Bob's arm. "Bob, come with me. We'll sit over here." She pulled and slowly he moved. She held tight, pressed against his shoulder when they were seated. She paid no attention to the others, ignored the sounds from the hallway, her every sense attuned to the man beside her.

A flurry of steps in the hallway.

Max nodded a welcome as Emma, Henny, and Laurel crowded into the archway. "Good of you to come."

Emma's bellow was stentorian. "I see everyone is here. All of us are eager to find out what happened to Ves. We appreciate being included since we tried to give her a hand after her fall."

Annie noted varying looks of surprise on the faces of the assembled guests, but perhaps there was a lessening of tension. The evening was taking on the aspect of a civic meeting.

Max said quickly, "We're a little short of chairs. I'll get some from the dining room."

Emma's light blue eyes scanned the room. Henny's expression was bland, an island leader attending a public gathering, ready to contribute if called upon. Laurel's quite stunningly lovely face was dreamy, as if she might soon follow a Tibetan path to a remote hut.

Max placed dining room chairs, two on one side of the archway, two on the other. The action seemed unstudied, unplanned, simply a man making provision for more guests than a room could comfortably seat. The fact that the chairs faced the earlier arrivals seemed unremarkable.

Emma walked majestically, a sturdy block of emerald green, to the far chair on the right of the archway. Henny slipped into the chair next to her, turned her face to speak quietly to Emma. Laurel moved as if she walked on clouds, sank into the far chair on the left and smiled at Annie as she settled beside her. Annie wondered how her mother-in-law could appear so utterly otherworldly, as if at any moment she might consult with a nightingale in flight. Max remained in the archway, Billy a little behind him.

Annie glanced at her watch. Five after seven.

"My hope tonight"—Max's tone was pleasant—"is to represent Ves Roundtree. Monday night Ves realized that Fred Butler was killed because he saw someone he knew at her house the Thursday afternoon she fell. For several Thursdays, Fred left work early, claiming a dental appointment. Instead, he came here to dig for pirate gold. He was here the afternoon the step was waxed on the staircase. Fred melted away into the woods, since he was trespassing. Fred was unaware of Ves's fall until she called a gathering here. That Wednesday was the night Fred drowned. His death was murder."

Billy cleared his throat, stepped forward. "I'd like to take a moment here to clear up some confusion." He looked at Max. "If I may?"

"Of course." Max was agreeable.

Billy said briskly, "We want to give the circuit solicitor as much information as possible about Fred Butler, and we realized we don't have an account of his actions as he left this house the night he drowned." He turned to Max. "Who was the first person to go outside that evening?"

Annie glanced at her watch. Ten after seven.

Max shook his head. "The guests went out together. I stayed behind to ask Ves if she wanted me to spend the night, but she said she was fine as long as she had her gun."

Billy looked around the room. "Can anyone help us out here?"

Gretchen's breathy voice was disdainful. "We escaped like a herd of gazelles running from a leopard. Have you ever had anyone accuse you of trying to kill them? Good luck on who saw Fred. Who cared about Fred?" Gretchen was imperious in a Queen Anne chair near the fireplace. One hand toyed with a sapphire pendant. Her fingers were long and bony, the nails painted a deep raspberry. "It took forever to get out of here. The drive is narrow, so we were parked behind each other. Curt and I arrived first so we had to wait until the other cars left."

"This scarcely seems worth talking about." Katherine's voice was sharp. "Fred didn't drown here. I hate talking about that night. What difference does it make when we left this hideous place? If you care,

Adam stormed out first and Fred was right behind him. Jane and Tim were in front of us. We went straight to Bob's car. I think Fred was standing by his car. The shadows were pretty dark. Headlights were on but it was a black night. Once we got outside, you couldn't make out where anyone was."

"Fred's headlights were on?" Billy asked pleasantly.

"Everyone had their headlights on."

Annie's watch read thirteen after seven.

Gretchen bristled. "It took longer than it should have. Fred's car was the last in the drive. I think he was behind Adam. I almost honked."

Curt gave his mother a sly look. "You sure did. I caught your hand, reminded you there was a nutcase with a .45 in the house and to simmer down."

"Anyway"—her voice held remembered pique—"it took Fred forever."

Billy looked at Katherine. "You thought Fred was standing by his car. Mrs. Roundtree says Fred's headlights were on. So"—Billy's tone was casual—"someone else must have been standing at Fred's window, talking to him. Who—"

The grandfather clock chimed the quarter hour. Steps sounded in the hallway.

Billy half turned toward the archway, but Max gazed into the living room to watch Curt Roundtree. Annie stared at Gretchen.

The steps stopped. Annie felt a presence in the archway, but she kept her gaze fastened on Gretchen.

Gretchen's eyes widened. Her lips parted. "Oh my God." There was shock in the suddenly slack muscles of that perfectly made-up face.

There was a melee of sound, the tone ranging from incredulity to amazement.

Ves Roundtree stepped into the living room. She might have been arriving for a chamber of commerce luncheon, a bronze turtleneck sweater, a checked wool skirt with a gather at the waist that created a cascade to one side, her signature high heels. But her face was hard and implacable.

Annie retained an indelible impression of Gretchen's initial response, utter and total amazement. Now she scanned the others.

Curt Roundtree gave a whoop. "I wish I'd known. I'd have taken bets. Is she dead or not?"

Jane Wilson came to her feet, her face a vision of happiness. "Ves, how wonderful. You're alive." Jane began to cry.

Tim Holt looked stolid, unmoved, broad hands planted on the knees of his jeans. Katherine stood, too, hands clenched, her narrow face eager, eyes burning with light and happiness. "This proves Bob was lying. This proves he's innocent. Let him go."

Bob gripped his cane, his fingers curled on the handle. He looked up at his wife. "I was frightened for you. The gun was gone. I thought . . . I guess I was nuts. I went from thinking you'd done awful things for me to knowing you were innocent. But I was afraid they'd charge you. Because of the gun."

"I threw the gun in the water." She sank down beside him. "Don't ever leave me." He drew her close, his good arm tight around her shoulders.

Ves moved forward. She stopped a scant foot from the red Victorian sofa, looked down. "You weren't surprised when I came through the archway. Everyone was shocked. Except you. You watched me without any reaction. You knew I was alive."

Laurel was at her elbow. "No reaction at all." Her blue eyes were stern.

Ves's voice was harsh. "You killed Fred and Adam, shot at Jane—"

A cry came from Jane.

"—but you knew you didn't kill me."

Tim Holt slowly rose, stood in front of Ves, muscular and powerful. His handsome face was amused. "I said you were nuts. That's what I told everybody. Nutcase deluxe. I don't get any of this. Asking everybody over here for what? So you can come in and accuse somebody, I guess. I'm the guy without any connections, so dump on me. I don't think so. You say I killed some people because I'm not surprised to see you. I don't give a damn where you are or if you are. You can do whatever whenever. I've had enough of this—"

Billy broke in. "Fred's cell phone had no calls that evening. His home phone had no calls. Fred took his car to the pier, met someone. How was that meeting arranged? Katherine saw someone at the window of Fred's car. It was here that he heard about the trap set for Ves. He was in the backyard, saw someone come. The night he died he looked across this room at you—"

Tim was sardonic. "Sure. Pick me. But it won't do you any good. He could have looked at anyone. Or maybe he already had a date for the pier before he came here. You can't hang this on me."

Billy continued, his voice heavy. "—and you understood that somehow Fred knew you'd been here. You didn't know Fred was looking for treasure in Ves's backyard on Thursdays. But you made up your mind to kill Fred." Billy turned to Jane, his voice deep, demanding. "Who stood by Fred's car window?"

Jane pressed her fingertips against her cheeks. Her face was tallow colored. Her blue eyes held horror and despair and sickening understanding. Shots in the night and Tim pressuring her to marry him immediately. Ves's money at the end of a dark rainbow.

Tim turned toward her. "I was with you. I didn't go up to the old geezer's car. Why would I?"

Jane slowly backed away from him, blue eyes huge in her young stricken face. Steps sounded from the hall, and Lou Pirelli was beside her, one strong arm around her shoulders. She turned, clung to Lou.

Ves's voice carried, clear, accusing, definite. *"Ecce signum."*

Annie glanced at Max and he mouthed, "Behold the proof."

Annie saw Jane's shoulders shaking. Jane knew. Jane was in Tim's truck. Jane saw him at the window of Fred's car. Tim may have been reassuring. *Hey, Fred, you and I need to talk. I didn't wax anybody's step. I went up to the door and knocked. No answer. I left. But you and I are kind of on the spot. Let's meet on the pier. Say half an hour. We can work out our times and go to the cops. We may be able to help them.* It wouldn't have taken long to say, then return to the truck, climb up into the cab.

Jane's voice was choked. "Tim said the old geezer, he meant Fred, dropped something and he'd hurry and pick it up and take it to him. When he came back, Tim told me people were sure funny. Fred dropped a rabbit's foot and was real glad to get it back. Said it was a good luck piece."

Tim's face turned an ugly red. "Jane, they've planned this. It's a setup." He started to walk toward the archway. "I'm out of here. I'm not going to be anybody's fall guy."

Billy, big, burly, immovable, blocked him. Billy shot a quick glance at Lou, who gave an emphatic nod. There was a satisfied look on Billy's face. He spoke in a measured tone. "Timothy Holt, I am arresting you on suspicion of murder." He gave the Miranda warning, gripped Tim's arm.

Tim turned a venomous glare on Ves. "They don't have anything on me. I'll sue you. You can't get away with this."

The confident look on Billy's face assured Annie that Billy was sure he had a case, could build a case, that Tim Holt was a murderer who would face trial and Ves was safe. Billy spoke to Ves. "You did the right thing to come out of hiding."

Ves spoke slowly. "I was frightened. Annie said you'd listen, but I didn't think you would believe me when I claimed someone killed Fred. That's why I left that night. I worked it all out. I have loads of frozen food. I packed up everything I needed and took it to Rufus's house. The electricity stays on year-round because we have occasional winter renters. Next I went to the shop. I was almost well from the fall, well enough to ride an electric scooter. I got a scooter at the shop, came home, and"—a flush stained her cheeks—"I made it look like something had happened to me, the chair knocked over and blood on the doorframe." Her lips twisted. "It's easy to bleed when you're afraid you're going to die. I jabbed an earlobe. I left the door open, the lights on. I used a flashlight and took a bike path on the scooter to Rufus's house. I never turned on any lights. I used my flashlight at night. I watched on the TV in the den. After Adam was shot, I felt paralyzed by fear. Then I started to wonder. Why shoot Adam? Everyone thought it was to increase the survivors' share of Rufus's estate. But I wasn't dead. I wondered if somehow Adam knew who Fred met on the pier. And I was right. Adam was in the car in front of Fred. He looked in his rearview mirror, saw Tim talk to Fred."

Tim folded his arms, his face defiant, his posture cocky. "Prove it."

Billy clicked handcuffs on Tim's wrists. "We know more than you think."

Ves had the last word. "I came back because I had to choose. *Aut vincere aut mori.*"

Max murmured to Annie, "Either to conquer or to die."

15

The place settings of hand-painted china made the dining room table elegant. Fresh gardenias in the centerpiece provided a sweet scent. Ves stood at one end of the table. "Thank you for being my friends when I needed friends."

Annie felt a glow. Ves's ivory silk dress emphasized the brightness of her red curls. Everyone looked festive, Laurel a vision of loveliness in a pale blue dress, Emma sturdy and commanding in an orange caftan reminiscent of a South Seas sunrise, and Henny regal in a high-necked velvet dress the same shade as the iris on the hand-painted china.

"I also wanted you to know that I spoke with the trustee. I can do what I wish with the corpus of the estate so long as it is distributed to some or more of the heirs who are alive during my lifetime. I thought about Rufus and those he wanted to share in his wealth. For that reason, I have provided a substantial sum to Bob and Katherine, Jane, and my nephew, Curt. All of us suffered because of Tim's greed. Money can't solve everything, but sometimes it smooths a path. And I used some of the income to reimburse the town for the search for me. And now, I'll serve—"

Emma cleared her throat. "Along that line, I wanted to say"—and her blue eyes were icy—"I don't like blackmailers." Emma's strong square face was as tough as any cowboy's boot. "Sometimes I have a soft spot for the reckless. Raffles was a good sort."

Annie pictured E. W. Hornung's famed safecracker A. J. Raffles, who smoked expensive cigarettes and wrote poetry when he wasn't stealing from the rich.

"I was thinking about Raffles the other day and happened to drop by the Perfumerie—"

Annie had difficulty imagining Emma in that haven of scent and unguents.

"—and it turned out Gretchen was most interested when I told her about my idea for a book about a blackmailer. The victim calls the blackmailer and engages in a back-and-forth about money and what will happen if a payment isn't made. The victim is recording the call. When it is concluded, the victim prints out the conversation. There is a neat technology that can do that. The victim calls again, points out possession of a recording of the incriminating call, and suggests they both walk away—unless the blackmailer is willing to go to prison." A satisfied smile.

"Reprehensible," Laurel chided, but she smiled.

Henny nodded. "I hope the recipient of your wisdom forgoes future thefts."

Ves laughed out loud. "Emma, if I ever take to a life of crime, I will consult with you first."

◆　◆　◆

Helium balloons, red, yellow, and blue, bobbed on a line tethered to the coffee bar to celebrate the publication of three distinctive chapbooks. In Annie's private estimation, the three literary efforts could also be described as amazing and she would say so with a very straight face, especially in her mother-in-law's presence.

"Beer Barrel Polka" blared from the sound system in deference to Emma's new title, set at a Czech festival. Death on Demand was jammed, blue-haired ladies from book clubs, bright-eyed retired professors, male and female, island gentry, island shopkeepers, some of the regulars from Parotti's, the Friends of the Library in full force. Of course, Emma's birthday cake, a triple decker chocolate cake with raspberry icing, had its own table.

Ingrid Webb, aided by husband Duane, manned the front cash desk. Annie and Max worked behind the coffee bar. Lines stretched from three tables set up beneath the watercolors. As Annie finished an orange slush, added a cherry to the top, she was grateful for small favors. She had seated the three authors honored tonight in alphabetical order, Henny Brawley, Emma Clyde, and Laurel Roethke. Emma *always* expected to be queen of the hill and took the center table as in the natural order of things. Henny was unpretentious and undemanding. Laurel was . . . Laurel.

Dark blue eyes perhaps spacier than usual, Laurel charmed customers, often taking a moment to gaze deeply into a buyer's eyes then speaking as if they shared a secret rapport. Annie overheard, "You remind me of a stag at sunset." The male recipient of this observation straightened his shoulders, pulled in his paunch, and swaggered away from the table with a half dozen chapbooks. To a sour-faced forty-year-old, she trilled, "I see you as a little girl. Serious but with such an impish sense of fun. Now, that is a great gift." And a miracle occurred and the sour look was replaced by a shy smile.

Emma, majestic in a swirling silver caftan and spiky hair silver as well, sported a beaded headband with a centerpiece of turquoise. The author was most amiable as she received awed tributes from adoring readers. A gruff chuckle as she modestly proclaimed, "Perhaps saying I'm better than Tey is an exaggeration. It's such a shame she wrote only eight mysteries." The implication: Poor dear can't match my one hundred and twenty. And counting.

Henny was elegant in a brown suede jacket and tan trousers and boots. She clapped her hands together in delight. "You've read Henry Calvin, too? *It's Different Abroad* is simply splendid."

Annie fixed two cappuccinos, held them out to Ben Parotti.

Ben nodded approval. "Could you shave an extra bit of that dark chocolate on top of this one?" He held a mug forward. "Miss Jolene loves your chocolate. She says she's sure it's Belgian."

Marian Kenyon slid onto a stool. "You look frazzled. Frazzled but happy. Quite a crowd. Make yourself a frappé and cool off and then I'll order."

Annie gave her an appreciative smile. "A touch of liqueur, even over ice, and I'd curl up like Agatha and not move. Agatha's in the storeroom, draped over my computer keyboard. That's how she makes a statement. I told her wall-to-wall pays for cat food. She wasn't impressed. But I'll take a minute and fix myself a limeade."

"That sounds good. Make four for us. I hate to tell you, but it's sweat town in here tonight. That's what you get when you jam in more people than the fire code allows. I estimate almost two hundred."

Annie poured seltzer over fresh squeezed lime, added a dash of strawberry syrup, took a huge swallow.

"Great covers." Marian held up three distinctive pamphlets.

Annie agreed though there had been big changes in cover format from her original plan of shooting stars for Laurel's *Merry Musings* and titles like spokes around a wheel for Henny's *Classic Crimes*. Only the huge magnifying glass for Emma's *Detecting Wisdom* had survived. Now the warm glow of a Tiffany lamp next to a stack of books added color to a rich mahogany desk in *Classic Crimes*. *Detecting Wisdom* featured scarlet letters against a gray background and a magnifying glass tilted over a footprint. The blue letters of *Merry Musings* floated in a swirl of pink. Annie was reminded of cotton candy but immediately banished the thought as Laurel had an uncanny way of reading Annie's mind. She looked toward the third table, saw herself regarded by a mildly inquiring gaze. *Not cotton candy. NOT cotton candy.* An abstract of a flamingo. That was it. *Flamingo, Laurel, flamingo.*

"Annie?"

She looked at Marian.

"I lost you there for a minute. Take several deep breaths. Gulp some more sugar and take your time to make our limeades. I'll bring you up to date on the jerk." Marian now referred to Tim Holt in all contexts, except in print, as the jerk. As she'd told Annie, outrage lifting her voice, "What kind of creep shoots at a girl, even if he misses, to bully her into marriage? Not because he cared about her. All he cared about was her portion of Rufus's estate." Marian's dark eyes glittered with malice. "Cocky is as cocky does. That's what Billy always says about perps. Would you believe they found the murder gun, the slugs match the ones in Adam's body, hidden in Holt's truck? They did. Damn near had to take it apart but they found it. And with fingerprints, no less. That was announced this morning. And"—she chortled—"I love it that the gun was found by Lou Pirelli. He's a truck nut. Has an old one he tinkers on all the time. He knew where to look and how to look." As Annie made limeades, Marian's restless gaze roved among the crowd. "Speaking of. There's Lou with Jane. Lou's got a good head. He won't press her. He'll take his time, make life fun for her again, and one of these days, they'll be Mr. and Mrs. Lou Pirelli. They're looking at the paintings. Here they come."

Annie put the last limeade on the counter.

Jane wormed through the crowd, Lou close behind her. She lifted her voice. "This is such a wonderful evening. I was looking at the watercolors."

"She knows all of them." Lou spoke with pride. "Her mom loved those books."

Jane's blue eyes held happy memories. "*The Man in the Brown Suit* by Agatha Christie, *The Black Goatee* by Constance and Gwenyth Little, *Murder's Little Sister* by Pamela Branch, *The Affair at Royalties* by George Baxt, and *The Shanghai Union of Industrial Mystics* by Nury Vittachi."

Chapbooks

Classic Crime by Henny Brawley

The Circular Staircase (1908) by Mary Roberts Rinehart, 1876–1958
Mary Roberts Rinehart was among the earliest mystery authors to include humor and a female protagonist. Her books reflect their times. Women wore hats. An unchaperoned single woman spending the night with a man was unthinkable. Rinehart was at one time the highest paid author in America. She was the first woman war correspondent to reach No Man's Land in France in WWI. She loved America's West and championed Indian tribes then in desperate straits.

The Thirty-Nine Steps (1915) by John Buchan, 1875–1940
Buchan's hero Richard Hannay is a gentleman adventurer—brave, stalwart, always understated in the finest British tradition. Buchan, 1st Baron Tweedsmuir, was once described as a man of unintimidating gay alacrity and a warmth of companionable charm. One of his

sons said a few years after his death: "Everything at home sprang into cheerful new life the moment my father entered the front door."

The House Without a Key (1925) by Earl Derr Biggers, 1884–1933

Debut of Honolulu detective Charlie Chan, a wise and philosophical man with a gift for insightful comments. A fascinating return to the Hawaii of the '20s and a fine introduction to Chan's understanding of the nuances of Eastern and Western attitudes. Chan is a fully realized character in the novels, unlike his depiction in movies.

The Murder of Roger Ackroyd (1926) by Agatha Christie, 1890–1976

Christie delighted in taking advantage of unconscious assumptions made by readers. She employs this technique as well in *Crooked House* and *Death on the Nile*. Discover her humor and charm in the autobiographical *Come, Tell Me How You Live*, a lively account of the daily routine on one of her husband Max Mallowan's archaeological digs.

Gaudy Night (1935) by Dorothy L Sayers, 1893–1957

An elegant exploration of the balance between love and independence, and a fascinating portrait of university life, its passions, prejudices, and sometimes, pain. Sayers was a remarkable woman for her time or any time, brilliant, clever, inventive, and fiercely independent.

Ming Yellow (1935) by John P. Marquand, 1893–1960

Marquand's literary novels explored the world of wealth and status. He received a Pulitzer for *The Late George Apley*. In a different vein entirely were the Mr. Moto novels, where the wily Japanese agent's efforts involved American adventurers. The early titles provide an understanding of China and Japan in the 1930s, and they are great fun.

Fer-De-Lance (1934) by Rex Stout, 1886–1975

The first Nero Wolfe and an introduction to the famous fictional brownstone on West 35th Street. While testing commercial beers, and to his amazement finding one acceptable, Wolfe says: ". . . a pessimist gets nothing but pleasant surprises, an optimist nothing but unpleasant." Wolfe and his assistant, Archie Goodwin, the narrator, unfailingly provide superb entertainment.

The Case Is Closed (1937) by Patricia Wentworth, 1878–1961

When all hope is lost, call on London's most unusual private enquiry agent, Miss Maud Silver. A man is accused of murder, convicted, and is now in prison, but his wife and her cousin believe in his innocence. Only Miss Silver can use her perception and guile to save him. Miss Silver often knits bootees for babies and is likely to quote Alfred, Lord Tennyson: "And trust me not at all or all in all."

Cause for Alarm (1938) by Eric Ambler, 1909–1998

A preview of the clash of fascism and democracy in WWII. Ambler revealed the dark heart of fascism in several of his 1930s thrillers. After the war Ambler became a successful screenwriter as well as a novelist. He had a talent for comedy, and *The Light of Day* (1962) chronicles a hapless rogue hero in desperate trouble in Greece and Germany. It was made into a movie entitled *Topkapi*.

Rebecca (1938) by Daphne Du Maurier, 1907–1989

One of the great opening lines in fiction: "Last night I dreamt I went to Manderley again." The tone captures the foreboding and unease that permeate the story of a second wife who lives in the dead Rebecca's shadow. Brilliant. A haunting novel about love and jealousy and cruelty. The author said of her work: "a sinister tale about a woman who marries a widower." Du Maurier's novels were often tinged with a horror that lingers in a reader's mind.

Above Suspicion (1941) by Helen MacInnes, 1907–1985

The adventures of a husband and wife team of amateur spies looking for an anti-Nazi spy in pre-WWII Europe. The background is based on MacInnes's journal entries while on her honeymoon in Bavaria and the darkening cloud of war that was fast approaching. Her husband, scholar Gilbert Highet, served in British intelligence in WWII.

The Norths Meet Murder (1940) by Frances and Richard Lockridge. Frances, 1896–1963. Richard, 1898–1982.

Frances and Richard Lockridge used their skills as reporters to create the Pam and Jerry North series, distinguished by Pam's intuitive leaps and Jerry's steadying influence. The Norths are among the early cool couples in mysteries, and the martini-bright style was influenced by sketches Richard wrote for the *New Yorker*.

Drink to Yesterday (1940) by Manning Coles, Pseudonym of Cyril Henry Coles, 1899–1965, and Adelaide Manning, 1891–1959

The first of the Tommy Hambledon British agent novels. Coles served in British intelligence in WWI and WWII, and Manning worked in the War Office in WWII. They also created four entertaining ghost novels, including *Brief Candles* and *Happy Returns*, about two cousins, one American and one British, who died in the Franco-Prussian War and return to help a modern-day descendant.

The Fog Comes (1941) by Mary Collins, 1908–1979

Murder in an upper-class family in fog-shrouded Northern California. Collins wrote six mysteries in the 1940s with intelligent, independent women protagonists. Each is a stand-alone and all are absorbing. Her last novel was *Dog Eat Dog* in 1949.

The Hollow Chest (1941) by Phoebe Atwood Taylor Writing as Alice Tilton, 1909–1976

Taylor was famous for her Codfish Sherlock, Asey Mayo, but under the Tilton name she wrote comic mysteries about professorial Leonidas Witherall. The spitting image of Shakespeare, he was known to friends as Bill. *The Hollow Chest* is a rollicking read with unexpected twists on every page. Tilton's books during the war years, such as *File for Record* (1943), depict the home front during WWII, from gas rationing to air raid sirens to junk drives.

Great Black Kanba (1944) by Australian Sisters Constance and Gwenyth Little. Constance, 1889–1980. Gwenyth 1903–1985.

Their only mystery set in Australia, a murder-struck journey across Australia by train. All but one of their books included *Black* in the title. The Little books were wacky tales with macabre twists and a laugh a page. Another favorite is *The Black Goatee* (1947). In the postwar housing crunch, desperate house hunters steal silently into the unused wing of a home to find homicide instead of comfort.

The Franchise Affair (1949) by Josephine Tey, 1897–1952

A chilling tale that shows how easy it is to enmesh the innocent with false accusations. The village turns against a mother and daughter accused of kidnaping a teenager, but the lawyer they seek believes in them. Tey's novels were imaginative and unusual.

The Chinese Chop (1949) by Juanita Sheridan, 1906–1974

The first novel to star writer Janice Cameron and her soon-to-be friend and champion Lily Wu. Three subsequent novels are set in 1950s Hawaii, when much of old Hawaii still existed. Juanita Sheridan was as adventurous as any of her fictional heroines. She wed often, traveled far, and claimed that her maternal grandfather was killed by Pancho Villa.

Man Running (1948) by Selwyn Jepson, 1899–1989

The first Eve Gill novel. During WWII, Jepson was a recruiting agent for SOE in Britain. He believed, despite his superiors' objections, that women made excellent agents, because the strong ones possessed a cool courage and could work alone. Winston Churchill gave him the authority to recruit women. Jepson's respect for women is reflected in his creation after the war of supercool Eve Gill as a protagonist in six imaginative tales.

Murder's Little Sister (1958) by Pamela Branch, 1920–1967

Disheveled, irascible *You* editor Sam Egan implores his staff: ". . . as a team let's have a stab at Misadventure, mm? If some swine's found a clue, we gradually introduce Suicide. Soft pedal it. Nothing of interest to a lurking journalist. Nothing definite, nothing chatty, nothing squalid. Remember, we don't want suicide and I absolutely refuse to have Murder." Pamela Branch entertains from the first page to the last. There are a great many clever mysteries, but few reach the heights of creativity and nonsense spun by Branch.

Killer's Wedge (1959) by Ed McBain, 1926–2005

The first in his magnificent 87th Precinct novels, the finest police procedurals ever penned. Police work is rendered accurately, with characters as real as the cop next door. In this superb book, life and death hang in the balance and tension ratchets to a tumultuous finale.

My Brother Michael (1959, 1960) by Mary Stewart, 1916–2014
The first sentence: "Nothing ever happens to me." An intelligent, intriguing woman is drawn into an adventure set against a background delineated with grace and precision. Mary Stewart is deservedly compared to the Brontës. Stewart's prose shines with erudition and charm.

Dance Hall of the Dead (1973) by Tony Hillerman, 1925–2008
Tony Hillerman grew up in Sacred Heart, Oklahoma, and attended an Indian boarding school for eight years, his introduction to a different culture. Warm, kind, and wise, Hillerman's mysteries, set in the Four Corners, depict the consciousness of Navajo and Zuni tribes. Hillerman titled his autobiography *Seldom Disappointed* (2001) in a tribute to his mother's dictum: "Blessed are those who expect little. They are seldom disappointed."

Crocodile on the Sandbank (1975) by Elizabeth Peters, 1927–2013
Mystery author JoAnna Carl takes a copy of *Crocodile on the Sandbank* to hospitalized friends, saying if that didn't make them feel better, nothing would. This first in the series featuring Amelia Peabody, a Victorian archaeologist in Egypt, entertains, educates, and delights. Elizabeth Peters (archaeology-trained Barbara Mertz) also wrote as Barbara Michaels.

Death in Zanzibar (1983; Originally Published in 1959 as the *House of Shade*) by M. M. Kaye, 1908–2004
Kaye's military husband was posted to various exotic locales, which she used as backgrounds for many of her suspense novels. Her most famous novel is *The Far Pavilions* (1978), an epic novel of British-Indian history. Kaye was born in India and educated in England, but her ties to India were deep and lasting.

Detecting Wisdom

BY EMMA CLYDE

Observations by sleuth Marigold Rembrandt and Inspector Houlihan:

MARIGOLD: A scared rat has sharp fangs.

MARIGOLD: If a woman thinks all she has is her body, life will treat her that way.

INSPECTOR HOULIHAN: Sex or money. Money or sex. If it's money and sex, all hell breaks loose.

INSPECTOR HOULIHAN: Don't hesitate to be tough.

MARIGOLD: Avoid mean streets. If you can't, be prepared.

MARIGOLD: Casual conversation has been the undoing of many.

MARIGOLD: How sweet it is when the good guy has more firepower than the perp.

MARIGOLD: If you have a secret, keep it.

INSPECTOR HOULIHAN: A good cop always has your back.

MARIGOLD: Pride is the serpent inside you.

INSPECTOR HOULIHAN: Everybody lies. It's up to us to figure out which lies matter.

MARIGOLD: In a tight spot, stare down your accuser.

MARIGOLD: A bad dream is your subconscious knocking on the door of a closed mind.

INSPECTOR HOULIHAN: Never take anything for granted.

MARIGOLD: Charm often disguises a weak character.

INSPECTOR HOULIHAN: Sex can make a man into a damn fool. Ditto for a woman.

MARIGOLD: Even a clever criminal isn't always on guard.

MARIGOLD: Watch out for wide eyes, a charlatan counterfeiting sincerity.

INSPECTOR HOULIHAN: Accepting a favor is the first step to corruption.

MARIGOLD: A man who cheats on his wife or a woman who cheats on her husband will cheat you, too.

MARIGOLD: When a perp panics, anything can happen.

INSPECTOR HOULIHAN: Listen for words that aren't spoken.

MARIGOLD: Self-absorption is the armor of the wicked.

MARIGOLD: The imps of hell clap their hands in delight when you e-mail in haste.

INSPECTOR HOULIHAN: Let people talk.

MARIGOLD: There are many different ways to tell the truth.

Merry Musings, Modest Maxims for Happiness

BY LAUREL DARLING ROETHKE

Happiness comes from giving, not taking.

Catch a falling star before it knocks you flat.

Indulge a friend's weakness for trite pronouncements.

Sufficiency for one is deprivation for another.

A cheater never knows the satisfaction of earning a win.

The prize isn't power, wealth, or privilege. The prize is
    love, which can't be forced, bought, or inherited.

A dog loves you because you are you.

Laughter lifts hearts.

It never hurts to ask.

Life is a cancan so kick as high as you can.

Everyone is important or no one is important.

Be kind.

In rattlesnake country, watch where you step.

Each person has a story.

A faraway train whistle tugs at our hearts.

A cat on politics: Nonsense will only be tolerated if seasoned with catnip.

A dog on politics: Will vote for bone.

Life is hard for everyone.

Is it true? Is it fair? Is it honest?

Listen for the distant laughter of angels.

Look for the saints among us.

God's gifts to us: a sunrise, the scent of the sea, snowflakes, a smile.

On a cold, gray day, imagine a July afternoon and the feel of sand beneath your feet as you walk on the beach.

Always wonder why.

If an elephant's in the way, find another path.

Of course there are unicorns.

A seashell is like a memory. The life is gone. The beauty remains.

Smile first.